MARIAM'S MEMOIRS

A catalogue record for this book is available from the National Library of Australia

www.brotherbrad.com

MARIAM'S MEMOIRS

A Sword Through My Soul

BROTHER BRAD SMITH

Dedication

To my mother, Gloria.

Just as you received a promise from heaven,
may heaven bless you.

Contents

~Prologue~

As the mother of Jesus, many people have looked to me as the model of perfect motherhood, a symbol of the love that *HaShem* — the Lord — has for the world. They admire me as one who has been granted a position of power, though I had no ambition to see myself as the God-bearer.

This role was assigned to me from the hand of an angel. My initial response was not to doubt or fight against it, but after careful consideration I was able to accept it with the words, "So let it be."

I had been accustomed to encounters with angels from my time in the Temple, though this is something which I kept to myself. When Gabriel approached me with this task I knew that this was a matter of importance in the heart of HaShem.

Little did I know the depths of pain that I would experience after accepting the word; otherwise I might not have undertaken this call on my life. I really don't know if history would have been much different, the way things turned out.

On a personal level I will share the heights of my joy and happiness, along with the depths of grief as I watched my Son's last breath taken before me.

Maybe you are also facing times of struggle, where the world is against you, and you feel that there is no way forward but to give up. Perhaps you are at breaking point through ridicule or bullying, or being despised as a single mother, or hated by members of your own family. Or maybe heaven has been silent and your prayers have gone unanswered.

If so, my memoir is for you.

As I share my private life in detail, your sorrow may become my sorrow, and my grief become your grief. Together we will be able to get through whatever you are facing and make it through to the other side.

Let me hold your hand.
Let me squeeze it gently to assure you that I am here.

Will you allow me to be a mother to you across these few pages that follow?

My memoir begins with my parents. It's from there that my life was shaped, and my call to service began.

My mother was faithful to her promise and gave me up to the service of the Lord in response to the vow that she had taken. Her story starts in Nazareth, a small town in the lower Galilee basin, nestled in rugged mountains.

Come, share my most precious and intimate moments together.

Mariam

Chapter 1

Mother

Inasmuch as I have treasured the memories of my son, having had them written onto papyrus and kept them close for many years, I felt compelled to arrange them into a historical account so that you may understand the calling of divine grace that I received to be the mother of our Lord.

I am no stranger to grief, as many of you would know. Although the call on my life was steeped in glory, you would know that many trials have been used to crush my soul. During these times I could only wait for heaven's help to get me through it.

And this is what I've learned: *The greater the glory, the greater the trials.*

As I recall these stories I have been blessed to be able to compile and share them with you, so that you may find strength and encouragement to lift you through difficult times of your life.

Sometimes, the glories follow the trials.

In many respects, whether you experience trials first, or glory, they almost always go hand in hand.

Please allow me to begin by sharing the first memories of my childhood. A miracle in itself, my arrival was welcomed with hearts of gratitude — though it was not without a struggle.

My parents, Joachim and Anne, were respected in our small Jewish community in Nazareth for following the traditions of the elders, the Law and the Prophets. They were devout, and maintained piety and distributed gifts to the poor, being careful to keep themselves from anything that might pollute themselves by the way they lived. They met regularly in our local synagogue and were distinguished leaders in our community.

Despite their life of devotion and reverence, they were unable to have children — and they had grown old.

Mother had prayed and wept and with desperate tears she called on HaShem. But as time went on her child bearing years came to an end, and it became evident that the blessing of motherhood was not going to rest on her. As she grew into old age, her heart was crushed with a burden of grief that she was expecting to carry to the grave. She carried a deep hurt of unfulfilled longing — and surely not unlike that which many women carry or fear today.

Behind the brave face presented to the community lay a depth of sadness that she kept to herself. In the open she stood boldly, believing that HaShem could change rocks into flesh — should He choose to do so.

Everyone understood and silently mocked her for being barren. The distant whispers, sideways glances and muted laughter echoed through the marketplace, avoiding real contact, attacking her with shame and disgrace. Granted that she was in the latter stage of life, it was not something that she could change.

Mother mourned this lost opportunity and had accepted that the family story was to be written without children. I remember her tears, when as a child I listened to her recount the way that HaShem finally answered their prayers.

"Mariam, my daughter, come to me," she whispered, with eyes of longing that filled the waters of my young soul with motherly love. I moved onto her lap while she held me close, wrapping her arms comfortably around me while the fireplace flickered soft yellow light around us. Her tender touch showed me her compassionate heart, and I knew I was loved.

"Mariam, please understand that you are no ordinary child. You are our longing fulfilled." Her voice was soft, and her hair stranded around us as I nestled into her shoulder. I was only very young, almost three years of age at the time she shared this with me.

Mother started to cry, and I was confused about what she wanted to share with me. Did I make her sad? Had I done something to upset her? I wanted to assure her that whatever was upsetting her was going to be okay.

Wrinkled hands cupped my face as she stroked my chin, helping to direct my gaze towards her face. I looked up as she wiped away a tear, took a breath, and then waited for her to continue.

"When the years had passed and all hope was gone," she muffled, "HaShem responded to our cries and mourning."

Mother's speech was slow and direct, gentle and with maternal authority. I let them sink in, not knowing that her words would somehow change my life in ways that my child's mind couldn't understand at the time.

"We had longed and cried and prayed for children. But as we grew older, time slipped away."

I didn't realise the level of emotional distress that they had experienced as a result of a desolate family life. The abandonment of heavens answers to prayer; the lack of joyful times that would have brought laughter and fulfilment as there were no birthdays, no celebratory events to mark the calendar, and no-one to pass on the history of our family or nation. Just an empty void that could not be filled by anything else.

"Mariam, despite all this, HaShem has mended our grief and brought us comfort in our old age." Tears of gratitude freely flowed down mother's cheeks, as she held me closely on her lap. Her embrace was to keep me secure forever.

"Mariam, please, remember this. Blessed are those who mourn." I had somehow caused to interrupt her, so she started again.

"Blessed are those who mourn, for they will be comforted."

Mothers words were a revelation to me, showing that a path of suffering is not always the final chapter of any story.

Indeed, I was their longing fulfilled.
Sent, as if, directly from heaven.

Her words became treasure in my heart and she insisted that I was to pass them on to my children, if given the chance, as words to live by.

With a more relaxed smile, she ran her fingers through my hair and continued, "When all natural hope dried up, an angel brought us the promise of a child. He told us:

"This time next year, you will be holding a child in
your arms.
Your daughter will be the servant of HaShem.
And you shall call her Mariam."

Having received such a divine encounter, they believed, and
I was born the following year.

Mother held her breath, savouring the memory of my birth
as she retold it. Other thoughts grew from this and swelled
her emotions to break a graceful smile that shone like an
early sunrise. Her long dark wavy hair formed a cover over
her ears and down my side, as though wrapping me in a
prayer shawl. I loved being in her presence for the times
like this.

Only later was I to understand that mother's story read
like that of Hannah, whose prayers were finally answered
with a son who was dedicated for a life devoted to
HaShem. And like Samuel, I was dedicated as a servant of
the Lord in the temple.

Little did they realise that their answer to prayer was to
form part of HaShem's unfolding story about His love for
our nation, our people, and the world.

His divine plan was to be revealed at the right time, and it
would take cries of sorrow and despair from earth to open
the gates of heaven.

Further, they did not realise that the world was waiting for
my arrival.

Why aren't our prayers answered when we want them to be?

I was not the only child that was born under miraculous
circumstances.

In similar circumstances to my mother, my older cousin Elizabeth was blessed at the end of her life with a baby boy. It had been well known across the Judean countryside that she was well past bearing children. Likewise, the disdain from others implied that HaShem was withholding His favour from them. They were adamant that they were not concealing some hidden sin, but were ridiculed as though they were.

As part of the priestly lines of Abijah and Aaron, they were treated with disgrace, just like my parents. Children were a sign of HaShem's blessing, and if this was not evident in their lives then how could they function with integrity in the temple?

But HaShem had other plans that changed their lives forever. As my uncle was selected to burn incense before the Lord, he received an angelic visitation.

> "Don't be afraid, Zechariah! HaShem has heard your prayer. Your wife Elizabeth will give you a son, and you are to name him John."

Elizabeth, being of the same generation as my parents, had savoured the stories that she had learned from my mother. She knew the struggle to conceive was deeply embarrassing and hurtful, and had grown to doubt herself. She struggled to ignore the disdain of others. However she also was inspired by the hope that HaShem gives comfort to those who mourn. And with an air of expectation, she also held the hope of motherhood tightly.

Within twelve months Elizabeth was holding a son in her arms, true to the word from heaven. Growing up, he brought a delight to their family and their hearts overflowed with gratitude. Finally they had been blessed and would not die childless. The taunts of the community were answered in a miraculous way, the crowd became silent.

Like my cousin John, I was indeed a miracle child, a longing fulfilled. He was born fourteen years after me.

So it is that when my mother gave birth I inadvertently joined the ranks of other children that had been born as a result of a promise, not through natural means. HaShem brought life from bodies that were as good as dead and changed the course of history through them. But it did not come without the grief that attended a life of waste, and the insults of the community that mocked the situation that they were in.

To keep their vows my parents placed me in the care of the temple leaders, where I was to grow up under their guidance. So I grew up in the Temple in Jerusalem, during the rebuilding.

It was there that I learned the significance of the history of our people, in relation to the promises of HaShem. And it was in the Temple that I grew to love the Lord and practise His ways, under the guidance and care of those whom He appointed to take care of me.

Each year my parents came to the Temple to participate in *Pesach*, that is, Passover, though they tried not to disturb me during one of the busiest days of the year. So they would also come at other times to be with their little girl and we would share the day together. I recall the stories of our family history, how HaShem had promised that someone from the family line of King David would someday rule the throne of Israel. And we looked forward to see that promise fulfilled.

My parents did not see me grow fully into the calling for which they had earnestly prayed. But I will always remember the times that they were able to share with me together, with gratitude.

I was saddened when it was time to say goodbye to my parents. First to my father, and then to my mother a year later. I was still quite young, and maybe I was not quite ready for them to be let go. They had been the expression of faith and love to me, having endured a life of trial of grief before they passed away.

As I grew, I treasured the things that were passed down, and how they received their reward.

Mother's words still ring in the background of my memories.

Blessed are those who mourn.

And even now, in my old age, the power of her words light my soul with hope.

For they shall be comforted.

Chapter 2

⁓Widow⁓

The circumstances of my extraordinary birth were orchestrated with divine accuracy, as if to align with a prophetic calendar. I did not realise at the time just how much this was to be a calling to something bigger. After my parents had dedicated me to the temple, my daily life became lessons in availability, willingness and obedience.

The Jewish leaders were overseeing the rebuilding of the Temple, a project that held promise for the restoration of our faith. It was widely accepted that King Herod was attempting to find favour with our nation and it was his duty to establish Pax Romana — the Roman Peace — in the region where he ruled. I was just three years of age when I arrived, and the Temple rebuilding had commenced a year before my birth.

This meant that although the Jews were to be my mentors and educators in the temple, they had little time to spend with me personally. As a result of their busyness, I was placed in the care of Anna, an elderly lady who regularly fasted and prayed in the temple courts. Affectionately, she became my *Bubbe* — grandmother — who filled the family relationship void in my heart.

Notably, she was recognised as a prophet in her day, one who shared deep intimate moments with HaShem and received words from heaven.

It was Bubbe who taught me not only how to hear, but also how to act on, a word from HaShem. From our time together she embedded a sense of reverence and royal duty in me, which I retained later in life. In a practical sense she raised me, and I was gifted with her beautiful and graceful presence to fill the role that was otherwise left vacant during my childhood years.

We grew close in a way that provided me with both kinship and a mentor.

Early one morning, Bubbe called me after early morning prayers, when the usual temple duties had been completed. She motioned for me to join her and was quietly waiting for me at a table outside the courts, under a tamarisk tree. Her aging face revealed years of perseverance that showed that she had been running a very long race, and her sense of determination was evident to all. Having been foretold by the Spirit, she would see the arrival of the promised Messiah.

"Mariam, my dear child," a smile widened as she spoke, "I am so blessed to have you here with me." She held out her hand to draw me in to her side as I approached, which I accepted and sat down beside her.

Her voice was soft, yet firm, and I snuggled into her shoulder to get closer, remembering that I had done the same with my mother. This helped me fend off the cool morning air as well as listen more intently to her voice. We often embraced in a mother-daughter relationship as we served in the temple courts. Her words wrapped around me with a sense of appreciation, bubbling in me a flush of humility that I did not expect.

Her eyes were aglow and her gaze was firm. There was something that she wanted to share, a message of significance which was not unlike her usual teaching, but this seemed like it would be of a more intimate nature.

She repeated herself.

"My dear child, today I would like to share a little more of myself with you." I took a slight breath in anticipation for what todays message might bring me.

"As you know, when I was young — a few years older than what you are now — I was married, as you would usually expect." Having known her for only a handful of years till now, it was hard to think of her as a young married woman. It's as if she was eternally at the temple fulfilling her duty to HaShem, and now also as a mentor to me.

"My father, Phanuel, had received a promise that he would see the face of HaShem — for that is what his name literally means. As I grew up, we lived in anticipation that the Messiah was to be sent soon. So our family pursued a life devoted to the Lord, to ensure that we would be counted worthy of being in his presence." She went on to explain how her family believed with conviction that they would be part of the blessing that was to come, and were taught how to fast and pray in order to receive answers from heaven.

I recall that she had mentioned previously that they were from the tribe of Asher. This meant that her family lived under the blessing of Jacob's final words, "Asher will dine on rich foods and produce food fit for kings." The family estate regularly produced fine fruit that was sent to the governors and rulers of the land. However as servants that were waiting for the arrival of the Messiah, they withheld dining on their own fine food, giving it up to fast for eternal rewards instead.

"Mariam, we were only married for seven years before tragedy struck. My husband — whom I loved and cared for while we were newly married — passed away suddenly. We never had children either, though we desperately wanted a family. Since then I have been living here in the temple, eagerly waiting and expecting the promise to be fulfilled."

The tears that swelled in her eyes showed just how much she genuinely missed her husband, but also revealed hope for the good things that were to come. Would she live long enough to see the completion of her family's promise? Her sorrow touched my heart, a wave of grief flowed over me. Would I ever know what it was like to experience the loss of a loved one?

I let her have her moment without interrupting. Then when she was ready to continue, she girded herself with a fresh sense of determination to deliver the story through to the end.

"At the time of my husband's passing, I dedicated myself again to HaShem. This was to be a fresh start for me, and I wanted to embrace my childhood revelations to see the coming of the Messiah. So after I had finished mourning I came here and made a solemn vow: I would fast and pray for the coming One. I would not leave to marry, or have a family, until the promise was to arrive."

A light began to glow brightly in my heart as she revealed what had been her motivation for some time.

This was no ordinary set of circumstances that led her to live a life of blatant humility, but one that she had committed to with dignity, honour and respect. Her eager expectation of their fulfilment was expressed through daily prayers and fasting, which she described as "knocking loudly on heaven's door." If there ever was a woman of faith that I could call on, it was my Bubbe, Anna.

Bubbe showed me, with deep sincerity, that living under a blessing shouldn't stop us from pursuing all the will of HaShem. And in doing that we should seek the kingdom of righteousness — there was no room for our own personal gain in realm of heaven. Our eyes should be focussed up, not looking at the things that surround us. We should pursue the call for which we have been assigned and not hesitate. Giving up what we hold precious on earth for a greater promise can result in a fulfilled life.

She continued. "Mariam, I have lived in eager expectation, based on the promises we received. I can tell you with certainty that those who hunger and thirst for righteousness will be filled. HaShem is faithful. I have this inner conviction that this will come about someday soon. That is, in my lifetime."

I understood what she meant almost intrinsically, having been with her daily and witnessed her way of life in the Temple. Her smile extended now, lighting her face in a way that swept away her grief. There was no sense of loss in her voice, as before. Her tone had become firm, and her face reflected a statement of assurance. Having put away fine food fit for a king, she embraced a humble life and lived with anticipation that one day this promise would come true: she would see the face of HaShem.

Her gaze was now in full focus within a hands breadth of my face, and I was waiting for her to break the moment which would let me step into the next part of my day. However it did not lift. It appeared she was searching for something in me that I was not aware of, something hiding in my heart. A bird flew overhead, landing on a branch of the tree that was providing a small amount of shade over us, concluding the end of our time together.

We embraced, and with a peck on my cheek, she smiled again, saying, "Remember my words."

"Yes, Bubbe, I will take them to heart."

Chapter 3

Change

Pesach brought many people into the capital each year with their offerings of unleavened bread and young lambs. I was appointed to assist those who came to participate in this celebration by providing assistance for their time at the Temple.

This was always a very moving experience, seeing the best looking lambs from the flock — selected to be without spot or blemish — be slaughtered and offered on the altar of sacrifice. This was done to remember the time that HaShem brought our nation out of slavery in Egypt, some thousands of years prior to this. Families would gather to roast part of the lamb offering and break bread before heading back to their own homes.

My parents had placed me in the care of the priests, and out of respect I carried out my responsibilities with diligence. When they had opportunity to visit, I took pleasure in describing the work I had been doing, as well as the care and attention that I had received from my appointed mother, Bubbe.

Each day I assisted the Jewish leaders to prepare for their rituals by washing their feet and helping them dress in their regal robes. I was appointed to collect towels and cloths used in ceremonies to wash and dry for later use. I had also been assigned a long term task to weave the veil for the temple, which would eventually be hung to section off access to the most holy place. This gave me exceptional delight and something to focus on to pass the time.

As a young girl, I had been instructed to accept the situation that I was in, and not to question the authority of my parents or the temple staff. To say that my mind was simple would be close to the truth, in that I did not have my own great expectations. I did not dare dream of taking on any higher responsibility, lest a title be awarded to me without cause.

During my formative years I experienced spiritual highs and earthly lows that created an air of excitement, as well as caution, which influenced the way I interacted with people in authority.

On many occasions, I met and interacted with angels, which became part of my lifestyle at the temple. They regularly fed me with heavenly bread during my times of fasting and solitude. They also taught me the Torah (Law), the Nevi'im (Prophets) and Ketuvim (Writings) that made up the history of my people, and revealed the promises of HaShem towards Israel. Although I did not have printed versions of these records, their messages became imprinted on my heart in a way that it felt like I had memorised them. I found it easy to recall each passage of scripture, the words of the angels were fresh in my mind from what they shared with me over time.

Although these heavenly encounters became quite natural to me, weaving the fabric of my life with spiritual events, over time I became aware that others did not walk in the same realm that I did despite their own dedication to the temple. I had anticipated that the priests and Jewish leaders would have normally encountered angels during prayers or while taking oaths — simply because I knew nothing different. However when I mentioned my own encounters, they raised their eyebrows in suspicion and became critical of what I shared.

"How can such a young uneducated girl know anything about our Law?" they snapped. I had explained how the angels were teaching me the very words that they had rote-learned for decades, reciting back to them word for word — and then explaining to them the text, just as was given to me.

In time it became obvious that I was walking in a completely different realm, and they had a changed attitude toward me. Instead of receiving me as a gift, which my parents intended, they showed signs of annoyance and became critical when I approached them. It became obvious that they felt threatened by my very presence — though I was unable to escape the angelic encounters that were occurring on an almost daily basis.

Under Bubbe's guidance, I grew to embrace a heart of poverty, which led me to keep quiet about my heavenly experiences. I did not want to end up like our patriarch Joseph, who revealed his dreams to his brothers and was sold into slavery. Why didn't everyone else have some level of experience similar to me? It seemed out of place.

Bubbe had developed a long-term relationship with the Jewish leaders, and had come to me later in the day after a special meeting with them. She had been appointed as their representative to discuss the delicate matter of my growing up in the temple, which was both a joy and an 'ongoing concern' to them.

"My darling, Mariam, I have been approached by the temple leaders to share with you their vision for your growing up." My heart raced and skipped a beat, feeling that they might somehow have colluded about my future.

"As you know, the priests are highly concerned and focussed on things of purity. They want to ensure that now — after hundreds of years where the word of the Lord has been silent — that we be careful to maintain the holiness of the temple, to prepare the way for the Messiah. They are observing the signs, and are hoping that the promises spoken by David and the prophets are to come true in their generation."

Bubbe drew a breath, as if waiting for me to question what this was to do with me in the Temple, but having remained silent, she continued.

"You are to me as my very own daughter, and soon you will be a young lady." Bubbe wasn't usually this hesitant when it came to explaining the things of the Temple, or of our history, or of the requirements of the law. Now it appeared that she was struggling to find the right words which would put my mind at ease and not cause me concern.

"As a young lady, your body will start to change so that one day you may become a mother."

I looked at her quizzically. Had she noticed the small bumps on my chest that had started to develop?

"That is, if you want to become a mother," she followed up on her words, not assuming that I wanted to pursue this role.

True, I had felt my youthful body start to materialise in changes that followed the same pattern as other girls who had grown past my age. So I knew what to look for and that I was not to be surprised with this news. I had always dressed modestly, as I had been taught, to keep a lowly state. From our times of sharing, Bubbe recounted the stories of Israel's unfaithfulness, where the temple was desecrated by indiscriminate practises that were performed to gods of other nations. This in itself brought uncleanness to the Temple, and dishonour to HaShem whom we serve, so I was careful not to be seen in ways that might stir the wrong thoughts in those who came with offerings for sin or guilt, or celebration.

Almost knowing my thoughts, Bubbe continued with the remainder of her briefing.

"In times of old, the Temple was used by those who had no regard for its purposes, and brought condemnation on us as a nation. People had prostituted themselves before the altar, as the surrounding nations had done when we were brought out of Egypt. And if that wasn't enough, they brought their newborn children to be sacrificed on the altar to Molech — desecrating our holy Temple, which was to be used for the worship of HaShem alone."

I could not imagine the altar being used in this way, having taken many humble people there over the years of my service to HaShem. A breeze brushed hair into my eyes and across my face, distracting me from what she wanted to say, as I dwelt on the forbidden practises that formed part of our sullied history.

The conversation changed pace quickly, from a history lesson to this current time.

Bubbe continued. "I have been asked to find a husband for you."

Although my focus had drifted into past events, she now had my full attention, and it felt abrupt and to the point.

"Mariam, when I met the leaders this morning, they expressed their concern that you were nearing the age where your body will change significantly. You won't simply develop outward features, but at some point in the next few years you won't be allowed in the Temple at all."

My look of confusion must have been what she expected, so she spoke more directly to the point at hand. Was it really their concern to find me a husband, or did they search for a reason to eject me from the temple?

"Your body will change to become a woman. But with that change you will start to bleed, once a month, and that can last about a week or so. Every woman goes through this; it is a cycle that enables your body to have children."

This was perhaps one of the most candid things that Bubbe had ever shared, and I felt in myself that I might not have been ready for it. However, at an intimate mother-daughter level we could share openly about things at times, and this was apparently one of them. I wasn't sure whether I was to look her in the eyes, but found myself looking towards the ground as if my emotions were digging for answers as to what this meant to my time in the temple.

"In our law, a woman who is experiencing her period is considered 'unclean'. Now this means that when your body changes and develops into a young woman, you will not be allowed into the Temple. This would otherwise cause this place of worship to be an unholy place, and put a hold on normal activities and rituals until it could be cleansed."

I was starting to understand, and it was personal. My thoughts and emotions struggled to keep up with what was being shared, as I knew that this would have a long lasting impact on me, and my calling.

"Mariam, after a long consideration, the leaders have decided that you need to be placed in the care of a husband who will look after and care for you. This will also bring you under proper authority, as they sense that their duty of care is almost complete, for the promise made to your parents."

The promise that my parents had made was that I was dedicated to HaShem in the Temple, just like Hannah of old had done. My sense of purpose was being challenged, and I was not sure how to respond to this. Were the temple priests scared of what might happen if I were to remain in their care?

Drawing a deep breath, I took a step back to check the full expression on her face. Was this as serious as she made it to be? I could see she was. This was no game play. And she was not seeking my approval to move forward — it was a directive that was to be put into effect as soon as possible.

Bubbe looked convinced; there were no other options other than to accept their request, and I could feel her heart break with mine as she knew that our precious times together would someday soon be over. There was only one response I could make, which I passed on to her to take back.

"Bubbe, as a servant of HaShem," I almost struggled saying it, knowing that my destiny and calling would be forever following a course that was something I didn't expect. "I am willing for them to find me a husband, if the it is the will of HaShem." Inwardly I knew that this wasn't their only cause of concern, but I needed to let the Lord be in control rather than the schemes of man.

Who was I to fight against the will of the Lord?

I had an awareness that allowed me to provide consent, knowing that whatever the outcome was going to be it would ultimately be directed by the hand of HaShem, not man.

With a nod that expressed my sincere approval of their request, she took my response back to the priests later that day.

I had not thought that the changes I felt in my body would somehow create such a disturbance to my way of life. A wave of grief fluttered through my body at the thought of the loss of my single life, which could come sooner than I had anticipated, if HaShem so desired.

My vow of singleness and wholehearted devotion to the Lord was being challenged. And my encounters in the temple were threatening others that did not experience this.

I rested in the assurance that all things would work together for good for those who love HaShem, and are called according to His purpose, knowing that this request may simply dissolve and I could continue with normal life at the temple.

But if the will of HaShem was leading them to find me a husband, then I would no longer be able to fulfil the calling which I felt was such a strong part of my life.

As a married woman, I would be concerned with the things of my husband, not of HaShem. And that is something that I would have to work through, not that I was quite there yet.

This dilemma left me with a personal determination that was not dependant on my own desires or wishes. That whether I am called here, or there, I would be HaShem's servant. HaShem's will be done.

My soul ached.

Chapter 4

The Appointment

The officers wasted no time to make arrangements to find
a suitable husband for me from a selection of eligible men
who would be selected by a divine ceremony. A call was
made that, on a certain day the following week, an assembly
should take place so that I should be given away.

The nominated location was the room of the Great
Sanhedrin, a place of business where matters of
importance were made on behalf of the nation of Israel.
I was a familiar with the room as I was required to keep
the floor swept and the tables fresh and orderly. I did
not realise that my betrothal would rank at the level of
importance to be held there, but those of higher rank
seemed to think so.

A podium was set up to allow the speaker to give details
of the ensuing process, and a make-shift altar with a

curtain circling it hung towards the back of the room. I was unfamiliar with this setup so I had to wait until the ceremony began.

Twelve young men, each eager to be awarded a wife, arrived on the day, about one week after the call had gone out, from the local towns in the area.

The speaker, Annas, commenced, requesting each young man to bring his staff and lay it in front the altar. The man to whom I would be betrothed would be confirmed through the process known as the budding of Aaron's staff. This would put an end to any objections as to who was to be my appointed life partner, and a betrothal ceremony would be arranged shortly after.

One by one, each man brought in his staff and laid it in front of the altar. When all twelve had placed their staff before the altar, the chief priest waved a bowl of incense in a circular motion in the air, and prayed, "Show us the one whom you have chosen to take the girl, by the budding of Aarons staff." The prayer circle agreed, "So let it be." The curtain was drawn and they were told to wait for the sign to appear.

The men were sent home and asked to return in seven days, allowing time for HaShem to answer. I watched the ceremony and eyed them from a distance, not knowing how this might work out. A level of uncertainty arose and created a pit of angst in my chest. Was I really agreeing to this? I had given my acceptance to Bubbe, but now the time was here I was starting to feel the impact it would have on my life. Did I have a choice in the matter, anyway?

One week later the men returned and gathered on the steps to the temple courts, waiting alongside the elders and priests. A few minutes later, Annas the chief priest arrived and called them together. His crafty smile enacted a sense of purpose was about to be accomplished, and once this was completed they could focus on the rebuilding of the temple without the distraction that I was presenting them.

Motioning to the group, they moved inside the building and the curtain was drawn, allowing each staff to become visible. Inspecting each staff closely, it appeared that none showed any sign to indicate the chosen one. I smiled with glee. Was this confirmation that HaShem did not intend me to leave the temple grounds? I could remain devoted to Him in the Temple and carry out my life call, as I expected to be.

Discussing this amongst themselves, the priests felt that there was something not quite right about the submissions. What might they do to make this plan work? Surely they weren't to keep the girl in the temple courts indefinitely?

The discussions ensued until Annas, having consulted with Caiaphas privately away from the group, drew the bemused men together and shared a story from Israels past.

"Fellow officers of the faith. We may have a shortfall in the men that were called to take part in this ceremony." Confused faces turned towards each other, their trimmed beards wagging as they muttered amongst themselves about what this might mean.

"In the days of the prophet Samuel, Saul had been rejected as king and the Lord was to appoint another in his place. Samuel was told to go to Bethlehem and select one of the sons of Jesse, whom the Lord would reveal." The story was familiar, and showed that divine favour rested not on external appearances — like stature or height — but on whom HaShem selects.

"After having each son appear before the prophet, Samuel felt that the chosen one was not in their midst and asked

Jesse, 'Are these all the sons you have?', to which he replied, 'There is still the youngest, but he's out in the fields watching the sheep and goats.' Samuel said, 'Bring him to me at once.' And when David arrived, the Lord provided confirmation that this was the man selected to be king in place of Saul."

All heads nodded in agreement, the story revealed how divine direction was crucial in the selection of the king of Israel. Annas continued, "It wasn't up to the physical appearance of the sons of Jesse, although Samuel was convinced that any number of his sons could be appointed as king, based on what he saw. Instead HaShem looked at the condition of their hearts to select the right man to fulfil the role. And we know how significant this has been to our nation until this very day."

The group of young men became silent, knowing from this statement that any hope they shared to win the temple girl would amount to nothing. Soon they would all be sent home with empty arms, but before that was to occur, there were more words to be shared.

Annas continued. "We have assumed that the girl, being so young, would be betrothed to a yet unmarried man." Looks of curiosity painted their faces with astonishment, as waves of disbelief swelled in their voices. "However this appears not to be the case. There is not one staff here that has shown the sign we anticipated. So we cannot proceed with this selection of men."

The muttering became louder; confusion created an awkward disturbance in the group. The plan did not deliver the expected result, as had been promised when they signed up. With a hush, and catching the eyes of each man in the room, Annas quieted the men so that they could continue to present details of the revelation. But it was at this point that Caiaphas took over the meeting.

"Friends, traditionally this ceremony is performed only with the single men who have not yet found a wife. However the result has revealed that no-one from this group has been selected. After consideration as to who fits the criteria under our law to marry the girl, it has become apparent that we did not invite the widowers to participate in this divine opportunity."

Once again, the silence was broken and the muttering resumed, with many shaking their heads in disapproval and disappointment of the outcome.

"Friends, I am sorry, but this ceremony must be concluded as we seek to invite another group of men from the district who can fulfil this duty by divine appointment. You may all return to your homes. Thank you for your time and understanding."

With that, the men were dismissed, and the priests conferred together as to how to call the next group together. The decision to halt the ceremony and hold it at this point meant that a new set of requirements had to be established. After some time, towards the end of the day, and before the sun hit the horizon, Annas called a meeting for how the ceremony would proceed back in the nominated room.

"As discussed, and of first importance, the temple girl is not to be handed over to any unholy or irreverent man. You will be required to provide the names of righteous men to ensure that the girl will be treated properly. This is what her parents charged us with when she was dedicated to the work of the temple, ten years ago. So we must find candidates that would be careful to uphold this agreement, so that we can transfer the weight of responsibility onto him."

All agreed that, in most respects, the new round of candidates would need to be known by them and have a demonstrated respect for the activities of the temple. And not only so, but also to hold a reverential respect for the girl.

"Second, he must not only be familiar with the law, but also be worthy to handle the matter of duty with great consideration. This is not a position to be taken lightly. As we accepted the duty of care from her parents, this has been an appointment that must continue once she is betrothed."

Nods of agreement followed, as they anticipated the final conditions.

"Third, whether the man has had children of his own — or none at all — this would not affect the entry criteria. Each man can be considered as a suitable applicant, regardless of the existence of any other children."

"Finally, we will impose no age limit. All men can be encouraged who not only have the desire but also the capability to marry the girl, so long as these first three requirements are met. We would however only want those who are physically capable and who have practical strength to be the man who fulfills this role towards the girl."

The list made sense, and was short enough to be able to encourage enough men to step forward who may consider themselves suitable to take home the bride. Having written out the directions on papyrus, it was distributed to the men to take it to the towns and villages that were no more than a days walk from the temple.

And so the process began once again to find a suitable list of candidates who would one day call me his wife.

Ten days later a gathering occurred in the courts of the temple and the screening process began. I was watching from the sides, this time with Bubbe overshadowing my interest in the men. Some came with their children, though most came alone. It was a long morning as the priests asked many questions, intending to narrow down the list only to those who would meet the criteria for acceptance. It was just before the evening prayers that a small group of eight men were selected to remain and the rest were sent home.

A solemn gathering was assembled and Annas called the men to order to enact the ceremony for a second time.

"Dear friends, we believe you have qualified to participate in the divine ceremony known as the budding of Aaron's staff. Through this process we will see which of you the Lord has chosen to take the young lady known as Mariam, the servant of the Lord. She has been entrusted to our care from a young age by her parents, who have since passed away. It is our duty and responsibility to ensure that she is cared for in the most appropriate way, since she will soon no longer be permitted to assist us in the daily running of the Temple."

The explanation was well known to the men, but to hear it directly from the chief priest at this occasion gave a solemn content and meaning to the group of well-intended men that gathered in the quarters.

Annas continued. "Friends, we invite you to place your staff at the front of the altar. We will wait seven days, and gather again in this place to see who has been chosen. The staff that shows signs of budding will be the one to whom we will delegate the responsibility of the girl."

The men were all smiles as they agreed to this setup. Though tentatively they knew from the former situation with the young unmarried men that this process may not be perfect — there may still be no result.

One by one, they stepped up to the altar and laid their staff, and when all had completed the task the curtain was fastened behind them. They all looked forward to meet together in one week for the final result, and then were sent home.

The evening prayers began, and I was required to assist with temple duties. The thought of my future husband being part of today's group of men began to cloud my head, keeping me from focussing succinctly on my role this evening. I was feeling nervous as to what might happen, given that I had no control of the outcome.

It was another seven nights of anxious wait before the group returned and assembled after the morning prayers and offerings. Would there be a result this time? And if there was none, was I to remain in the temple, as my parents intended?

I was anticipating the same outcome, and secretly hoped and prayed that the priests had misunderstood the situation. In the Temple, I felt I was doing the will of HaShem; to consider anything outside of this was beyond my level of comprehension. However under the care of my appointed foster-mother, Bubbe had shown me a life of self-sacrifice, and I learned to be willing to accept the things that I could not change. "So let it be," she taught, enabling HaShem to perform His will without a fight in any circumstance in which I found myself.

Calling the men together, Annas gave a small briefing as to what might happen when the staffs were revealed in just a few moments from now. I slid into the side hallway near the front, just within earshot of what was being spoken, to capture their reactions when the curtain was drawn aside. Some of these men I had often encountered at the Temple due to their diligence in respecting the laws and regulations,

and I had only met others at occasional ceremonies. All
were single, older men who had lost their wife. Some had
children, some had none. All looked physically strong and
capable — according the regulations that had been adopted
for this second round. If it were up to me, I would not
know who I should choose. So let it be.

The tension in the room grew as silence prevailed. Only
their breathing was heard in anticipation as Annas stepped
up to unclip the holds. Sunlight from a nearby window
made the curtains shimmer, reflecting the deep blue and
purple embroidered threads in the daylight as they were
drawn aside. All eight staffs lay on the ground with the
sun's rays splashing on them, bathed in a golden swathe of
natural divine glow.

The men edged closer to take a look, leaving me to stretch
and see if any staff had budded according to the tradition
of Aaron, or if I was free to remain as the temple girl
forever. This was not something that I was looking forward
to, and my heart clanged loudly in my chest waiting for
an outcome. What would he be like? Would I really have
to submit to a man, when I have already promised myself
wholeheartedly to HaShem?

Annas bent down, picked up a staff, and held it in full view
of everyone to see, who by this time started to pull back. The
staff had indeed budded, showing a growth of leaves and
flowers from the top of the stem, revealing HaShem's chosen
man from the ceremony. Seven others remained unchanged.

A sense of awe filled the room, with the miracle in plain
sight for all to see. This was no ordinary answer to prayer.
This was, as had been hoped, a direct answer from heaven
which would change the course of history forever. That is,
my own history!

The priest eyed everyone to gain their full attention, and then stopped at one man to call his name. By now my heart was racing, and had to accept that the priests had heard correctly about my betrothal, which would result in my exit from the Temple. Unconsciously, I bit my nails which snapped loudly in my mouth, creating a shock wave that made me fully alert.

"Joseph, come forward."

The circle widened to allow him through. A quiet cheer and hand claps rose from the small gathering. The eyes of the priests focused in. This was the one who was going to take responsibility for their girl and become the betrothed.

The unsuccessful others could only look down, attempting to hide their disappointment at failing to win a wife.

"Friend, she is yours. Please come back in ten days, and we will arrange the ceremony."

With a look of gratitude, and some sense of trembling, Joseph nodded in agreement. "Thank you. I will."

Taking a breath to puff his chest, he also looked down to avoid eye contact with the others and then headed out the door. I had been away from the scene to quietly watch the outcome and avoid being involved in any way.

Within seconds I realised that Joseph was heading straight towards me, I had not moved from the entrance. At this point I could not run, and kept my arms covered near my side as he approached to leave.

Stopping just short of me, together we allowed our eyes to connect. For me, this unusual feeling of being observed and admired was not something that I was used to. Our worlds were so different, there was a lot that I needed to learn before the betrothal ceremony. Who was this man standing before me? Was this really the will of HaShem to get me to care for a man whom I knew absolutely nothing about?

Our gaze seemed to last for a while, though in reality it may have only been the span of three or four shallow breaths where a world of thoughts circled my mind within. Finally, Joseph found purpose beyond our immediate encounter, and gave me a gentle nod.

"Mariam," he spoke softly, almost stammering. I shuffled slightly to the right, into the hallway, indicating that the gap to the door was freely available; I didn't want to force him to stay with me any longer than he ought to.

"Joseph," I said in response to his greeting, and broke our connection by looking down to his feet. I kept my head bowed as he moved past me through the door and out to the open courtyard. Without looking back, he continued off the grounds to make his way home.

The next ten days would give us both time to prepare for what was to come, though I still had misgivings about it.

Finally, taking a deep breath and straightening up, I searched for Bubbe who I saw at a table outside and headed her way.

She would know what happens from here.

There were many things to discuss.

Chapter 5

Waiting

The nine days that followed created a stir in my thoughts and dreams, leaving me with butterflies in my stomach that did not want to land. I had never felt pressured to take on things beyond my level of control, even when my parents had passed me into the care of the temple priests at such a young age.

The appointment was changing the course of my life significantly, and I was hesitant to accept that this was all part of HaShem's plan just yet — though the miracle of the budding staff confirmed that His hand was divinely creating a path in this direction. I was sifting through a wide range of emotions before accepting what lay ahead, though a quiet peace overshadowed me, allowing me to continue to process the everyday things in an orderly way.

Bubbe assisted me to sort through my belongings — not that I had much to wear, or many possessions to my name — in anticipation that I would need to carry whatever I could hold to take with me on my exit journey from the Temple grounds. My life was simple, as was my duty to perform the functions allocated me on a daily basis. I did not need jewellery, nor any fashionable clothes, and I had just two pairs of sandals: one that catered for official duties in the Temple precinct, and the other worn outside the grounds.

"Bubbe, what is it like being married?" I asked.

My young mind had not entertained the thought of boys, though my developing body indicated to me that changes were ahead. I would need to learn how to embrace the role of a married woman as the child-bearer of society, amongst other things.

She smiled, knowing that I would not be able to understand more than the immediate preparations, and began the conversation starting with the required formalities.

"Mariam, tomorrow we will attend the *kiddushin* with you. The ceremony itself will be kept brief, as in your case you do not have your father here to give consent to the arrangement. This has been delegated to the priests, and they will allocate a suitable guide to assist in this matter."

This was not in any way a reflection of a normal betrothal. Usually the groom would approach the parents of the bride with the proposal to marry, with a bag of coins containing gold or silver as the bride price. In my case, I was not sure if a dowry would be paid, and if so, who would receive it?

Bubbe continued. "Then, after consent has been granted, which in your case has already been decided by divine lot, then the *ketubbah* — the formal agreement — will be produced. This document lists the terms of the marriage, and once signed, it is assumed that you will be married in the eyes of everyone."

This first stage is a legally binding agreement and commitment between the couple, but they are not allowed to live together, and certainly no depth of intimacy is allowed. The second stage of the marriage ceremony would take place about a year later, allowing the groom sufficient time to put things in place and prepare a home.

"The *ketubbah* includes the terms of settlement for divorce, if required, and would only be allowed if either of the couple were known to be involved in another relationship. If that happens, the bride price would be refunded, and they would be allowed to divorce. This however takes serious discussions with the bride's parents, and it cannot be done in haste. So it rarely occurs."

I had never heard of anyone going through a divorce. There was a level of shame and disgrace associated with this, and it was seldom talked about. If the intent to marry was not followed through with propriety, it would bring upset on the two families and the community would find it difficult to live together harmoniously. So this was considered a legally binding agreement where both parties would not be able to turn back, once the *kiddushin* had taken place.

Our betrothal was quite unlike any other — with my parents already passed away there was no-one to provide consent to the marriage, so the dowry would not be received by my father. On Joseph's side he was already an older man, his wife having died some time previously, and with children of his own. He already had a house in the rocky hills of Nazareth in the north, though it had been taken over by a majority of Gentiles. There was no need for him to do much in the way of preparations, so it would be acceptable for us to marry when I had come of age. And like other girls my age, that time was approaching fast, it seemed.

Understanding this, led to my next question. "So … where should we live from tomorrow? The priests won't want me in the temple any longer." I was unsure about the arrangements, and having a deeper clarity about the next steps would make it easier for me to understand what might take place.

Bubbe hesitated, the question catching her almost off guard, as if she was the one who had undertaken the preparations and it had not been added to her list of things to do. She dropped the towel she was folding onto the bed, and stared into the ceiling as if to gain inspiration. Was this going to be a rushed marriage so that the natural course of events could be sped up? I was expecting a more instant reply, but it did not seem to come quickly. After an extended time she offered a suggestion, though she made it clear that this was her own idea and not a word that she received from above.

"Tomorrow, after the *kiddushin*, we will collect your items from this room. You will spend your final night here tonight. Mariam, you will need to say good-bye to your old life and this place, and be prepared for change in your new life. You won't need to return here anytime soon."

Clearly she was avoiding my question, reinforcing the process while trying to work through the practicalities in how this might work. I let her continue, as she often brought forward words of wisdom that provided a clearer picture though I could not see past tomorrows impending formalities, and the living arrangement that would be required.

"Normally, the ceremony would not be held at the Temple or a synagogue, but this arrangement with you is different and the priests considered that this would provide an ideal location to celebrate your work here amongst them.

During the ceremony they will seek to bless you both, being sanctified toward each other for the purposes of marriage."

The course of my life was unfolding one word at a time, though it was slow for me to grasp it in its entirety. I took a seat on the mattress and tugged on Bubbe's sleeve, trying to get her to focus more clearly on answering my question. Whether this worked or not, I am not sure, as she continued to work through a course of events which would be followed by any normal couple, as was the situation when she was married many years ago. She pressed in with more details, and tried to clear the path for me to accept what she was saying.

"Tomorrow, the *kiddushin*. Then when he is ready, the *nissuin* — your formal marriage ceremony."

"Yes Bubbe, but when? And where will we live from tomorrow night? How are we to live together, and yet apart?"

My mind was searching for answers while my heart panged at the thought that I was entering into a period which might put my holy calling in jeopardy. What if he was to take advantage of me before we were married? I panted with exasperation with so many unanswered questions, uncertain as to whether I wanted to hear it anyway.

She spoke softly, reassuring me that I could put away my anxiety.

"My daughter, there is no need for angst, it will all unfold naturally. Joseph will have thought about all this, and I am sure he will honour you in the sight of HaShem and the community."

I wanted to believe her kind and encouraging words, she was my overseer and trusted friend — and she spoke from experience. I breathed out slowly, closed my eyes, and prayed for a clear mind.

When I looked up again, she continued. I was clear of mind, but my heart was set to flee.

"There is no need to hold a burdened heart. This will be a time of joy for you. And it's the next stage of your life calling, so you need not be afraid."

She stopped abruptly when she realised that her words had broken through my shield of caution, as though I had accepted them as a word from heaven.

"It's the next stage of your life calling," she repeated.

I swallowed and cleared my throat.

This was not the answer I was seeking, but it became clear that I needed to hear it.

"Mariam," Bubbe wrapped her arm around my shoulder, gently rubbing back and forth in an act of consolation to give me assurance, which gained my attention.

"Trust HaShem. He is faithful. He has called you to be together. There is no reason to be afraid. Trust HaShem."

Fighting within myself, Bubbe's words calmed me, and I surrendered my thoughts to accept the things that I could not change. Stepping into a pose of submission, and looking to my beautifully mannered and godly mentor, my mother for the last ten years, I accepted this as a word from HaShem.

I wanted to show her that despite my lack of involvement in the decision process, that I would embrace it without causing a disruption. My inner conflict would need to submit to my decision to follow the will of HaShem.

Breathing out slowly, and then fluffing my hair as I exhaled my last puff, I responded. "Tomorrow, I will betroth Joseph. I will be his. And he will be mine. And we will walk this path together — wherever HaShem calls us."

Bubbe smiled, and drew me in to herself with a reassuring embrace. She drew me in and simply held me by her side, as if to suggest that this was part of our final good byes. Her warm and tender arms wrapped around me until they grew tired, letting them drop by her side. Scruffing my fringe with her hand, she wanted to brighten the mood — it's not as though someone should have died — and confessed, "I think I am going to miss you around here."

Certainly I would miss our times together; there was no line between our work and our personal lives. Both of us had been drawn to live and work in the Temple, and through it our lives had been enriched.

Dappled light broke through the open window, lighting on the folded clothes and other belongings that were now wrapped in towels on the bed, forming two bundles that could be tied onto the back of a mule for our journey after the ceremony. Only the bedding needed to be wrapped into a bundle, to make it easy to carry and be kept clean.

"Tomorrow. Tomorrow!"

So let it be.

Chapter 6

~Preparations~

The day of our betrothal arrived and I noticed a distinct change in the air, which I took to indicate that a new season in my life was about to begin. I didn't sleep too badly, and despite my thoughts my heart seemed to rest. But before the ceremony there were our usual chores to complete — assisting with the morning offering, ensuring that the grounds were tidy, and to be prepared for service if any priests called for assistance. The *kiddushin* was planned for the fourth hour of the day, that is, four hours after sunrise.

My room started to feel empty and small, even lonely, despite living here for the last ten years — it was where I called 'home' for so long. And the place where we were heading after the ceremony was not yet revealed to me, though Bubbe assured me that it would all unfold succinctly and to simply trust that Joseph would have it all under control.

Laid out on my bed were my service clothes which I would wear for the last time, and when I had finished the mornings duties these would be handed to Bubbe for someone else's use. The long dress had been specifically designed for duties around the temple, and had been extended each year to cater for my growth spurts, until a new one was required. Indeed this was my fourth dress while here, and I embraced it with humility as an act of service. But now this dress would no longer be needed as I left the temple to became a woman bound to a future husband.

The difference in my daily clothes would be a constant reminder and an outward expression of my change of role in society. My sandals also, would remain. That is, my service sandals for use in the temple. As they were not allowed outside the walls of the precinct, these would remain for others who could use them. I would only be taking my outside sandals, and would wear them during the *kiddushin*.

Other young ladies had recently been betrothed, and I smiled to myself when I realised that their hair was fashioned beautifully in a braid and intertwined with fresh flowers, giving off an aroma over the couple during the ceremony. Although I could have planned for this, I felt that there really was no need to go to any trouble with my appearance. I liked being 'plain'; to me there was nothing to gain with braided hair, wearing fine clothes or pearls. What mattered was a pure heart, and I did not want to draw attention to myself in any way, though Bubbe assured me that I was already a genuinely beautiful young woman.

The priests had provided me with a fresh linen tunic, with an additional handspan of length — rolled up and sewn at the base, which made it a little bottom heavy — that would be let down in the event that I was to grow any taller. It graced me from head to toe and kept me both warm and modest. A woven reed belt was also provided that kept the tunic together at my waist, though when it was hot this could be removed to allow air to circulate.

An outer garment, a cloak, woven with wool from the sheep in Bethlehem, was also provided, that I would use in the cooler months as a second layer to keep me warm. Finally, a veil, this one made of linen to keep things light, was provided to cover my head and shoulders — mainly for modesty. Together this completed the picture of the new me, and would be my daily dress until we settled and other clothes could be acquired.

My time of contemplation was broken with the ring of Bubbe's voice echoing through the door, announcing her arrival. "Mariam, today's the day!" She walked briskly into my room, halted at my bed, and eyed me up and down to check how things were progressing. After a short inspection, her outstretched arm on my shoulder indicated that there was something on her mind. So I stopped, pausing for her to speak. Instead she sat down on the bed, drawing me to her level to share what was on her mind.

"This morning you have been given back time, and are not required to attend to morning duties. Instead, they want you to prepare for the ceremony, since it is your day of betrothal." My service clothes lay neatly next to me, ready to be used for the last time. But now they were no longer required. I felt a mixed sense of relief and loss, indicating that my service here had already been completed. I drew a deep breath, and looked up to Bubbe, who was waiting for my response — though I was confused as to what to reply.

This meant that I now had time to myself, though I needed no additional preparation time as my new clothes were ready also. A short bucket wash would provide me enough time to slip into my undergarment and into the fresh tunic. My sandals were already well worn, and completed the picture. And I would fasten the veil to cover not just my head and hair, but for this event it would also cover my face.

"I'll get ready soon," motioning to Bubbe that it wouldn't take long, though instinctively she knew that I was already pre-prepared for the event. The bells rang out across the Temple grounds, indicating that the morning offering was to begin. Bubbe rose to leave, but before departing she wanted to share with me her closing thoughts.

"Today will be a beautiful day, made just for you." Her gracious smile and tone, full of encouragement and wisdom, wrapped around my heart in ways that I did not want to see unwind.

"Mariam, it has been an honour to train you in the ways of HaShem, and for service in the Temple."

Her gaze firmed up, capturing my full attention. This woman of dignity embellished me with her life of humility, faith and perseverance, displaying depth and strength that formed the foundation for my own spiritual growth.

"You have been made for this."

And with that, she was off to fulfill her calling.

Chapter 7

~Kiddushin~

People started to gather in the temple courts in the break after morning prayers had been completed. Chimes rang out across the grounds to indicate that the ceremony would begin shortly, and an attendant ushered the handful of religious community and guests in to the Chamber of Hewn Stones, the meeting place for the Sanhedrin. This room was attached to the rebuilt temple, and was partly embedded into the northern wall of the Temple mount. It had been used for the divine appointment of the budding of Aaron's staff, where Joseph received the charge to take me as his betrothed.

I had not seen Joseph enter, though I was assured that he was already inside awaiting my arrival. I expected none of my direct family to be in attendance, so I was pleasantly surprised to see my cousin Elizabeth and Zechariah waiting patiently near the door for my arrival. Zechariah had been informed of the betrothal from the network of community leaders, and mentioned this to Elizabeth just before the last full moon. Having received confirmation of the date for the ceremony, they both wanted to be there for the event.

Elizabeth was my closest family member that remained in contact with me during my early years and we shared a special bond. Like Bubbe, she held a deep respect for Jewish law, and lived an honourable life in this respect. Zechariah was a member of the priestly order of Abijah, which was required to periodically carry out duties, as arranged by the Sanhedrin's religious calendar.

Before entering the building, we made a point of greeting each other with an embrace The ceremony would follow shortly, and I was unsure when we would see each other again after that. It felt so good that they could be here with me, which helped settle the butterflies in my stomach.

And then it was time.

Unusually, there were no seats set up in this building today. It was large enough to handle the number of people in attendance with ease, and they shared small talk amongst themselves until I came to the entrance. A hush ensued at my presence, as I waited for a sign from the officiator to welcome me in. There was no-one to walk me into the room.

The kiddushin is never usually held at the Temple, nor a synagogue, the exception being mine in this case, although we weren't actually inside the Temple but in a building next door. It was large enough to cater for the 71 Sanhedrin that were present, plus family and others who were there to assist. All up, the group numbered 83.

The seats had been pushed back against the walls to allow for a quick ceremony, creating an atmosphere which urged everyone to complete their duty and enable them to return to their daily life as soon as possible. This was not an extravagant affair, more of a formality.

As silence ensued, I was scanning the room from the doorway and found Joseph towards the centre, enclosed by the men, and some women, who routinely came to the temple.

Other than my cousin, the only other family I had in attendance was Bubbe, and she was quietly off to one side near the front of the room as if to assist with the ceremony. With a slow and gracious nod, the officiator welcomed me in to stand near Joseph, so I shuffled to the centre of the room to stand by his side. I could hear every beat of my heart resounding in my ears as I waited for the quietness to break and the ceremony to begin.

It's as if time stood still.

Standing next to Joseph — we had only briefly met during the selection period — I did not realise how tall he was, as I had been watching him mostly from a distance. But here, in this moment, standing next to him to be his future wife, he was a good arm length taller than my frame. I was impressed, and felt a sense of security next to his side. Gratitude started to rise within me as I thanked HaShem for providing a man who at least looked like one who had the stature to take care of me. Especially since I had not ventured into the world beyond the temple for any length of time.

He was well-dressed and looked handsome in his modest flowing tunic that also appeared to be as fresh as mine. I could see the strong muscles of his arms and the outline of his shoulders although he was much older than me. My thoughts of marrying an old widower were waning, and I began to grow in confidence.

I looked up with a brief stare to capture his attention.

He smiled and lowered his head to a tilt, giving me confirmation to proceed.

We were really going ahead.

The officiator, seeing that we were ready, motioned with a raised hand.

Scanning all eyes within the room, the ceremony began.

"Friends, welcome to the kiddushin as witnesses for the betrothal of Joseph, the one chosen by divine lot and appointment, to our temple girl, Mariam, who has assisted faithfully in her duties here for the last ten years."

The gathering focussed in on Joseph and myself, with smiles from the elderly men breaking through their beards. I had grown to know most of them through assisting them with errands in the temple, at some point or another. They looked genuinely happy to proceed.

"As you are aware, we received Mariam as a gift entrusted to our care by her parents, who dedicated her to service in the Temple. She has been the Lord's servant here in many ways amongst us and we have been blessed with her aid during this time. As she is now coming of age, we felt it best to find her a suitable husband from among the eligible men in Israel. After many weeks of searching and beseeching the Lord, it was revealed that the man before us today, Joseph, is the chosen vessel for this task to marry the bride."

All agreed that Joseph fit the candidate requirements to make a suitable husband, and that the appointment could only have been a result of the divine answer from heaven. Their heads nodded in agreement with a hushed murmur from the pious crowd, as we waited for the officiations to continue.

"Now let us begin the ceremony. Joseph, would you like to start by offering a gift?"

Accepting the invitation, he turned to his friend next to him. This was to be the symbol of Josephs love and commitment to me. I would treasure it until he prepared a place for us to live during the *erusin* period — the year or so that it would take to establish a home for us, while waiting for the day that we would be married.

The grooms friend produced a ring, gold and shiny, though worn, and handed it to Joseph. This was not the first time that he would hold the hand of a young woman, having done so many years ago. With the presentation of the ring came his claim of ownership on me, something that I had not heard before, or expected to be said, in front of all the witnesses present.

He stretched out his hand to invite me to be his betrothed.

I lifted my right hand so that he could place the ring onto my finger, and, gently taking my hand into his, he spoke words of consecration over me.

"Behold, you are consecrated to me with this ring, according to the law of Moses and Israel."

We took a moment to commemorate this first act of togetherness, lifting my eyes to meet his as the ring slid gently on.

I was later to understand that this was the ring he had given to his first wife, but it had originally been the ring forged by his grandfather that was presented to his grandmother, on the day of their betrothal many, many years ago. This had been passed down from one generation to the next, three generations of father-son relationships that had pledged their commitment to their betrothed, who would later become their wives, through this ring. It therefore held significant family heritage, and was a testimony to be kept by the wife for later generations. Today the ring represented the pledge, demonstrating Josephs' commitment to love and care for me.

The officiator allowed us a moment, but wanted to continue in a more efficient manner that would step through the process and allow them to move onto other duties for the rest of the day.

With a voice of authority, he called. "Please, distribute the wine."

Bubbe stepped forward, bringing to us two cups of red wine that had been prepared and were resting on the solitary table that remained inside the room. We accepted the gift, lifted the cups to our lips, and shared them together. This first drink demonstrated a life commitment, which would bring two separate lives together as one.

This was the first time that I had tasted wine, and the strong flavour filled my cheeks in a way that I could not have been prepared for, rising out of my nostrils and forcing me to exhale. I drew a deep breath to replace the aromatic flavour in my mouth. I caught sight of Elizabeth, who gave a small chuckle, trying to keep herself composed so as not to disrupt the flow of proceedings. After exhaling in a more controlled fashion, I straightened up and we continued.

Today, everything felt different and new.

Notably, the only thing I felt was missing was my own parents, having died some years previous. If mother was alive today, would she have approved? Would father have been there to bless us with gifts of clothing, jewellery and other items to send us on our way together?

I could not arrive at an answer to the questions that were now circulating in my mind. Caught in this moment, I had drifted out of the present, offsetting the path that I felt would have been a more natural outcome. But this ceremony was not a normal event, and I had grown not to expect a normal way of life, like others my age.

As the taste of wine lingered, Joseph stepped up and brought forward the *mohar* — the financial gift that would normally have been provided to my parents as part of the betrothal. In this case, the mohar would be presented to the temple, being the place to which I was entrusted when my parents dedicated me to the Lord. A small sum of coins — tied neatly inside a leather bag — was offered, received by the officiator, who then passed it on to Bubbe who was standing nearby. Although she was not the treasurer, she would ensure that it would be placed in the right hands after the ceremony.

Lastly, the *ketubbah* was presented to all in the form of a scroll that listed the terms of our betrothal, and future marriage. Those present would be the witnesses — and also the ones that would be our judges if either of us were to be unfaithful during our betrothal period. In this case, the entire Sanhedrim along with a handful of family members and close friends were present. This was legally binding, and if found guilty the penalties could lead to death. But usually, any form of infidelity led to a divorce and infused disapproval from society. As such, this made the commitment difficult to break, and ensured that both parties were bound to do the right thing until the marriage would take place.

At that point Joseph stared hard, his eyes penetrating into the depths of my soul, and announced this vow, "… and if either of us turn away to another, or found to be with child from another, then we will be loosed from all marital rites or obligations."

Silence.

Although this was implied as part of the ceremony, it was not typically a written form of the agreement.

An uncomfortable air developed, the faces of the encircling men not knowing whether this was part of an infused act in the scene, or if what Joseph was saying was intended to be included.

It just 'happened'.

Finally the officiator closed the ceremony, and gave the indication that the betrothed could now leave the building.

Holding hands, we faced the array of witnesses and guests, and proceeded with a low bow towards them and each other. We were met with a round of applause, and a path opened up so we may exit the building through the door that I had entered just ten minutes earlier.

Pausing briefly, I wanted to capture the moment, realising that it would not last forever, or be repeated. Elizabeth's eyes were wet with tears, and Zechariah had his arm around her shoulder as an act of support. Together they were quite old, having been married for many years, but were without children.

Bubbe faced me with an affectionate smile from across the room that hid something deeper that she was holding on to, creating in a me a curiosity that would not be answered at this moment. We would have to speak at a later stage about that, I reasoned.

As the group widened further, we headed out the door into the sunlight.

Officially, we were betrothed.

The next steps I would take were a mystery.

Chapter 8

~Bethlehem~

The bright sunlight bathed us in a natural golden glow
as we exited the building, its warmth shrouded us with
approval. Although I did not know what to expect from
here on, I had to let Joseph take the lead to handle the
events that were likely to arise in the next twelve months.
We both knew the importance of taking the vows seriously,
and how it would look in the eyes of the community if we
were to break them in any way.

A donkey had been prepared and was standing with my
packs tied up and already in place. I learned later that
Bubbe had secretly collected my things in the short space
of time before the start of the ceremony, and passed them
onto a friend to load up. This included my bags that were
bundled in cloths, my bedding and other small items.

The donkey was loaded with as much as it could handle,
and I blushed at the totality of possessions that I had

acquired. There was therefore no need for me to return to my room to collect anything, the items that were to remain were for exclusive use within the temple, and would be passed on to another in the course of time.

Joseph broke my hesitant stance, motioning with his hand to indicate that our journey would proceed for the half day walk to Bethlehem. We expected to arrive in the early afternoon, well before dark, which was important as the following day was to be a Sabbath and no-one was to walk further than the permitted 2,000 cubits else they would face accusations of working on the Lord's day. The Sabbath commenced once the sun fell below the horizon, which meant that the journey could be made safely in time, with my possessions loaded on the back of the donkey.

The path to Bethlehem was not straight like the other roads that the Romans were working on between the other major towns throughout Judea. This continued to be a well-worn track, beaten down through the upper layer of dirt over hundreds of years. The nostalgia of our fore-fathers formed part of the area that we were travelling through, and I had seldom ventured abroad outside the temple grounds, other than to visit Elizabeth who lived about a day's journey from me in the Judean countryside, where I was escorted to stay for a night every so often.

Our first real time together began on this journey. It allowed me to ask the questions that were burning in my mind, and which Bubbe instructed me to 'just trust' Joseph to work it out. Once we had left the city limits and felt comfortable to talk, I proceeded with my enquiry.

"Joseph," I was hesitant and didn't want to assume that I could talk without permission. However there was no rebuke, and his eyes confirmed that I could continue.

"When I was at the temple, Bubbe told me to implicitly put my trust in you, assuring me that everything would work out. And I do, that is — I do trust that you have everything under control — though I have some questions about where we might be staying until we are married."

The *erusin* period, the time in waiting, was the usual time of preparation for the bride to make wedding garments and to get ready for married life. The marriage ceremony itself, the *nissuin*, would be celebrated when the couple were ready to come together, and usually celebrated through their consummation, which signified the end of the *kiddushin* period. There was going to be not an insignificant amount of time that we were to remain holy and separate, dedicated to each other until Joseph would announce the *nissuin*.

Understanding my concerns, Joseph took my hand and kissed it gently, his beard rough on my skin.

There was nothing to be frightened about.

"Mariam, I did not know that the Lord would respond to the budding of my staff the way He did. I was not in any way expecting this result, and am quite surprised at the outcome, to be honest."

This was when I learned that Joseph was not eager or expecting to be betrothed to me, and I felt slightly alarmed at hearing it from his lips. After seeing the disappointment on the faces of the young unmarried men who had attempted to win my hand the first time, I had assumed that every man partaking in the ceremony had the same level of desire towards me as the rest. Apparently, I was wrong.

When Joseph received the call for widowers to be part of the second round, he did not rush to sign up immediately. He had been taking leave from his home town when the invitation was sent out, having stayed with relatives in

Bethlehem to grieve through the passing of his first wife. He was hesitant because he was already raising children of his own, who were still under his care, and was not sure that he wanted to marry again, though he was encouraged by others to be part of the application, as maybe that would take his mind off things? I was to learn of all this later. In short, he was ill-prepared and somewhat reluctant but felt obliged to respond anyway.

To his surprise, the outcome raised questions that he could not bring up with me at the time. His staff had indeed budded in front of all the officials, and he was charged to follow through with it.

It turned out that this was an unexpected journey for both of us.

We shared a mutual silence for several hundred paces as we worked through our own emotional responses to the way the betrothal had come about. Had we been pushed into this? Surely, this was the hand of the Lord when Aaron's staff budded to signify the assignment of Joseph as my betrothed. Were the priests really forced to push me out of the temple to keep it pure, as they had told me?

Finally, Joseph continued the conversation, which started to provide me a new level of assurance that the steps we were taking were going to be accepted by our community. We wanted to live right before everyone, not just in the sight of HaShem.

"We are not far from Bethlehem. I have relatives there who have offered to provide us accommodation. They understand that we are in the *erusin* period, and have therefore arranged separate rooms for us. We will stay there for two nights, and then we will continue to travel on to Nazareth."

I breathed an immediate sigh of relief.

The few early years of my life growing up in Nazareth seemed like such a long time ago, and it was where my parents returned to once their time had finished in Jerusalem. This was a place of grief, where they were to settle to see out their final days, and take rest away from the hurtful crowd. They did not know at the time that they would someday be holding a young baby in their arms, who would be their child of promise — their longing fulfilled. I was an unexpected gift.

The trip to Nazareth is one that I had never planned to take; indeed, I had not travelled any further than Elizabeth's place in Judea. This would become a new adventure for me, though in my mind I was still the Temple girl. I had to learn to let go, and it would take time to adjust.

Further, I did not have opportunity to visit Bethlehem, either, despite its close proximity to Jerusalem.

Joseph continued. "My relatives were born and raised in Bethlehem, and are descendants of the line of King David, who, as you would know, was once a shepherd in those hills." He was pointing with an elevated arm towards the distant hills which had been cleared of trees some generations previous to this, and which provided a good amount of grass and protection on the slopes. He stroked his beard to contemplate how this might relate to our current situation, thinking things over, but without words.

I had hoped to meet Josephs family at some point in time, and didn't realise that our first day together would provide an opportunity to do so, especially since none came to the celebration earlier in the day. I smiled at the chance to live a normal life like other girls my age, rather than be tied to the courts where I served. I looked forward to being part of a loving family that could take us in, even if it was going to be just for the two nights, as he said.

We passed through the town square, where merchants were starting to close their stalls as the day drew to an end. It would be inappropriate to attend the house and bring nothing, so we stopped to pick up bread, fresh fruit and a half a hin of olive oil. This would be gifts to contribute to the meal with this family who would adopt me as one of their own, in a way.

That evening we were greeted with open arms, kisses and formalities to welcome us to their humble abode. Over the meal I faced an inquisition that led me to share how I was working in the Temple courts since I was a small child. They listened with interest as I told them how I assisted on site with offerings, keeping things tidy, and generally being available when help was required. I found it nice to be called "Joseph's wife" even though we were only betrothed.

They understood the importance of handling the *erusin* period with utmost care, and in that short time they became my self-appointed guardians to uphold my cause. Laughing heartily, they joked to Joseph that his room was out in the back stall with the donkeys and sheep, because they couldn't keep both of us under the same roof. I had never experienced such warmth of family love till now, other than from my own Elizabeth — whom I knew cared deeply for me.

Finally we found rest, and I was awaked to the shrill of a rooster outside the window where I had been sleeping. I jumped awake. A morning call like this was not something that I was used to, and I didn't want to become familiar with it either. Where did my peaceful life go?

By the time I dragged myself up from the floor mattress and slipped into yesterday's tunic, a fire had been kindled and the aroma of burning olive timber permeated the low-set building. For my first morning away, this gave me a satisfying sense of freedom as I slowed my breath to infuse my lungs with the scent. I was to learn that Joseph's family and relatives were builders, and the kindling was the result of offcuts from projects that were no longer required.

The two nights and days blended into each other, and eventually our joyous time together came to an end. As the new week began we packed to head to Nazareth, which was to be five more days of walking, with donkey loaded as before, until we reached our destination.

My heart released a sense of sadness as we departed, possibly because I was leaving a newly established family relationship that accepted me without question, and had been close to where I was living until now. I also felt slightly emotional that, once we were to arrive in Nazareth, the *erusin* period could take twelve months or more until nissuin. This seemed to be an extraordinary amount of time to wait, although there were no signs yet of my coming of age, and it would be more than inappropriate for Joseph to become my husband until my body had sufficiently changed.

We were not planning to return to Bethlehem anytime soon.

The five days ahead of us would get us to Nazareth before the Sabbath, so we said our goodbyes and hugged, then commenced the journey.

With chin raised and chest determined, we pushed on.

Chapter 9

~Nazareth~

These few days travelling together gave us our first real sense of appreciation for the calling that was on us. It was obvious that we came from distinctly different paths, and from an earthly perspective this would be considered a very unlikely union, if we were given a choice in the matter.

But we resolved that HaShem's plans were higher than our plans, and His ways are higher than our ways.

We had to allow HaShem to be HaShem.
We had to learn to keep in step with Him.

Believing that our marriage was ordained from heaven, we continued to travel as a soon-to-be married couple to live in the region of Galilee.

From Bethlehem we travelled north of Jerusalem to reach Jericho, where we stayed the night and gathered supplies for the journey ahead. The trip between Bethlehem and

Nazareth was shorter and more direct to go through Samaria, however a more comfortable route, with loaded donkey, was to walk along the low lying plains of the Jordan River, despite the extra distance. It gave us a measure of protection as well, since bandits often pounced on travellers along the Samaritan route and were not as present along the Jordan.

On our first real night alone, Joseph found some basic accommodation consisting of two separate rooms. In Jericho, the hotel was used to hosting betrothed couples, but there would usually be a chaperone in attendance so as to avoid situations such as this. Once we were beyond Jericho we would have nothing but our own integrity to live by, I reasoned. We knew that HaShem had arranged the components of this marriage into which we were called to be active participants, and had sworn to uphold the sanctity of our betrothal vows to each other and to our witnesses.

Jericho, known this day as the city of palms, was more renowned as the city whose walls were crushed by Joshua upon entry to the promised land. As part of the defeat, Joshua released a curse on the firstborn son of the man who was to lay the foundation stone to rebuild the walls of Jericho, and a second curse on the youngest son when the gates would be installed. Miraculously the curses came true upon a man named Hiel, and both his children were killed, wiping out his entire lineage. We were therefore keen to ensure that there would be no reason for curses to be called down on us from these people. This was no place to stay for any length of time, given its history.

Before we departed, Joseph arrived with some fresh bread and small goods that would be enough to see us through to Bethshan, a town at the entrance to the Jordan Valley where we would stay on the fourth night. He also arrived back at the inn with a chaperone, who would accompany us for the two nights along the valley route. This would provide us with assistance, if required, and also kept us in a position of honesty.

The second and third nights were quiet with the stars shining brightly as we camped along the foreshore with a fire. After the second night under the stars we paid and dismissed the chaperone who returned back to Jericho, as we travelled on to find an inn at Bethshan. Thankfully, Joseph was able to locate separate rooms. We would need a good rest before departing on the final leg of the journey, given that it was the longest and steepest part of the expedition to date. We managed to eat and sleep quite well that night, fully prepared for the day ahead.

From here, our last day would take us through Jezreel, before ascending the hills to arrive at Nazareth by evening. As we started on our way, Joseph shared that there were several significant events in this valley that shaped our nation.

The first was Gideon's victory over the Midianites, who were camped as numerous as grasshoppers on the open plains and had assembled to destroy our nation. In response Gideon led a small band of just 300 men during the night with trumpets and bright lights, smashing clay jars with a shout "A sword for the Lord, and for Gideon!" In terror, the enemy slaughtered each other, and the threat of attack dissolved without further incident.

The second story of significance involved the death of an innocent man, Naboth, who was being pressured to sell his vineyard to King Ahab by his evil wife, Jezebel. She had orchestrated the murder of the prophets of HaShem and introduced Baal worship in Israel. As a result, Elijah had prophesied the death of Jezebel in the land of Jezreel, and the end of Ahab's reign as king.

The history stirred in us a sense of discomfort while traversing the area, and we were sure not to delay our travels. We needed to arrive without fear or incident, and locate a place to stay for the evening. Perhaps I might have a relative that could host us for the evening? Not that anyone knew that I was coming, that is.

Nazareth was a rocky and mountainous town located on a hill with a hollow basin. Mount Tabor was in the distant south east. We were enclosed by terraced hills and pasture, and visibly known for its olive groves. The town itself was a mixture of Jews and Gentiles, though more Gentiles than Jews at this stage, that managed to live together with a level of harmony. The Gentiles had come from the north and settled in Nazareth hundreds of years prior to our arrival, and offset the once Jewish community with their traditions and religious practises. From time to time there was a spirit of unrest and unease between the competing cultures, though for the most part they were tolerant towards each other.

Puffing as we made the last hundred paces up the rocky terrain, we stopped to take in the sights of the small village that was called Nazareth. My first impressions were that there really wasn't much here — no impressive buildings like the capital where I was brought up, and only a few people in view in the fields. Joseph was squinting to locate someone that he might recognise, but I was not sure who that might be. There had been no mention of family in this region, other than my own parents living here before they passed on. So I was surprised when Joseph led the way, pointing to a small cottage in the distance, where we were to attend.

"Over there, that's where we are going." Although the sun was still above the horizon, the cottage was nestled in a ticket of trees, and smoke emanated from a chimney to indicate that the evening meal was being prepared. "Let's go."

I was amused. And annoyed. Where were we going? Why wasn't Joseph saying anything about this? I felt left out of the plan, though I decided to maintain trust in what was unfolding. He had not let me down yet.

As we approached the front of the house, a middle-aged man of similar stature and appearance to Joseph appeared. Standing several steps away, I watched as they embraced and called the others from inside to form a welcoming committee at the front of the house so I could be introduced more formally to the family.

Joseph's introduction was brief. "Everyone, this is Mariam." The faces of a number of young children — all younger than myself but some only by a few years — looked at the foreigner from the city. Their unwashed hair and grubby hands made me feel somewhat unclean, although their smiles showed a definite air of welcome to their clan; they remained silent.

"Mariam, meet my brother Clopas." The situation became clearer, although that was to change after further rounds of introductions. I was pulled forward in an unsolicited embrace to meet Joseph's younger brother, who tapped me on the shoulder as a friendly gesture, and welcomed to the family.

Clopas responded with further introductions, "Please meet my boys, James and Joseph. We should call the younger one Joses while my brother is here." They were young ruffians and sure to be trouble, if opportunity permitted. I could sense that they had little regard for their father, and were only here because it was insisted that they meet the new girl.

Further rounds of introductions followed. "And this is my wife, Maria. Actually, she is not my first wife — and neither am I her first husband." Clopas coughed heartily as he strained to control his laughter at what he just said.

I returned with a wry smile and a quizzical look, trying to understand the joke.

Maria stepped forward, more ladylike than I anticipated, but nonetheless a genuinely friendly older woman, and courteously exchanged a hug for a greeting. I could tell that she was the mainstay keeping the family together, and without her effort the place would surely fall apart.

"You two!" Clopas whistled inside. "Come here and meet the new guest." The shuffling of feet grew louder towards the door as the boys came into view.

"Finally, meet Simon and Jude. They don't belong to me, but are Maria's boys."

My head was filling with all the names, trying to make the connection as to who was who, but there was one question that I could not solve at this opening meeting.

Not attempting to be rude, I asked impromptu, "So, what happened to Maria's husband?" The link wasn't obvious, as although she was introduced as Clopas' wife, with the two boys of her own, I was curious as to their history.

Maria bit her lip gently before responding and glanced at her husband to gain approval to speak. "My first husband died suddenly a few years ago, leaving me to raise these two by myself." A wave of compassion and sadness struck and made me realise that I had jumped in too soon to ask such a private question.

Maria continued. "I was struggling to survive, until one day Clopas arrived in town with his boys, and I learned that in a similar fashion he had lost his wife. They were living to the west of Jerusalem in a town called Emmaus when she died, and had travelled here to find respite from the grief he was experiencing. In time we married, so we were able to provide support for each other, and our larger combined families."

Maria provided a succinct and thorough background as to the circumstances that led them together in this communal family gathering, though the amount of information which I received in those few short breaths was almost overwhelming. I came to learn later that it was permissible for widows in their situation to marry without the traditional erusin period, and in fact that they consummated their marriage very quickly to bring about stability, without enduring the disdain from the community.

Given that the two families were only fairly recently joined together, I reasoned that they were still probably working things out together.

I carefully eyed the group, whose embattled strength seemed to be reflected by the rugged hillside, along with a number of other families in the area, now called the Nazarenes. In these unforgiving hills you would need resounding inner strength to survive, it seems. Would I be asked to fit in here, and become part of this family?

My instinct told me otherwise.

But regardless of this, Joseph broke the now awkward silence by clearing his throat, and pressing through the formalities to address the subject of our arrival, and turned to speak to me directly.

"Clopas and Maria have kindly offered you a room to stay, during our *erusin* period."

My stomach churned at the thought.

This was not going to be a case of happy families, was it? Leaving a house of cleanliness and order and dumped into the back blocks of a remote community, to be taken care of by a distant relative, was not what I was expecting. Is this why Joseph held back talking with me about this? Did he know it would be less than ideal?

Nazareth was not known as an inviting place.
And now I could see why.
This was not going to be easy.

I grimaced in a sort of appreciative and hope-to-be humble sort of way, to demonstrate a level of appreciation to the proposal that I was just offered. The looks on the faces of both Clopas and Maria seemed to be just as overwhelmed as it was for me, wondering how another mouth to feed was going to work.

Straightening up, Joseph wanted to smooth over the atmosphere that was developing into a somewhat unpredictable weather pattern, and insist that this would work out in time.

"Maria, thank you for accepting my call for help during this time. I know it comes at great cost to you, both of you," looking at both his brother and wife by shaking his head side to side, "and be assured that I will repay you for all you have agreed to do for us."

They waved their hands palm down in a joint effort to assure me that it really was no trouble at all to accommodate me, and that there would simply be some adjustments to make all round in order for everyone to become comfortable.

My stomach churned with unease and I sensed that it wouldn't be without a struggle.

Was my presence actually welcome here?

I prayed, "HaShem, am I in your will right now?"

There was nothing but silence.

Drawing a deep breath and holding it in, I exhaled slowly to calm myself.

So let it be.

Chapter 10

Breathe

My first night under the roof of this strange but welcoming family was not what I expected, or hoped for. After we had shared a meal, Joseph excused himself for the night with the promise that he would be back first thing in the morning. There was some family business that he needed to attend to, now that we had arrived back to his home town. Leaving me alone with his family might have been considered an initial good outcome to maintain propriety, however I also felt a slight amount of panic with him gone.

I had been provided a guest mat in the room with the children, and somehow I managed to sleep through the night enough to wake as the sun cracked through a silhouette of the morning trees.

It was now over a week since our betrothal, and my usual early morning prayer-time routine had completely disintegrated as a result of the need to travel, seeing new faces and generally trying to keep up with situations that came my way each hour of every day. I was feeling exceptionally disconnected from my normal way of life, and distant from the practises that I had adopted under Bubbe's care in the temple. I desperately needed time alone to settle my spirit in HaShem's presence.

The four young bodies around the room looked rested and peaceful when asleep, which was not the state which I encountered upon my arrival at last night's introductions. The rest of the house had not stirred, and the early morning air seemed inviting. The smell of timber smouldered from the fire place, but no flames were visible.

Quick, before they stir, I will take time for myself outside in the fresh air.

I slipped on my sandals, wrapped my shawl around me and tiptoed over the bodies that surrounded me on the floor, being quiet so as not to stir anyone, then slid through the entrance to the kitchen and finally out through the semi-closed front door.

I had never felt freer.

Now I had a chance to enter into my morning routine and find peace in personal prayer.

Fresh sunlight splashed on a patch of ground under a nearby tree, away from the wood pile, which was cleared and looked inviting. I did not need to take anything other than to present myself to HaShem and rest in His presence. There, away from the others, I would find my solace, and reconnect with the One who knew me.

The ground was slightly damp, but I managed to fold down my tunic so as to create an additional barrier while I crossed my legs and took a deep breath, resting my back against the tree. Closing my eyes, I searched for heaven's acceptance. Had I been so far away from HaShem that I was now considered 'unclean'?

From my time with Bubbe over the years, I had been taught the practise of communion. This is something that she held dear, and had explained that through fasting and prayer she had learned to hear the words of the Lord clearly. Indeed, she was a recognised prophet within the temple courts, and was well respected for the way she handled the words that she received.

I breathed again deeply, taking in the fresh morning air, and exhaled slowly. Then I opened my prayer time with the *Shema* in the traditional way.

"Hear, O Israel. HaShem Elohim is HaShem."

My meditation was focussed on the name of HaShem — the proper name of the self-existent and eternal Divine One, who is also our ruler and judge.

I repeated the *Shema* three times, slowly, allowing the words to make up a picture of worship and respect that had been missing from my routine for the last week. Finally, my heart reached a place of peace.

Then I took another deep breath.

The atmosphere changed, and I felt enveloped by the dew from heaven.

I allowed my eyes to focus, while still closed, until the picture of a river soon developed in my mind. There were trees flourishing on the side of the bank, and the scene unfolded beautifully and alive. The first psalm came to mind, which I recited through a whisper, under my breath.

> "Blessed is the one who does not walk in the ways of
> the wicked
> Or stand in the ways of sinners
> Or sit in the seat of mockers

> But whose delight is in the law of HaShem
> And on His law he meditates day and night."

How I had missed these times of meditation, when I could delight in the law by listening to the early morning prayers that filtered through my window in the Temple.

In my mind I could see trees growing steadfastly and unwavering by the water with a variety of fruit trees ready to harvest; the sun shining overhead, and animals coming in to drink from the waters that provided life and vitality to support the environment around it.

> "He is like a tree planted by streams of water
> Which yields its fruit in season
> And whose leaf does not wither —
> Whatever he does prospers."

Pausing, I reflected on the psalm, allowing my soul to experience the newness of life that came with the heavenly water that I was drinking in. My soul bubbled up with renewed strength and was refreshed in this time of meditation, watching the picture unfold in my mind's eye.

> "Not so the wicked.
> They are like chaff that the wind blows away.
> Therefore the wicked will not stand in the judgement
> Nor sinners in the assembly of the righteous."

I stopped and held my breath.
Judgement was not mine to enact.

I needed to apologise to HaShem for the way I had been thinking about the situation I was in with Joseph's family.

Had I been difficult and offensive to them? I hoped not.

I wanted my heart to be clean and free from stain, to find my own innocence again.

And I wanted to be able to show them gratitude for supporting us through this time.

Above all, I did not want HaShem to cast me out of His presence.

I wanted to stay connected to Him, with a right heart.

> "For HaShem watches over the way of the righteous,
> But the way of the wicked will perish."

The psalm concluded, and with that I also bowed my head, asking forgiveness for my thoughts, as I adopted a change of heart.

I listened to the air flow from my breath become the only central thing in my ears again.

Exhaling slowly, the scene in my mind started to fade.

I laid back gently into the tree, and listened to my surroundings take over my natural senses.

A clang emanated from inside the cottage door.
I heard stirrings from inside as the family arose.
The family was getting up.

It was time for me to return, and see how I may be of assistance.

I would later seek other times of the day where my heart could once again settle and find peace away from the duties of family life and responsibility. This was definitely a different way of living, and I was not sure how long my pious life could last out here.

I felt clean again, at least for now, and longed for more of the Lord and of His word.

Chapter 11

New Beginnings

I did not realise that such a dramatic change would come so quickly to the temple girl, who was now Joseph's betrothed.

My world had changed very quickly.

Previously, I had identity and purpose each day I served in the Temple courts, with an eager expectation that I would see in the coming of the promised Messiah — a dream shared by Bubbe that had rubbed off onto myself.

But yielding to the role of a betrothed woman — and whether I could still confess that this was the will of HaShem or not — was a concept that still was so distant in my mind that I realised that there was a lot to learn.

Having completed my first real attempt at prayer and meditation since my departure, and with the household starting for the day ahead, I headed back to the cottage to see how I may help. After all, I felt that I was not simply HaShem's servant but also to assist in every practical way where I was required.

Maria came to the front entrance, scratched her hair as though she were stirring up a rat's nest, and exhaled with a wake-up yawn. She looked tired.

I must have caught her off guard, perhaps she was thinking that I was still resting amongst the boys, when I appeared just around the corner. Maybe she wasn't used to others being awake at this time of day? Shrugging it off as if it never occurred, she dusted her clothes down in the cool morning air to get her arms and legs moving for the day.

"*Boker Tov,* Maria," I greeted her with a quiet good morning phrase. "*Boker Or,*" came a brief and concise response, spoken under her breath to keep noise to a minimum.

This morning I felt a wave of compassion come over me towards her, and the family that resided within. Granted that she was no Bubbe to me, well not yet, I started to dream about how we might grow to learn from each other over the course of time that I would be living here. Would I be here for the full twelve months of our betrothal?

Questions lingered in my mind, but I didn't expect to resolve them any time soon. We would need to take one day at a time until my wedding day. Thinking of that, where was Joseph? He wasn't present, like he promised.

His seat was noticeably vacant from the morning scene, having become so much part of my new life over the last week that his absence seemed unusual. He mentioned that he would be back in the morning, but did not explain what he needed to take care of last night. After dinner he had stayed just a short while, and with a quick embrace had left me in the care of his sister-in-law and brother. Was he always going to be distant like this, or did he have other pressing things to take care of?

I was to find out sooner, rather than later, as before we could enter into any further discussion I heard a faint whistle echo through the trees. A familiar tone, I looked up to see Joseph a small distance away down the cleared path, and was heading our way. He had spotted my movements as I was approaching Maria, which gave him opportunity to alert me to his arrival. My heart pounded, now assured that he was a man of his word, quietly humming to myself that my security was being restored, though tried not to show it. With a glance I raised an eyebrow at Maria, and turned to shorten the distance between myself and Joseph.

I approached with outstretched arms to accelerate the reconnection of our overnight distance apart, and offered a *"Boker Tov"* welcome to him as well. We stopped at the place of prayer, where I found my peace against the trunk of a small tree, and gave a short embrace. With everything so unfamiliar I needed him to be by my side to ensure that things could unpack in an orderly manner, although I'm sure he was working things out along the way. Though having already been married, this is not something that he should struggle with, I reasoned. He would know how things would progress from here, and I could rely on his faithfulness and capabilities to be able to set up our home together.

I was again struck by his towering height. It gave him an aura of strength, however he took pains to lower himself closer to me, drawing me closer to him. I sensed that he wanted to explain why he departed so early last night, so I pressed in.

"Mariam, welcome to my Nazareth." as if to introduce me to an old friend, describing the village as though it were part of him. Was his quiet nature a reflection of the town in the way he spoke and handled himself?

"This is where I lived with my wife and children." My breath caught in my throat. Wasn't I about to be his wife?

"My former wife, that is." I relaxed my guard, realising that he had misspoke, re-affirming what I had already known, as he had described to me on the trip here, that his wife had passed away not too long ago.

I gave him time to reconcile his thoughts, and allow him to share the story that had been on his heart — the reason why we ended up in this place.

"When my wife died, I was left to raise our children on my own. The plague that hit Nazareth was devastating." His words were slow and melancholy as he relived the tale of what had occurred.

"Nazareth is home not only to Jews, but to Gentile invaders who had settled amongst us. One of the gifts that they brought was a disease from the north that none of us had encountered, making most people in the village very sick. Many people died — including my wife, Clopas' wife, and Maria's husband."

I held my breath.

I had heard of the plague from my time in the Temple, but fortunately it had not reached as far as Jerusalem. Therefore I had concluded that HaShem's judgement and punishment was on His enemies but His favour rested on the city of David.

How wrong I was to think like that!

Now I could see the impact that this had at a personal level, as Joseph described the scenes in a very low voice, how it left a wake of destruction and blankets of tears as it indiscriminately took people who stood in its path.

This was a town fighting for survival.

Sad history is not something that people want to talk about. But since this was to become my new home, it was better that I learned it sooner rather than later. Is this why Joseph kept to himself for most of the journey here?

The depths of sadness that this town had experienced now showed in the grounds, lurking under the trees, as if hiding in plain sight. Eerily, it seemed as though there were people listening to what was being shared. Was there someone observing the arrival of the temple girl in 'their town'?

I was starting to understand that life was not always easy or joyful, and that there would be circumstances that occur which are outside our level of control. Even life itself can be threatened by an unseen wind that is carried from one person to another, although that mystery is one that would have to be given over to HaShem if it ever entered our lives. Would I be susceptible to the plague, if it was ever to return?

"Come. Let's spend time today with Clopas and Maria, we have lots to discuss. And let's get ready so that you can stay comfortably with them. And then later, let's say after the Sabbath, I will show you my workshop."

His tone changed, and I picked up a spark of excitement in his voice at the mention of what seemed to be a passion in his life. My curiosity caused me to raise an eyebrow, and I awakened myself staring into the sky considering what the workshop might look like.

Today would be full of surprises, for sure.

Chapter 12

~New Arrangements~

We arrived at the cottage to greet Clopas and Maria at the
timber table outside, preparing food for the day ahead.
There were two long bench seats, one on each side of the
table, which easily accommodated six people on each side
of the table, so we took opportunity to greet our hosts and
sat ourselves down before any little bodies came outside
to join in. I admired the handiwork and detail of table and
benches, it was stylish, impressive and sturdy. Was this a
family heirloom?

We continued last night's conversation and shared some
of the fresh bread that Maria had prepared. We wanted
to delve deeper into how the next twelve month's living
arrangements might look. The focus of discussion was
broadly about the practicalities of our living arrangements,
meal preparation, help around the cottage and assisting
with the children. However there was also a natural
undercurrent flowing through our conversation, which
came from my appointment as the temple girl: that is, how
do we bring honour to the Lord?

Josephs brother, as it turns out, was devoutly committed
to our Jewish customs and practices. Like myself, he loved
to meditate on and discuss the Torah, the Psalms and the
Prophets. As head of the family, he would lead the family
to the local synagogue each Sabbath — which was not
too far from home. Traditionally, someone from the town
would be called upon to read through an allotted passage
of scripture, and when finished they would provide insights
for the text that they read.

Importantly, tomorrow was the Sabbath, where we would
have the opportunity to gather at the synagogue, and I
could see how spiritual life outside the temple functioned
in the smaller Jewish communities and towns. Maybe there
could be opportunity for me to become more involved in
the synagogue during my stay here?

The mornings planning meeting ran into lunch time,
with a series of breaks in between while we handled the
practicalities of children, and other interruptions. It wasn't
until after lunch that we concluded the session to come to
an agreement as to how I would participate in the running
of the family, daily duties, and the timing of the marriage
that was to come. It seemed that extensive plans were
needed so that the community, not just the hosts, would be
able to warmly accept me into their day to day lives in this
somewhat isolated and obscure little town.

It was agreed that Joseph would build a room as an
extension to their house, which would be my living quarters
until the end of the erusin period. He would commence
this the day after the Sabbath. This would be my personal
space and the children would not be allowed to frequent the
room, which gave me a sense of privacy and peace. This
also meant that I was not to have any guests in the room,
and that all meetings would be held outside on the timber

table and bench seats where we had been talking all day. The room would take a few days to build, perhaps a week, with assistance from Clopas and the children, as required. As an interim measure, I would need to sleep inside amongst the bodies that were scattered across sleeping mats. Uncomfortable, yes, but only for a short period until things were in place.

I would also assist Maria with the running of the family, a role that would prepare me for married life in the event that I would have children of my own one day. Bubbe's words flashed back into my mind at that point, "That is, if you want to become a mother," I recalled her saying, almost hesitantly, at the time. Back then I was too young to consider being a mother and having children; but moreso the call to motherhood didn't appear to be on my life, especially when I felt appointed to serve HaShem in the Temple. Regardless, I was now on a different course and the dust of Jerusalem had fallen from my sandals, being quickly replaced with the dust of Nazareth.

Being physically separate from Joseph during this time meant that I had to have reason to see him, and hence make it intentional, if we were to catch up in any way. Joseph's home and workshop was over a thousand paces from Clopas' cottage, not too far in reality, and the villagers would be settled once everyone got to know me. Maria assured me that no-one would lay a hand on me as they understood that Joseph had a new wife on the scene. Joseph himself was respected in town for reasons I would find out later.

So a formal arrangement was made — not that I was unfamiliar with formalities and tradition — but we agreed to set aside a certain hour of each day for me to be able to meet Joseph in his workshop, not in his house. This would be how we were to operate during this time of life together, yet apart. We agreed that I would visit Joseph at a set time, that being the sixth hour of the day, allowing me to bring fresh food that I would prepare that morning. This would give us some 'together time' to talk and plan our future event, where I would learn to be by his side and support him. After our meeting I would return home and help Maria with afternoon activities, which would normally be manufacturing or mending clothes, educating the children with stories and prepping everyone for things that they would need the following day.

I could see that Maria and I would need to form a close friendship, and it amused me that our names were so similar. I would learn to be like her in every way. Would she become a sister to me? Although I was missing Bubbe's company and instruction, she was more of a mother-figure than a sister to me. Now there was opportunity for me to be part of my own family and have a real sister, and brother! A quiet gap in my heart seemed to fill with the thought that I would be accepted here, if this were all to work out for good. Finally, I would have a family that I could call my own.

Although Maria and Clopas were much older than myself, the discussion led us to the conclusion that as Joseph's bride-to-be I should be treated with a level of authority and rank in the family that the children should look up to. To be seen in this regard, I would share the parenting responsibilities with Maria, and although not my children, they were told to respect me as their own mother. In this way they elevated my status. This in turn created the situation where their children would be accepted to be my children. In short, their four children became part of my family responsibility, and I co-parented them with Maria. I had a thought: What about Joseph's children?

The family unit was to develop over time, and consisted of Joseph and myself being tightly integrated with Maria and Clopas, such that we gave and received support from each other as required. In time the relationships became natural, and we functioned as a single family unit living under this roof, though of course Joseph had his own place to stay, and his own children to take care of. We were all aware that once things were ready, Joseph would take me under his roof to be his wife, though that time was a while off yet, it seemed.

The sun was nearing the horizon for the day, which meant that we were entering into the Sabbath and no more work could be done. Having already lit the fire inside for the evening, we shared a meal for the second night together and prepared ourselves for the day ahead. Clopas mentioned that he was called to lead the synagogue reading tomorrow, and the passage of scripture was already pre-allocated. He would be handed the scroll upon entry, and when everyone was settled he would share with the group.

I turned to Joseph, who was rising to leave for the evening, and caught his eye before being able to take hold of his tunic. I raised myself up to give him an embrace, and thank him for bringing me here to Nazareth and for working things through with Clopas and Maria.

Although he didn't say much, he held me in a firm gaze.

His eyes were as dark as the night sky, and penetrated the depths of my soul to let me know that all was okay.

Everything was going to work out just fine.

In time.

Chapter 13

Synagogue

I slept another night on the floor, however this time it had been arranged for me to sleep in a corner of the room and a light curtain had been raised to provide me a sense of privacy. This was an outcome from yesterday's discussion, and they felt it was right to start implementing the plan straight away, as it was felt that it was not right to keep me in the same room as the boys.

Last night's meal time provided the opportunity for Clopas to instruct the boys about me, that they were to obey me as *Ima*, their own mother.

"Mariam will be with us for a while, and this means that when she gives an order it's as good as *Ima* or me saying it. Got it?" All nodded their heads in agreement, accepting that despite me being just a few years older than them that I now held rank that was equal to their mother. But would they really listen to me, being so young? I guess time would tell.

Rising on the Sabbath has always been an exciting time for me, and now that I was away from the temple practises I realised just how much I missed the routine. To prepare myself for the day, I slipped outside as the sun was emerging and found yesterday's spot against the tree. I was eager to meditate again to settle myself for the day ahead. Being a Sabbath, I would normally be a lot busier once my quiet time had ended, but today there were no morning prayers or offerings for me to provide assistance, and I was left with plenty of time to myself.

So with my back against the tree, like yesterday, I entered into my personal time and thanked HaShem for daily provision, blessing His name. I waited until my heart rested in the peace of heaven, a tangible peace that stayed over me throughout the day. The peace provided me a sense of security whereby I was not easily shaken by any circumstances that would arise, from which I drew strength and purpose. Bubbe's instructions and teachings had kept me hour by hour in HaShem's graceful presence, and I was grateful for her role in my life.

Breakfast duties required light meal preparation for which I was called upon by Maria to assist with, given my new role and status within the family. I stepped in to help eagerly, cutting a bag of freshly-picked olives in half, breaking goats cheese into bowls and slicing fresh fruit into sections so the children could find them easy to eat. We all sat outside at the bench table, with fresh cistern water each.

Clopas was keen to get to the synagogue — it was an honour to be selected to perform the reading, and he craved this opportunity to read to the community. Today's passage was a reading from the prophet Isaiah. There were no scrolls available at their home, so he had taken time during the week to visit the synagogue so as to access the passage, and contemplate its meaning. When everyone looked as though they had finished their food, I was asked to help wash the children's hands and face, and then it would be time to leave. We were to travel by foot and it would not take much time at all, given the Sabbath regulations for how far we could travel.

Upon arrival, there were several striking features that made this building stand apart from others in the area, although the building itself was of quite plain appearance. This was a Jewish community hub where people could come to study the Torah, perform worship and deliver their ceremonial rites. It was a place of learning, and a place that was to be respected. We were expected to be courteous and formal, and acknowledge those leaders with rank and position.

The entrance was quite wide, and being a rectangular building it was oriented towards Jerusalem to incorporate an act of divine respect to our capital. The centre of the room was an open area with a small timber platform, the *bema*, where the readings and teaching could be delivered to all in attendance. A replica *menorah*, similar but smaller to the actual menorah in the Temple, provided a source of light to those who would perform today's reading.

The floor layout was arranged so that people of importance would be offered the chief seats, which were pressed up against the three sides of the building, and which also looked just like the timber benches around the table at the place where I now called home. The poorer people sat on the floor to listen to what was being said, the floor itself being made of flagstone, a random collection of slate pavers that were set in a pattern. I wondered if there was any divine meaning behind its layout, though no immediate imagery came to mind.

Joseph had arrived early, and was seated inside with his children, who were in fact much older than Maria and Clopas' children, and myself, but had not been married as yet. We glanced at each other across the room, my eyes gave a quick dance to show my excitement at the meeting ahead, and headed in to allow Clopas to sit near his brother.

Before entry, everyone were required to wash hands at the *mikveh* — the ritual bath — located near the front door, as a symbol to cleanse our hearts before entering the room. This observance was the beginning of our spiritual duties once we entered the synagogue. Once completed, the boys were instructed to sit on the floor at the rear of the building, with Clopas and Maria on the bench seats above them. We would be required to wait patiently until the meeting was called to attention, and keep all talking to a minimum.

Eventually there were no more people coming through the front entrance, and the synagogue leader called us to order. There were around eighty people in attendance this morning. He stood on the bema, raised his arms and lowered his hands to create absolute silence. All eyes lighted upon the aging gentleman in flowing robes, waiting for him to speak.

Once again raising his hands, in a strong and authoritative voice, he opened the meeting with the shema. "Hear, O Israel. HaShem Elohim is HaShem." We bowed our heads in reverence to accept these opening words, and waited for him to invite todays speaker.

"Friends, today I would like to invite elder Clopas to read a passage from the prophet Isaiah, and afterwards share his thoughts on the subject. Please remain quiet as he shares this passage with us." I eyed Maria gleefully, knowing that such an honour was rare, and we shared a pursed smile. He stepped down from the bema and sat near the front to keep watch on the proceedings.

Clopas rose and took position on the platform, and sat in the Seat of Moses. This is reserved for the reading of the Torah, although for special occasions the seat was also allowed to be used as the Seat of Honour, where the most prominent guest would be invited. Another elder opened the Torah cabinet, sifted through several scrolls to locate that of Isaiah, and stepped up to hand it to Clopas, which he accepted with a gracious nod. There was an air of expectation from the temple-dwellers, and we each held our breath until the opening words were shared.

The passage was located towards the front of the scroll, and the smooth rolled handles enabled the passages to flow easily from one location onto the next, until the passage was ready to read. Once upon it, Clopas paused to make eye contact with the observers, gave a smile, then looked down to read. I didn't realise how well-versed and refined he was at reading scripture, not unlike the priests that I had assisted in the temple; and it was evident that he had a high regard of self-respect as he spoke.

Clopas began.

> "Later, HaShem sent this message to King Ahaz:
> "Ask HaShem for a sign, Ahaz. Make it as difficult as you want—as high as heaven or as deep as the place of the dead."
>
> But the king refused. "No," he said, "I will not test the Lord like that."
>
> Then Isaiah said, "Listen well, you royal family of David! Isn't it enough to exhaust human patience? Must you exhaust the patience of HaShem as well?

> All right then, the Lord himself will give you the
> sign. Look! The virgin will conceive a child! She will
> give birth to a son and will call him Immanuel (which
> means 'The Lord is with us').
>
> By the time this child is old enough to choose what is
> right and reject what is wrong, he will be eating curds
> and honey.
>
> For before the child is that old, the lands of the two
> kings you fear so much will both be deserted."

The reading ended with solemn grunts of approval from
the synagogue leaders, which was the queue to invite him to
continue with an explanation of the passage — in his own
words. This would give everyone something to talk about
and focus on until the following Sabbath day. The scroll
was handed back to the elder, who rolled it back up and
placed it carefully inside the cabinet alongside the rest.

Raising from the seat to stand on the bema and talk to us
directly, Clopas began. "My friends, as we know, Ahaz was
an evil king in HaShem's sight. He was self-absorbed and
he had no regard for authority." His speech was slow and
intentional, scanning the room to lock in nods of approval
before continuing to share his thoughts.

"Today we read that HaShem pressed Ahaz to request a
sign to demonstrate that nothing is impossible for Him to
do. He wanted to express His power in a way that gave no
room for debate or questioning. Just like He brought Israel
out of Egypt, HaShem sought to gain acceptance from His
people and for them to respect His power." A quietness
around the room indicated that there was no debate about
what was being said.

"But Ahaz refused the invitation to ask for a sign. In this
way, he defied a divine request, which lined up with his

character. And his stubborn refusal meant that HaShem would provide His own answer to the query from the Holy One." Clopas stopped, thinking through what to say next, as if to wait for divine inspiration of his own. We gave him time, and when he was ready, he continued.

"Friends, HaShem does not want us to harden our hearts, like Ahaz, that, although he was king of Judah, refused to respond to the royal invitation. When HaShem appears to us and makes it obvious that we are to be involved in the work He is doing, we would be wise to respond favourably, rather than test His patience." There were nods of approval from the synagogue leaders, indicating that he had interpreted the meaning of the passage correctly, which were then reflected by the attending crowd.

He continued. "As a beloved people, our hearts should be open to Him doing a work through us, and in us. There is no reason to be frightened or run away, whether we encounter an angel, or a prophet were to stand among us. We should be tender and responsive to what is being asked of us, weigh it up, and consider how we should act. An appropriate response is an act of divine service to HaShem."

The synagogue ruler rose and gave hand signals to indicate that the key interpretation of the message had been delivered correctly — and that there was nothing further to add. Clopas had done a fine job presenting the challenge that arose from this scripture, and was being dismissed from the bema to return to his seat beside us.

However, Clopas continued.

It's as if he was struck with an epiphany, and could not help point out the rest of the passage to the eager gathering, and in response raised a hand to stop the leader from approaching the platform until he was finished. This brought a small jeer of surprise from the other elders, which needed to be silenced before continuing. The leader hesitated, and graciously sat down to allow him to continue.

"This passage promises that one day the Messiah will appear among us. There will be a virgin, who will give birth to a son, and the boy will be called Immanuel — which means, 'the Lord is with us'. Ahaz's stubborn refusal to respond appropriately meant that he missed this sign, in his generation. We ought to be careful not to miss it, in our generation." He spoke confidently, and eyed the room. There was a peculiar air of authority in his voice as he left us with these concluding remarks, stepping down from the platform and handing the meeting back to the synagogue ruler.

To take hold of the meeting like this, after he was being dismissed, was an act of disrespect, a blatant abuse of the role that he was invited to perform, and everyone knew it. We were silent as he approached the bench, and Maria eyed him as if to ask, 'Why did you have to say that?'. This was no time for showmanship, especially since he was a fellow elder in the town, and protocol was expected.

Clopas face remained steadfast. He did not know why he said that, it was a flood of words that he could not control. Above the silence there rose a small murmur until the remainder of the meeting would be concluded.

Given the situation, we didn't expect to learn anything else from the Sabbaths teachings today. Ultimately, this could have grave consequences on our standing in the community.

Somehow we lasted until the end of the ceremony and then edged home together under a vow of silence.

Would we talk about this at home, or simply move on and forget about it?

My heart burned to think that this could be the start of rejection from the community.

Joseph, where was Joseph?

I needed desperately to find him and talk, but he was missing.

Was he also ashamed at his brother's actions?

This was going to take some time to resolve, it seems.

What was the real undercurrent of how this community operated?

This was nothing like my normal Sabbath morning experience, and I wanted to forget it!

Chapter 14

~The Workshop~

The uncomfortable walk home did not last long and the resulting activities upon our arrival allowed the closing remarks from the meeting to be put aside, at a family level, at least for now. It was something that we needed to sleep on, and with the falling of the sun that evening we managed to shrug it off as an odd incident, but we all knew that there were likely to be repercussions — we just weren't sure how or when this might be felt.

The next day was the start of the week, and after my morning quiet time and breakfast ritual were concluded, a man and his children appeared on our doorstep. It was Joseph, the elusive one from yesterday's meeting. He had promised to take me to the workshop at the start of the week, and I was eager to visit. I had not seen the work of an artisan first hand, though we used their items every day in the Temple, the utensils were used every day in homes and palaces alike.

Joseph eyed his brother carefully, who was seated on the timber bench outside the cottage, and they exchanged morning greetings with some caution. Josephs immediate absence after the meeting caused some concern, indicating a level of disapproval had arisen between the siblings. Would they broach the subject today, or leave it for another time? I side-stepped around the two to stand alongside Maria, and have the boys take their seats at the table. With more family members present, there was another round of introductions to be made.

Hesitantly, Joseph motioned that he would like me to meet his daughters, so I put aside my morning duties to come and meet them. Understandably he had already briefed them about my arrival, and the circumstances under which we were betrothed, so there was no further background to add at this point in time. Instead, he kept the greetings formal and to the point, and I could sense that this was making him slightly uncomfortable given the nature of the circumstances that had unfolded over the Sabbath.

"Mariam, please meet my two daughters. First, my eldest, Abigail, who is nineteen years old." He paused to allow us to exchange greetings. "*Shalom lakh*," we said in unison speaking over each other, which provided a giggle, and exchanged a customary bow.

"And this is Tirtzah, my youngest, who is sixteen." This allowed me to perform a second welcome ritual to demonstrate my acceptance.

They were very pretty girls — not that they were girls, but were indeed young ladies — and who were themselves waiting for a husband. Their names held meanings of significance amongst the Jewish community, with Abigail's name meaning "my father is joy" and Tirtzah's meaning "delight". Together with Joseph, whose name meant "HaShem will increase", these provided a sense of identity for the family unit that seemed incomplete without their mother, who was never discussed. I was about to enquire about her to the girls, as Joseph had failed to make any mention of his former wife, other than to acknowledge that she had already passed away, on our sojourn to Nazareth. Maybe this was a point of grief that he was still working through?

I was not sure how the first time meeting with Joseph's children would work out, but to me this looked like it would unfold naturally and we would be able to find a common ground that would work for all of us during the erusin period, and afterwards.

Clopas broke through our pleasantries, and created an air of urgency to allow us to be on our way. "Mariam, today is a special day for you, having travelled all the way to Nazareth, you have been with us for a few nights now. Maria can handle the rest of the duties this morning, so please spend the rest of the morning with Joseph, and the girls. If you are able to make it back by the sixth hour, then we will have something for you to do by then."

It was clear that he needed some space between himself and Joseph at this time, and his tone of voice indicated that sooner, rather than later, would be a preferred time to leave for the workshop. So I quickly washed my hands, stepped inside briefly to gather a few items, and with a glance towards Maria I handed over my morning duties for her to fulfil. She smiled, knowing that without my calming presence this day could be long. She showed genuine appreciation for how my day might work out. "Go in peace," revealing a small amount of envy in her tone.

My attention turned towards Joseph, who with Abigail and Tirtzah started towards his home.

We arrived after only a short walk to another small cottage that lay close to the centre of town, just outside the central square. At the town centre Joseph had a constant stream of people who would visit the workshop to inspect his work, and ask to build them furniture for their home or business. The cottage was attached to the workshop, which in turn had a small room as a shop attached to the front, which made the entire length of the building much longer than an ordinary dwelling.

Three functional and large rooms under one roof aired the aroma of freshly cut and stored timber throughout the building. The fragrance aroused my senses and I appreciated just how beautiful Joseph's handicraft would become. It wasn't just delightful artisanship but the fragrance enveloped my entire being, inviting me to participate in some way.

This would become our home. I liked it instantly, and started to imagine myself here. The girls left us alone, providing their father the space to talk with me privately and show me around. Joseph was still unusually quiet, and I hoped to be able to tease out his thoughts and bring to light what was on his mind.

"Mariam, let me show you my workshop, I spend most of my day here." He pointed out the logs that were curing over a rack of shelves which he had retrieved from elsewhere in the district over time, and which would be cut to size and length when the job required them. There was quite a variety of different timbers, both large or small, all which had to be fashioned by hand to create people's requests.

He pointed out with a sense of pride the tools that were available for his craft. They had been passed down from his father, and his grand-father, and possibly even beyond that. The work of a carpenter was a trade that was passed down from one generation to the next, and it was fitting that he would inherit the family business and would continue to supply ornate furniture for the local population, as well as those travelling from abroad.

As he was explaining this to me, it became clear that there would be no-one to pass the family business on to, since he never had a son. Joseph, being much older now, and with no-one to succeed him in the event of his passing, was aware that his business was not likely to survive once his daughters were married — their husbands would follow their own family tradition rather than take on new skills.

This in itself left an impression on me, and I was curious as to whether we ourselves would have children, given that our marriage was expected to be sometime in the next twelve months. I raised my eyebrows, considering the thought. I was not quite ready to take on the role of motherhood just yet, as Bubbe suggested I might at some point in time.

Time in the workshop was cut short by the *shrier*, the town crier, an official who rang the bell to indicate that the sixth hour had passed and my time at the workshop was at an end. I needed to start my way back to the cottage and help Maria with preparations for the rest of the day.

"Tomorrow," Joseph began, "I will bring the timber down and start on your room. I just need a little more time to myself today, though I was hoping to get to work on it as soon as possible." I nodded and provided a small smile of gratitude in response to Joseph's schedule, showing my appreciation and approval of his offer to build the room. This would enable me to have my own space, and allow Maria to have the room in her cottage back for other purposes, as the place itself there was quite small — especially given the number of people living under the same roof.

Heading for the door, and before exiting, I whispered a quiet "*Shalom*" into Joseph's ear, to give him the assurance that all was ok, despite how he was feeling towards his brother. I was convinced that this would work itself out in time, as all things normally would. He bowed his head heavily, knowing that Clopas' disrespect in the synagogue would make it hard on us in this community.

"*Shalom*," he responded, although not fully paying attention. Instead of being a time of excitement, as I had thought it might be, the visit fell a little flat. I closed my eyes briefly to suppress my thoughts, needing to realign myself with what lay ahead, and exhaling in a slow controlled breath.

And with a small bow, I turned to leave for home.

We can work through this tomorrow.

Chapter 15

~Detached~

Joseph's attitude was now playing on my mind, and I lost clarity around how I could help Maria once I returned home. The tension between the brothers was quite tangible, and I wondered if some other incident had come between them previously. If I was to live here until we were married then we would all need to work out how to get along. I was not one to live in a disruptive environment and liked the order and routine of the Temple, where people came with an attitude of respect to bring their offerings and sacrifices to HaShem, where matters of the heart were dealt with in an orderly way.

This situation was new to me, and I needed to work out how best to navigate through murky family issues that had arisen, though it didn't appear to be my responsibility to have to work out a solution for this. Was this also part of a normal family life that I should be aware of?

As the sun was heading towards the horizon we sat around the fireplace to discuss the usual days activities, and share some insight and meaning to what we had accomplished. After some general small talk, the tone became serious as Clopas led the discussion. Clearly there was something that he wanted to bring up, and he did not want the sun to go down while he still felt an air of anger was present.

"Maria, Mariam, I need to talk about what happened yesterday, in the synagogue, if that's okay with you?"

I could hear the concern in his voice, suggesting that there was something more to the situation than what we had observed. Maria, by nature of the fact that he was the husband, expected him to continue, while I gave a sincere nod of approval.

"Thank you, please hear me out. This is not something that I planned, and it was a most extraordinary experience for myself, at the time." He was referring to interrupting the flow of the meeting with the abrupt hand signal to the leader who was ushering him off the platform.

"I know this looked like a sign of disrespect, but at that moment I had what seemed to be a message that I could not hold back. The words just flowed from my mouth!"

Maria turned to me, with a giggle, and we both bit our lips in unison. Clopas' attempt at a confession was a little clumsy in its delivery, though we got his point. We turned back to the man who was now facing the floor, in deep contemplation of his own feelings about the matter.

"Please understand that when I prepared the reading during the week, I did not have any follow up words to share as I closed my time. They simply fell out of my mouth. I really had no control over them. It's as if they were meant to be shared at the time. It was beyond my control!"

Together we giggled, causing Clopas to become even more unnerved. He was expecting a high level of criticism as a result of his actions, but it was becoming evident that his time on the bema was an ordained calling. We allowed him to continue, though we were convinced he need say nothing further about the matter.

He waited for us to settle, which took little time while we allowed the flickering fire to consume our attention, and our legs to warm up. The boys looked sleepy, and Maria suggested that they head to their mats and find rest, and leave us alone for further conversation. With a round of good-night hugs to all three of us, they headed inside and let the adults continue to talk.

Clopas continued. "And then there's Joseph."

We stopped our giggling short, knowing that family issues were presenting themselves, and we ought to be engaging more appropriately to what was about to be shared. My eyes widened towards Maria and we both looked at Clopas to listen to him more intently. What was going on between the two?

"For a long time, I've felt that he never accepted me. Ever since I was young, he was the one who always had to be right. So when small things happen, like they did yesterday, he expresses strong disapproval to me — he didn't even stay to the end!"

He was getting upset, his quivering lips showed that this was an issue that had long-affected their relationship. I had not seen Joseph walk out, nor his daughters — he was simply not present when his brother finished, and I had not observed how these two events were connected.

Maria edged closer to her husband in order to provide moral support, but wary that he might hold anger that could snap if she wasn't careful. He looked up, softened his deranged face, and beckoned her over, and which she came to his side with an embrace. He needed time to clear the air before moving on.

"Joseph always thinks that he is the most important person in the room. Just because he is the oldest son, with some years between us, he often wants to pull rank. There is never any room for me to demonstrate any type of leadership, because he often steps in to take my place. It's always been like this — he always has to be the centre of attention."

Clopas was no longer looking at the floor, but directly towards me, in a stare that appeared to look through me instead of at me. I don't think he even realised that I was there, lost in his world of thoughts and imaginations. He looked so badly hurt and upset that he must have found it hard staying in the present. When he realised where he was staring he shook himself awake.

"Oh, sorry Mariam, I wasn't meaning to inflict this on you."

His tone softened and his darkened features started to ease. This was quite a heavy topic for him to work through, and must have been a burden for many years, which had now come bubbling to the surface. Clopas wasn't looking for revenge, just acceptance and equality. He didn't want centre stage, but to be able to hold a position with respect from others, especially his brother.

I could hear the pumping of his heart resounding loudly, almost screaming at me, with thumps that showed that this was a heart-crushing situation. This wasn't going to be solved in a day, it would be something that they had to work out together. The uncomfortable thing for me was that I was stuck in some unseen war between brothers, with whom my betrothed was due to commence building a room the following day, which meant that he would need to be here every day over the course of the next week — or until the room was prepared and ready.

This was going to be awkward.

As if reading my thoughts, Clopas returned to almost normal levels of conversation, though hesitant, to bring up the topic of the room.

"The room," he commenced.

"Tomorrow, if Joseph is up to it, he will bring timber to fit the walls and roof for you. We will add the room over there, attached to that part of the house." He pointed to the nearby vacant ground, and with a variety of other gestures explained how it would work in with the rest of the house. There was to be no additional flooring, no fireplace, the ground would be flattened to allow a raised bed with room for a seat, and table near a window, which would have external shutters for the weather. In time, Joseph would also make a clothes cabinet and other items, to make my life comfortable during my stay in waiting. This was only to be a temporary measure, though it would remain afterwards for the family use as they see fit, once I left.

With that off his mind, Clopas started twitching his fingers in a way that showed that he was still thinking about things, and would need time, so we left him with his thoughts. Maria and I came back to the bench seats and started to make more official conversation around the practicalities that would present themselves later today, namely food for the children. At least we could detach from whatever Clopas was going through and find mutual support in each other by attending to the necessary running of the house.

I started to see that it might take a little while for Clopas and Joseph to work through their issues. If they followed the instructions provided by the synagogue leaders then they would need to go through the process of *teshuva* — that is, repentance — as a path towards reconciliation. This helped to bring about peace in situations that had escalated by identifying the actions that were harmful towards each other, confess that they understood how it had impacted their relationship, and provide a commitment not to repeat the transgression.

To do this took a lot of courage, and would normally be performed with another by their side during the procedure. It's not something that could be rushed, both parties would need to be ready to engage in teshuva. The recipient — the aggrieved one — would need to be in a position to be able to handle the confession, and respond in a way that demonstrates acceptance to show that both parties could find peace. It does not always solve every issue, but it provides the ability for people to work through things one issue at a time. Sometimes this would have to be done numerous times a day, or week, until the relationship was restored. But the synagogue leaders only required teshuva to be completed seven times — after that it would be too much effort, and it would be better to disconnect from the relationship altogether.

For lifelong family issues, such as this, it would likely take more time, due to the level of sensitivity required on the parts of both men. They seemed to be worlds apart from where they should be. Would this be something that I could help both of them work through?

I contemplated the possibilities, though realising that I was simply a guest at Clopas' home and not in a position to be the one to negotiate terms of peace in this short time. I blew my fringe out of my eyes, and let out a sigh.

There was always the practical side of living that would require a show of mercy.

This might not be easy.

But it had to be done.

I gritted my teeth, determined to work out how to bring this to a head.

"HaShem, give me wisdom, I pray!"

Chapter 16

~The Room~

The following day arrived and after my now-established quiet time I returned to assist Maria with preparations for the morning. The heaviness of the former day had lifted and I was hopeful that today would run smoothly. The children had arisen and it was almost the second hour when a dray carrying a range of timber beams, posts and supports came rumbling towards us down the winding path. It was Joseph, with both daughters in attendance. I was pleased that they could come, and hoped that their presence would soften the atmosphere between Joseph and Clopas, and also provide me with the opportunity to get to know them further.

As it turned out, Joseph was a very private man. He had kept the details of his wife and daughters to himself, as if waiting to reveal them at the proper time, I thought. However I sensed that Clopas would argue that he wanted to maintain a level of control by not sharing information like this with others. No time for arguments now, I reasoned, so I quickly shelved those thoughts and focused on the two pretty girls in flowing tunics and long dark wavy hair that approached me, with their father a few steps behind the dray.

"*Shalom.*" I greeted them as they approached within hearing distance of the cottage. "*Shalom,*" they responded, almost in unison. Their faces reflected friendly and happy lives, content with what they had, and appeared to be genuinely pleased to be here and help build the structure.

Joseph arrived from behind the timber pile, unaware of the escalating tension that had been the focus of yesterday's dilemma towards him. "*Shalom,*" he greeted us all, acknowledging that we would have a long day ahead. Clopas looked up, and with a small amount of effort managed to mutter a quiet "*Shalom*" back to his brother through gritted teeth, who responded with a quizzical look, though let it slide.

Maria would not be directly involved in the building work today, taking on the responsibility for the boys, and she would call on me to assist with providing fresh food and water for the workers. The bench would be well used today, a common place where we would take rest every so often during the process of construction. We sat down together for Clopas to give instructions as to where the room would be built.

Joseph led the conversation and Clopas immediately showed signs of anxiety. "I have brought the timber for the room, and could not work out how it might work attached to your existing cottage — as that is already quite old." He had a momentary pause, not at all wanting this to be a swipe at Clopas' living conditions, though agreeably the cottage needed some maintenance.

"Instead, I have been thinking that a standalone room, just off to the side of your main residence, would be easier to build and would not require us to disrupt your existing roof and wall structure."

In a flash, Clopas showed signs that his plans had been dismissed, over-ridden by his brother without consultation. It seemed that he didn't know whether to express anger now in order to just get the room built so that I could be established, or to suppress it until an opportune time. He hesitated for a few moments before answering so that it didn't come out the wrong way.

"That sounds fine. Let's do it your way." His words were somewhat abrupt, though his eyes drifted up to Joseph to provide a form of consent to commence the project. Joseph's plan actually seemed like it might work, as there would be no destruction of their cottage while the new room was built, so the night dew and any changing weather conditions wouldn't have opportunity to threaten their dwelling. It made sense.

Together we walked over the ground where the room was proposed, looked up into the nearby trees, and marked the edges of the building on the ground, along with the location of the door and window. When laid out it seemed quite spacious, was not too far away from the existing building, though was able to provide sufficient privacy and within earshot if a call was needed. Joseph might know what he's talking about after all.

Building commenced, first by laying out corner posts into position — some of which required further clean-up with the axe, shaving off some rough edges, to provide straight neat poles that would carry the wall structure. There were six poles on each side, with stronger poles in the corners to provide additional strength. They would stand upright by digging down into the earth and inserting them knee deep, then compacting the soil around them. It would take until the sixth hour for the holes to be dug, the additional hands helped to accelerate this process so all the poles were standing in position by lunch time. It was coming together quickly.

We stopped for a hearty meal of roasted goats meat, bread, olives and beans. I sat next to Abigail and Tirtzah and thought it was particularly nice to be able to eat with new friends, who would become family to me at some point. The girls had assembled at the far end of the table, and were entitled to sit, being the elder of the children present, whilst the boys took it in turns to take a seat amongst themselves on the available space on the bench seats, alternatively standing near the family.

Everyone chatted about how well the room was progressing, and how far we would get until the end of the day. There were other duties to fulfill, Joseph and the girls would need to leave in early afternoon, and we would continue to work tomorrow, and the next day, so long as the weather held up.

The room was being designed with a single sloped roof, allowing water to drain towards the rear of the building. The roof would provide an overhang of about an arms' length off the walls all around, and a window would be placed on the southern side wall to allow the sun to provide natural light during the day. The entrance faced west, allowing the afternoon sun to provide natural light inside the room, and which would provide a direct path back to the main building. A hinged door would ultimately be hung from the sturdy side wall pole that was placed into position for that very purpose.

We started again after lunch, this time focussing on the roof section by lashing the appropriate poles across each side at a height that only Joseph and Clopas could reach, at a stretch, and with the aid of chairs. Once in place this gave the building a solid outer frame, and it would be tomorrow's duty to fill in the walls with more flexible poles to allow the mud-brick to be applied into position.

Long solid timber poles were lifted into position on top of the roof structure, and fixed with flax rope that the girls had made previously. This seemed to be a natural time to break, so it was agreed that we all stood down for the day, and debriefed about the success of the day's activities over a feed of fresh fruit. We were all quite relieved to get to this point on the first day.

The brothers appeared to be talking to each other again, well, in a way that did not express cynicism or contempt. If they learned their trade together under their fathers direction, then they would have had to work closely on similar projects in the past. I wondered why Clopas had not continued as a builder, rather than to seek his own line of business, maybe something I would ask about later?

The sun set and with good weather the building continued the next day from the second hour. I was impressed with the progress, and how soon I would be settled into my own place to give Maria back her space — although I would not be distant from raising the boys.

There was ample time today to weave the second dray's flexible timber poles into the frame of the structure, and with four of us working on it, each having a partner to work on one side of the building together, the walls had been completely set in place by lunch time, marking another milestone. Some more solid timber was fixed around the window opening which provided a sense definition to the building, showing how it would look in its final state. Joseph stopped at lunch time to pursue other things, leaving the roof thatching and side walls for the remaining days ahead.

The third day started just as the others, with a delightful cool breeze flowing over the Nazarethan countryside, the trees dancing as they waved overhead. The sun shone in splendour, but it was not too hot to work. Today was to complete the roof thatching, and Joseph's daughters brought the dray fully laden with pre-cut reeds that they had collected in the afternoon of the previous day. Now it made sense that they had other things to pursue, but I felt a little left out of the process. The reeds were lifted into position, just enough to cover the entire roof, but did not provide any form of water resistance so the entire building would need to be covered in mud plaster.

The mud was collected after lunch, and this time Joseph made a point to let me know that this was not on my list of duties, and that he and the girls would do this together. I could see that they enjoyed working with their father, and how much he cared for them as they worked. This was no obstinate man that had his own interests in mind, but a very caring father-figure with a protective personality. He guarded what he cared for most, which in this case was evident before us.

Several trips to the clay pit would be required, along with water to soften and mould the clay into position, and by the end of day it became apparent that this was going to take a longer amount of time to be completed. Indeed it was a very slow process, as we allowed the men to take charge of the dirty work with the clay and the girls assisting only when called upon to provide water or carry tools back and forth between the brothers.

As it turned out, the plastering took an additional day
to complete the walls of the room, plus another day for
the roof. All up, five full days and the structure looked
complete — albeit missing the door and window at this
point in time. It would then be in liveable condition once
the mud had set, and I would be able to use it from early
next week.

The final day of the project saw Joseph work alone, having
let the girls do their own thing — they had contributed
greatly and had brought a spark of joy to the work group
that might have reduced any friction that had been dormant
from the time leading up to this, not that they seemed to
be aware of it. This morning the dray had a selection of
light timber pieces and work tools, and would become a
work bench where the door and window would be created.
With the other sets of hands missing, I was eager to help
and was encouraged by Maria to step in and help with the
building instead of assisting her with daily duties. She was
keen to see the end of this building project so that life
could return to normal.

I began to appreciate that Joseph was in a very unique
position, having had children late in life but had also lost
his wife only recently. He was not planning to wed any time
soon and had responded to the invitation out of empathy,
and because he happened to reside in the area briefly.

Joseph was a learned man, a teacher of sorts, who took
time with people to explain how to do things properly. This
is a role he enjoyed doing, and his eyes shone with delight
to be able to share with me the process of designing and
constructing the door that we were working on together that
morning. After several slight amendments to the design, we
managed to hang it into position in time for lunch.

In a similar fashion, after lunch we completed the window, which was pinned at the top to allow it to be pushed out and up, held in place with support poles that would touch the ground when opened.

Towards the end of the day, we stood back together and admired the creation. Six days it took for HaShem to create the world, and six days it took to create a room for me. We both laughed at how the timing of things ended up being this way.

This play on words created a buzz in my mind as this would be my own creative place, where I could not only find my solace and routine, but also position myself to be the wife of Joseph once we were married. I could sense a divine peace descend on the completed project, and it was agreed that we allow the building to dry out and I could move in the day after the Sabbath, which was the following day.

In the meantime I was the guest of Maria and Clopas, able to sleep on a mat in the corner. It was sufficiently warm, and comfortable, but having a room that I could call my own was starting to look a lot more like home.

As the sun neared the horizon, its rays peering through the leafy trees atop the little village, I noticed the look of satisfaction on Josephs face suggesting a sense of achievement. It wasn't simply the building work but also that he could now see how the next twelve months would work in relation to keeping us 'close but apart' during our erusin period. For that we were grateful to both Clopas and Maria for enabling us to be part of their lives and extending their welcome. They were integral to being able to make this work, and it would be nice to have a family that I could call my own.

Joseph reached out his arm to rub my shoulder in a way to tell me that he appreciated my help to complete the door and window today, as well as my assistance all this week. We were both dusty from working with the timber, the shavings had brought a peculiar smell to our clothes and we would need to bathe and change before retiring for the night. Fortunately Maria had been able to loan me some clean night attire to add to my otherwise small selection of clothes, which worked well at night but were too big to be worn during the day. A bucket bath was in order.

"Mariam," Joseph whispered. "When the time is ready, we will be together in our own place. But here is where you will have to call home for now."

Although I had already worked this out, he wanted to be sure that I knew that this was not a permanent thing, and to be ready for changes ahead. Since leaving the Temple, my role and duties had changed and I was learning how to run a home, be involved in family life and care for children. The changes in my body were a physical sign that ran alongside the progress of these other events.

Although things were developing quickly, I felt a lot younger than Josephs' girls who seemed to be of a much more marriageable age.

My eyes blinked twice in agreement, and with a short "Thank you" and a hug, we said our good byes for the evening.

Chapter 17

⁓Two Moons⁓

The next six months came with an incredible amount of grace. I now had my own room, and could enter into my personal time without impacting the family life of my hosts. Such a blessing! My time with Maria was indispensable and we intimately grew together with a common cause: to co-parent the four boys, including Clopas, and maintain the running of the household. She was a true sister to me in every sense of the word, and I could see we would share a life-long friendship, despite that we would someday soon be officially related to each other.

My morning and evening times were filled with the presence of heaven as I meditated on the scriptures and prayed. I fasted one day a week — just like Bubbe had taught me — and sought to establish myself as a loyal and faithful servant of the Lord, knowing that these days as a single woman would soon be replaced and I would be responsible to care for a husband. I was nervously excited about the future, and had wondered how this would work itself out over time.

Joseph and I met regularly, planning not only our wedding but also to find suitable men for his daughters who were well overdue to have families of their own. First, as Abigail was the oldest, Joseph had been meeting privately with parents of the eligible men of the town to determine if any might be a suitable candidate for his daughter. After several proposals were considered, both families eventually agreed to an arranged marriage from a Levite clan, with a very short *erusin* period.

Tirtzah was the younger daughter, and I could sense that he did not want to let her go so soon, being of similar personality to himself. Joseph took his time, and met with several families in Nazareth and further afield in nearby Cana, to look for a suitable husband for his daughter. This was going to take some time. I was not too concerned for his daughters, though I found it a little difficult for me to say good-bye when we were just getting to know each other. Joseph was in a dilemma. He wanted to provide for me and for us be a proper married couple, without the presence of his daughters. And he was pressed for time to make this happen.

This in itself was a long process, taking almost a full twelve months to send his youngest into the arms of another man, but finally he was freed from his fatherly duties and was again able to live life as a single man. That is, only for a while. It would not be acceptable for me to marry until I was of age, and those days were surely getting closer. Not that I wanted to hurry things along, my life was already well placed with daily scripture devotion and meditation, experiencing HaShem's peace upon me constantly so that I could bring peace to others.

The time that we would be apart from each other was narrowing, and with his daughters now gone we had the opportunity to prepare the place in a way that took my likes and interests into consideration. Together we walked through the workshop, looked at the layout of the meal room and sleeping quarters, and I asked about the possibility of making a few changes that would enable us to step into married life with minimal fuss.

Joseph did not say much, and was observing what I was saying to allow me to paint the picture of what we would look like as a married couple. It wasn't until I was adrift in the details of making some significant changes to the building, knowing that he was quite a capable man, that I realised I was alone in this conversation. I stopped, holding my breath and came back to stand beside him, waiting to hear how he would respond to my suggestions. Had I offended him with my ideas?

Eventually he came around, and I was not expecting the response he provided.

"Mariam, I can see how excited you are about our marriage, and want to acknowledge that HaShem has indeed brought us together for such as this." Blessed, I was reassured that Joseph was holding onto our future direction and waited for the "but" that would come at the end of what he was about to share.

"This place has been my childhood home, as well as my father's, and his father's. There's a lot of history and a lot of memories bound up here, which I am truly grateful for." Indeed I could see, smell and touch the living history that had shaped the walls, the benches, the ceiling; there were generations of life experience carved into this place. I had started to accept that this would be my home, my daily visits allowed me to see Joseph at work in his workshop and I was learning much of the history of this place during the lunch times when he could break to see me.

"But I've been thinking that I want a change, from here, that is." I frowned quizzically, not sure where this conversation was going, and ran my fingers through my hair.

"I was considering that we should start our marriage together in a new town, a place which we could call our own. We could get a fresh start, and with my daughters now having left home we have the opportunity to relocate." I could see that he was struggling to bring this up, though he was now moving past most of his emotional barriers and was getting to the point. My face relaxed, and I held out my hands to grasp his wiry fingers to assure that I was not objecting to his thoughts. His breathing slowed, and then continued with the proposal, holding my hands firmly.

"My great-grandfather was born in Bethlehem, and just outside and northwest of Jerusalem is the town of Emmaus, where he first met my great-grandmother. They lived there in their early years before they moved to set up the workshop in Nazareth. I have always wanted to return to that area and learn the history of my family roots. His tone raised with an air of excitement as he shared of the opportunity that this presented, which would allow us a fresh start together. I began to think that this would be a good thing, and let him continue with his vision.

"It is the same distance from Jerusalem to Bethlehem as it is from Jerusalem to Emmaus, though Bethlehem is to the south of Jerusalem. I have always longed to go back to my roots and live out my final days in that area, where some of our family remain." It was apparent that Joseph had been thinking through this for a while, and I was now feeling that his plan should be accommodated and built into our family life together, just as he was suggesting.

It was my turn to talk, now that he had broached the subject.

"Joseph," I rubbed the back of his hand to reassure him that he had my support. As head of our marriage, he was responsible for planning where we would live and how that would work out in our everyday lives. And there really was no reason for us to continue in Nazareth, if he could make plans for us elsewhere.

"I appreciate what you are saying, and am happy that you have thought about things in such depth. This gives me assurance …" I cut myself short, not really knowing what to say, but the thought of raising a family came to mind.

Nodding his head slowly in agreement with my words, Joseph gave my hand a firm squeeze to relay his response, and we stopped without words to live in the moment. A change like this would be significant, so it would be better to make the move early and integrate it into our married life, rather than become established in Nazareth and attempt to move at a later date.

In that short moment we found common ground, and it was agreed that we would move to a suitable location and leave Nazareth behind. It would be harder for him than for me, having to pack up a lifetime's worth of tools to establish the workshop elsewhere. But it would take some amount of time to do this, and the date of our marriage was surely getting close to hand, though Joseph, being the husband, was responsible for when we would proceed. In any case, this sequence of events would need to happen quickly.

Joseph responded. "I would need to take time to visit the location in order to find an appropriate property, and this could take one or two moons." I could see that he was almost going to ask my permission to leave, but then realised that he did not need to ask but simply make the way comfortable for our future transition. Before he could say a word more, I responded, accidentally cutting him off.

"That is going to be fine. Whatever you do, I am sure HaShem will lead you. When would you plan to leave?" The question was hard to ask as I was somewhat hesitant, although I knew that Joseph was capable of setting things up in a way that would make us comfortable together.

"After the Sabbath," he replied. His tone of voice was firm — he had already thought about this. This meant that he would leave three days from now, allowing us a short amount of time together and that he would be away for up to two moons.

My spirit settled, and I felt the peace of heaven overshadow me.

"Let's ask HaShem to mark your steps, and lead the way."

Together, we prayed.

After a short hug, we each let out a deep sigh and looked out the doors of the workshop to the community. It would be sad to leave, I reasoned, having expected to live out our days together here.

Joseph would be away for a reasonably short amount of time, and when he returned it would be likely that we would be in a position to marry from that point on.

In the meantime I would prepare for married life and learn as much as I could from Maria and Clopas, and be able to find solace in the room that had been built especially for me.

It would not be long before we married, and our lives would be brought together in a new way, and in a new town.

Though the thought of my vow remained silent in the backdrop of my mind.

Had HaShem overlooked this, for a time?

Chapter 18

Visitation

Spring was now visiting us, the month of Sivan was filled with beautiful flowers in the field, and a mixed aroma in the air filled my senses with joy. I found time to take in the freshness of all this season would bring, roaming the hills and fields around Nazareth as time permitted. The natural fragrances added to my excitement and anticipation that had been built around Joseph's departure, which he shared with the community after the Sabbath proceedings, and was now two nights down the road to Emmaus in search of a property.

We had shared our goodbyes together in a family breakfast with Clopas, Maria and the four boys, and waved to see him off with a donkey packed with food supplies, a change of clothes and his rolled up sleeping mat to see him on his way. Joseph had planned to take the shorter route down through Samaria, and without my presence he could complete the journey over two days to arrive at his relatives place — most of whom he would not have met in many years.

This was going to be just a short time away, in reality, while he prepared a place for us to live, enabling us to get established. My time would be filled with daily household duties, teaching the boys of the history of our nation, explain the importance of the sacrifices and offerings held in the Jerusalem Temple, and generally how to live a life worthy of the calling that we had received. I was, however, not as good a teacher as I had in Bubbe, or so I thought. Oh how I missed our times together! I used everything that she taught me — as much as I could remember or practise — to impart into the boys, to train them spiritually for their lives ahead.

Now established in my own room, my daily practise and routine echoed what I was taught in the Temple, allowing me to pray, meditate and fast as often as I felt led. My room was simple, and there was no real need to collect many other items as we would be moving away as soon as we were married, and we really didn't need much anyway. Joseph already had a lifetime's worth of furniture including benches, chairs, kitchen utensils, and everything required for the running of a home, without the need to acquire anything further.

Three days after Joseph left, the cool morning air called me into my time of worship as the sun's rays broke the horizon, splashing on the drapes through my open window, and I entered into my quiet time. My desk and chair had been arranged as usual, and I meditated quietly on scripture while waiting for the atmosphere to shift into the presence of heaven. I was always filled with peace that overshadowed me, which would remain with me through the rest of the day.

This was a peculiar morning, one that I will never forget.

As I was concluding my prayers and meditation, an angel appeared. His body shone like lightning, filling the room with glorious light and majestic power.

"Greetings, favoured woman. HaShem is with you!"

The majestic presence in my room made my heart skip a beat, my mind racing. What could this mean?

"I am Gabriel, the angel of HaShem. I have been sent because you have found favour with Him. Don't be afraid."

I was overcome with the radiance of the heavenly glory that surrounded this awesome being, I was sure someone would see the glow from outside the room.

The angel continued. "I bring you a message from the Almighty." Bubbe had mentioned that in her times of prayer and fasting that she had come into contact with angels, who gave her divine strength and wisdom, and this encounter felt just like she had described to me.

I bowed my head in reverence to allow him to continue.

Gabriel continued. "You will conceive and give birth to a son, and you will name him Jesus." At that moment I knew that I was receiving a promise from HaShem that appeared to line up with our divine appointment and betrothal. However there was an air of immediacy in the angels words that sounded like I was to become pregnant very soon — perhaps while Joseph was away? I started to ponder why I would be given the child's name, when the naming ceremony was the responsibility of the husband?

"He will be very great and will be called the Son of the Most High." The angel seemed to interact with my thoughts in a way that did not need any words to be spoken, understanding his voice in my heart. I had understood that any message brought by angels binding, something that could not be challenged, as this was a word from heaven itself. In essence, I would be carrying the child of the Most High, the life of the world, in my body. The possibility of what this meant was not immediately clear to me.

"HaShem Elohim will give him the throne of his ancestor David, and He will reign over Israel forever. His kingdom will never end!" I was receiving a very clear picture of how this message connected all the prophecies from Israel's past to usher in the arrival of the Messiah. My days of learning scripture flashed through my mind, indicating the fulfillment of those words. But why am I being involved? I am just a servant of the Lord, and don't amount to anything in title.

It was now my turn to interrupt the angels message, and he raised an open palm towards me to allow me to speak.

"How will this happen? Joseph and I have not come together yet. I am still a virgin." The thought of involving our betrothal vows weighed heavily on me, if I were to become pregnant.

Gabriel replied. "The Holy Spirit will come upon you. The power of the Most High will envelope you. So the holy baby to be born will be called the Son of G-d."

These words brought immediate clarity to my concerns about breaking the betrothal — I would conceive, but not through natural means.

My mind recalled the baby miracle of Abram and Sarai, how their bodies were as good as dead and yet were provided a child of promise after the encounter with the angel, in their day. In my case, I knew that my body was not quite ready to have a child. Bubbe had described this to me, and I was watching out for signs that my body was maturing — and knew that sometime soon my body would change.

My heart searched for some form of evidence that this was going to come to pass. Not that I had doubted the angel's words, but like Gideon I considered that HaShem could provide assurance through other means that this would indeed happen, to back up His word. Again, instinctively, Gabriel responded to my query without me uttering a word.

"Let me confirm to you that my words are true. Your relative Elizabeth has become pregnant in her old age! People used to say she was barren, but she has conceived a son, and she is now in her sixth month. For the word of God will never fail." He smiled to pass on the ever-enduring fulfillment of grace that He had received from the Throne of Heaven.

Elizabeth, pregnant? This was surprising news to me. I knew how much they wanted a baby, and how they wanted to adopt me as their own, but even that was not possible. This could only be from the hand of the Lord, a miraculous act of HaShem. My eyes fixated on the thought, not realising that I was staring straight through the messenger, until I drew my thoughts back to the present and looked up into the face of the angel who was waiting for me to respond.

I drew a deep breath, understanding that a favourable response would initiate the release of heaven's promises, and enable the fulfillment of the calling on my life. I was not simply a temple girl, nor just Joseph's future wife.

"I am the Lord's servant. May everything you have said about me come true."

My response was accepted, as if recorded in the books of heaven, to be returned to the Almighty.

And with a flash, the angel left.

Chapter 19

The Caravan

The angelic encounter left me in a state of flux, though altogether beautiful and satisfying.

The atmosphere in my room had been charged with an oily liquid that draped over my head and shoulders in a way that I cannot describe from an earthly perspective. What's more, the covering remained on me, as if by the angels words I was already being overshadowed by the Almighty. I certainly felt different, my spiritual senses having been immediately released from the apparent limitations that were on us in this realm, and I could see and feel in ways that I had not sensed before.

Life was going to be different from now on.

As a result, the visitation brought meaning to many things that I had been experiencing and I considered what life would look like for my cousin, now pregnant in her old age.

Could I get to see her during this time? It was certainly a long way to walk by myself, all the way back to the Judean countryside where they lived. That would be a four or five day walk for me, and not to be done by a young woman all alone over that distance. My trip from Jerusalem to Nazareth, with Joseph, and a chaperone, was done over five days. A return trip of a similar distance would be quite risky — how would I get to see her?

The morning routine called for my presence to attend to breakfast activities, and I managed to keep the experience to myself without blurting it out to Maria and Clopas, though I had an overflowing joy that expressed itself plainly across my face. Finally, Maria noticed my radiant expression, drew me aside, and wanted to know the details.

I kept my response simple, not quite ready to give away my experience. "I would like to visit my cousin, Elizabeth, who was there on the day of my betrothal. Would you mind if I went to see her? She has been my only family to me that has stayed close, although we have never spent too much time together."

Maria was puzzled as to why I wanted to leave so soon after Joseph's departure, but could tell from reading the look on my face that this was something of great importance to me. "Let's ask Clopas," she replied. As Joseph was away, he was my appointed caregiver, and took on the responsibility for my well-being.

"So you want to go away, too?" he mused. I hoped that my request did not seem like an insult to him, and I found it hard to read his expression. We were seated on the outside benches, with the sun shining overhead on a typical clear Nazarethan day. I waited for him to think through the implications of what this might bring as there were many things to take into consideration. How long would I be gone? How would I get there? Who would assist Maria to run the place while I was away? But he didn't ask any of those questions, and rather provided a solution that seemed to work things out perfectly.

"I'm happy for you to go, you seem like this is urgent and have been with us for over twelve months already. There is a caravan heading down which will pass through the area, leaving tomorrow. I will introduce you, and provide the allowance for the trip there, and back. They travel all through the land of Israel, now that the Romans have built some excellent roads, and pass by here once a month to collect items for sale in other areas. The return journey is set at certain times of the month, usually coinciding with the phases of the moon."

Tomorrow was going to be the full moon, and those with goods for sale would provide them to the caravan who would receive a commission and bring the remainder of the money back to those who provided the goods. I could stay with Elizabeth and travel back on the phase of a new moon. This plan could work, as it would provide protection and a means of travel without having to be separated from the group. Clopas looked pleased with the arrangement, and the timing was nothing short of a miracle.

It was agreed. I would travel with the caravan in the morning and stay with Elizabeth.

My day was filled with anticipation, knowing that the words of the angel would provide me certainty of Elizabeth's promised baby, and also my own, when the time was to come.

Chapter 20

~Pregnant~

We had been travelling for four days, stopping off briefly at towns along the way. The townsfolk knew that we were on the way because a herald had been appointed to ride ahead of us and stir things up, so that when we arrived we already had an expectant queue of eager shoppers. In turn, the merchants of that town had brought some of their wares, which we collected on their behalf, to add to our journey. This was a well organised business, and my time with them was drawing to an end as we arrived near Zechariah's home.

Gabriel's words echoed in my mind, causing my face to beam brightly with enthusiasm. "For the word of HaShem will never fail." I was eager to see my cousin's swollen tummy, the fulfilment of promise. Their home appeared ahead, and at that point I gave the caravan leader a courteous bow, and we confirmed that I would be ready on the new moon to travel back with them to Nazareth. All they would need to do was drop past the place and I would join them there. Travelling with the caravan was both entertaining and safe, though it interrupted my morning routine so I was waiting to establish myself once settled in at Elizabeth's place.

There was no need to knock on the door, as the elderly couple had it open to let in sunshine and had heard the merchants arrive to the noise of the swaying bells and tinkers that were attached to the bridles of the donkeys and camels. They knew what to expect around this time of the month and had stayed inside, not needing to buy anything at this stage of life. So it was with ease that I entered the open door and called out, "Elizabeth!"

Our faces met across the room, it had been over a year since we met at the betrothal and they looked happy. At once, Elizabeth buckled under an immense kick from her baby within, causing her to fall onto a nearby chair. The unborn appeared to be excited when I called her name. Oh what joy that must have felt!

Elizabeth took a few seconds to catch her breath, fanning herself and starting a dry pant with short breaths. "Don't rise, let me come to you." I motioned, asking her to remain seated so that I could give her a hug.

At the moment we embraced, the Spirit fell from heaven, and the sensation of an oily substance came upon her, just as it had done to me when Gabriel had announced that I would be pregnant. It was during the embrace that heaven and earth came together, forming a new dimension, and the house was filled with an atmosphere that was simply indescribable, like a low cloud had entered the house — although we could not see it.

Together we waited to let this substance became somewhat normal, and it did not fade away. This was the new normal, living in the presence of heaven.

I took a chair and sat next to Elizabeth, and waited for her to catch her breath before I gave away the reason for my visit. "Why am I so honoured that the mother of my Lord should visit me?" she enquired. What revelation did she hold of me in that statement?

I relayed my story. "The other day, during my prayer time, an angel appeared to me and told me that I was to have a baby. And not only that, he mentioned that you also were pregnant and encouraged me to see you!" I could barely contain my excitement, my face beaming with joy as I stared into her eyes.

She looked intently at me, with a fresh understanding of the realities of heaven that were now becoming manifest in her living room, and let out a loud exclamation. "Mariam, HaShem has indeed blessed you above all women, and your child is blessed!"

I knew nothing of the child within me, other than believing that the angels words would come true at a future time, though Elizabeth seemed certain that I had already conceived. Our eyes danced together and our faces lit with joy at this knowledge. We were both pregnant at the same time! We really didn't need words to express how we felt, and what we experienced during those initial moments together.

She continued. "When I heard the sound of your greeting, the baby inside me leapt for joy. You are blessed because you believed that the Lord would do what He said."

Her words were powerful and encouraging, and I felt strangely overwhelmed with the heavenly substance that was sticking to us like glue. My soul started bubbling with joy, a new song rose within me. It was a song of the Spirit, fuelled by Elizabeths words which carried a prophetic utterance.

"Oh, how my soul praises the Lord.
How my spirit rejoices in G-d my Savior!

For he took notice of his lowly servant girl,
        and from now on all generations will call me
        blessed.
For the Mighty One is holy,
        and he has done great things for me.

He shows mercy from generation to generation to all
who fear him.
His mighty arm has done tremendous things!
He has scattered the proud and haughty ones.

He has brought down princes from their thrones
        and exalted the humble.
He has filled the hungry with good things
        and sent the rich away with empty hands.
He has helped his servant Israel
        and remembered to be merciful.
For he made this promise to our ancestors, to
Abraham and his children forever."

Elizabeth was mesmerised, her eyes fixated on me.

This was no ordinary song — it was a psalm of praise
that rose from within me, overflowing and wanting to be
released. I did not know where the words had come from,
and it summarised the history of the coming Messiah that
had been promised for generations.

There really was nothing more to add, and we held each
other in a holy embrace for some time.

When it felt like we had held long enough, Elizabeth let go
of me and spoke just one word.

"Magnificent!"

Chapter 21

~Kairos~

The caravan arrived as expected to take me back to Nazareth two weeks later and I went out to greet them. Elizabeth and I were having such intimate moments in the grace that was upon us that I didn't want to have to leave, so I asked if they could return on the next full moon to collect me instead, which they graciously agreed to. They also offered to pass on a message to Clopas for me: to mention that all was going well, and that I would plan to return on the following moon. Nodding graciously and bowing low to the ground, he observed my request and took it back home.

Four weeks later they returned, but even then I felt it was too soon to go back, so again I asked if they might care to return on the next new moon, and I would travel back with them at that time. Again, they politely agreed, and returned with a message to Clopas that I would be just a little while longer before returning home. I also dropped an indication that Zechariah and Elizabeth were having a baby, which was growing close to the point of delivery, and I wanted to assist her with household duties up until that time. Faithfully, they took my message back to Nazareth.

I was looking forward to when our children could play together — perhaps after Joseph and I were married? We would certainly be a lot closer when we moved to Emmaus. My presence was genuinely appreciated as I helped Elizabeth around the home. She was finding it difficult to maintain the usual meal preparation and running of the place, given that she was already past child-bearing age and now entering her final month.

Her husband was not unable to help, and he chipped in where he could, but due to his silence we were not able to speak much with him. So we talked among ourselves, enjoying the maternal glow associated with being with child. There was only one thing that Zechariah stressed to us, and anyone that entered the house: that the name of the baby would be called "John".

"But, darling, there is no-one in our family called by that name," Elizabeth protested. Despite this, Zechariah motioned on a board that the angel had directed him to be called John, and this was to settle the matter. Convinced of this, the child would be named at the circumcision ceremony and Elizabeth would name him with what he had been assigned.

Our time together was beautifully mutually enriching, but I was unable to stay for the arrival of her baby. I felt that since I had already deferred twice, the expectation to be back home would lead them to anxiety if I wasn't home soon. I was also conscious that it was time for Joseph to return — and I didn't want him to be alarmed. Further, my body started showing signs of significant change, demonstrably pregnant, responding to the angels words.

It was time for me to return.

There was peace over the household right up until the time of my departure. Each morning I entered into my quiet time with HaShem, praying and meditating on the promises from scripture that we had received. With the presence of heaven resting on us so strongly, we gained revelation and deep understanding, knowing that the words of the prophets and the law were directing us to the coming Messiah. We were now part of the storyline, being overshadowed by the glory of heaven.

What were our children to grow up to be? We accepted that John was the name of their baby, and the angel had announced to me that my child was to be called Jesus. "John and Jesus," I mentioned under my breath to my cousin, both of our bellies swollen, though mine much less so than hers. "I hope they don't keep us awake all night with their incessant kicking!" giggled Elizabeth. We both laughed, knowing that the boys were already communicating with each other, and we were sure that they would grow up with sincere friendship when time allowed for visits.

"There is but the matter of my return," bringing up a topic that I was somewhat hesitant to discuss.

"Yes, that." she agreed, knowing that my absence from Nazareth would be noted and they might start to worry for my safety — or perhaps I had run away and did not want to proceed with the betrothal after all? "Yes, I will have to return home soon, and won't be able to be here for your baby. But we will catch up in time," I assured her.

Joseph's time at Emmaus was to be only a short while, and he would have had reason to return to Nazareth once things were planned and underway. I sensed that he was already on the journey back home, if he wasn't already, and would be concerned for me. So we agreed that I would return with the next merchant caravan so that I could travel safe back home.

"So … how do you think Joseph will respond?" she asked with a rising tone in her voice. The situation — although borne of HaShem — meant that Joseph might want to terminate the betrothal. I had been dwelling on this for some time, but did not want to mention it, understanding that since this was a situation beyond my own control I would need to rest in the One who started it.

"I'm not completely sure how he will take it," I responded. I had secretly hoped that he would understand that an angel had visited me and spoken words of life into my body, but unless the Lord had provided this revelation to him ahead of time then it would take some careful wording to ensure that he was able to handle the message.

Elizabeth took my hand, held it up, and said, "Let's pray." Together we committed my departure and subsequent arrival at Nazareth, the meeting with Joseph, to the Lord; praying that all would go well and that we would be covered with divine grace and mercy.

After a nights rest, the caravan returned to collect me, this time without my protests to stay, and we travelled on to Nazareth after a session of hugs and tears. Elizabeth's baby was due any day now, and I felt I was forced to leave when she could have benefitted from me most.

However, it was time.

This was the moment that we had to depart, and commit each other to the Lord and His purposes. We knew that the babies to be born us were part of the great plan for Israel, and that we would be overshadowed by the Almighty.

We simply needed to be faithful.

From my departure we travelled the five full days through villages and towns to eventually arrive in Nazareth just before sundown, where I was deposited at the door with Clopas, Maria and the boys all looking out for my arrival. They were pleased to see me. It felt naturally warm to be home, to my own room, and in the presence of family that welcomed me with open arms.

Maria had prepared dinner, which they all gave me a small portion from their plates, enabling me to join them, and she eyed me carefully. Did she know that I had changed? Could she see that I was different?

It wasn't until after dinner, when Clopas was sleepy and the boys had found their sleeping mats, nestled together around the flames of the fireplace, that she brought it up.

"Mariam, we really missed you." she started, stroking my hand in open empathy. Her face reflected the warmth of the fire, and the aroma from the smouldering timber presented the memories of home.

"I'm pleased you are back with us after such a long time away. We were starting to be concerned for you, though we know we shouldn't have been." Her caring tone wrapped around my heart in a way that opened a longing for me to be here again. I nodded graciously to accept her words, before responding.

She was fixated on me, and her eyes were drawn to my belly that was starting to reveal a small bump under my tunic while seated in the chair. She knew.

"Well?" She asked hesitantly, not knowing if, or how, I would respond.

I took my time, drawing a deep breath, and confirmed her suspicions.

"Yes," I responded in a hush voice.

No more words were said that night, we simply gave each other a hug as tears welled in our eyes. How was I going to explain this to Joseph?

Right now, it was time for bed.

I headed to my room, and needed to pray.

Chapter 22

Surprise

Morning arrived all too soon. I didn't sleep at all well through the night, knowing the difficulty of the message I was to share with Joseph later that morning, knowing that he had already arrived several days ahead of me. I slipped into my home routine early, and assisted with morning duties as was expected, and prepared myself as quickly as I could to see my future husband at the workshop. This was to be no ordinary meeting, and I held a quiet inner peace knowing that the outcome was inevitable. I took a deep breath before announcing my arrival. Would I be faced with a clash of hostility, or moderate acceptance?

Arriving at the front door, "Joseph — I'm back!" My voice led with a raised tone to present a call to see if he would come out, or if I was to come inside. Peering in, I could see the pleasant orderliness of the tools aligned on the walls that he had grown accustomed to. Not even a length of timber seemed out of place while he worked on projects, he had a peculiar style of workmanship that demonstrated pride and efficiency that others could not compete against.

The dappled sunlight through the trees gave a pattern on the front wall of the workshop. The sound of feet shuffling inside to arrive at the front door gave my heart a leap. He stood a few paces inside and took a good look at me while running his hand through his beard — had he noticed the bump under my tunic?

"*Shalom*. Come in, come in." he ushered, insisting that I was no stranger, ensuring that I received a hug on the way through. He was relaxed and happy to see me. I took another deep breath to keep my peace.

"*Shalom*. It's so nice to be back." It was indeed good to be home again, to smell the fresh timber shavings in the air. A quick look around the workshop confirmed that he had already started a new project. The atmosphere was quiet, and a sense of anticipation from our lengthy time away was building between us. I wanted to hear about his time away, how he would be building a new home for us, and when we might travel after our wedding. My mind drifted into our future life together, wandering off as he spoke about a farm that he had purchased for us to relocate to, in time.

I may have not been fully aware of what he was saying, when he stopped abruptly to snap me back into reality. He wanted to hear from me.

"And how was your trip to see Elizabeth? Maria mentioned that you have been away for some time." His tone was not harsh, and showed a genuine interest. I quickly brought him up to speed with Zechariah and Elizabeth's baby, the practicalities of travelling with the merchants to and from Nazareth, and the rush to arrive home.

He listened intently and seemed to enjoy the sound of my voice, allowing me to speak freely and openly. Was there more to add? His face invited me to continue, as though there was something missing that needed to be shared, and he tilted his head down to press me further.

Deep breath.
This might be uncomfortable.

"As I mentioned, I hurried to see Elizabeth because I had a vision of an angel that said she with child in her old age. But there was something more that the angel shared with me — the real reason why I needed to leave quite quickly."

Joseph was now standing alert, his pose was set to fight or flight, not knowing what I was to say next.

Breathe, Mariam. Breathe.

Somewhat nervously, my words came out all at once.

"The angel shared with me that I would become pregnant, but not through a man. This would be a miracle. This child would be called the Son of the Most High. And he would be given the throne of David."

I stopped.

Joseph froze.

His eyes scanned my body to see if what I was sharing was true.

Blinking rapidly, I could see a look of confusion across his face, so I did not say any more about it.

Instead, I put my hands over my belly and pressed my tunic flat over the area where the bump was starting to appear. My young body was providing definitive proof that the words of the angel had come to pass, and I lifted my eyes to seek his acceptance of what I was presenting.

Joseph's breathing got louder, indicating frustration, so I waited for him to respond.

"You're with child?" His swallowed deeply.

It seemed as though time stopped.

"Seriously, you're *pregnant?*"

I nodded my head slowly to confirm that what he heard from my lips, and seen in my body, was indeed true.

"You're PREGNANT?!"

I could see fear mixed with anger rising within him. His body became erect and fingers were twitching uncontrollably. His face flushed red at the thought that this event was beyond his control.

"Who is the father?!" he demanded.

It's as if he did not hear my story about the angels' visit, his mind racing to seek a solution for the problem. This was unexpected news, and was a situation that would affect both of our lives forever in a way that he had witnessed happen to others. He would be labelled an outcast, and we would live miserable lives together, becoming the scourge of society. Or he would not accept the situation, sending me away to bring up the child alone as a single disgraced mother in a community where there would be no support. And certainly no approval.

His clenched fists indicated that this news was hard to accept, and I didn't want to interrupt his thinking, sensing that he needed time to get through this.

Taking two steps back and with shame and anger, he uttered just two words to indicate what I should do.

"Please leave." He raised a finger, pointing to the door, and poked the air twice to affirm his words.

Bowing to his wishes, I lifted my tunic slightly off the ground and ran home to my room, the door closing firmly behind me.

This had not gone well.

Would he want to break off the betrothal?

My heart thumped in my chest — was it really okay to accept this instruction from the angel after all?

I could but ponder over what would happen, and wait for an outcome.

"HaShem," I prayed, "am I really in your will?"

Although heaven was silent at that point, I cried to myself on my bed, and did not leave the room all day.

Chapter 23

~The Decision~

It was two days before Joseph made an attempt to see me, and I had kept myself calm to let the situation work itself out naturally. My heart was filled with a quiet confidence that, despite his strong reaction, the words of the angel would over-rule any earthly condition that we were experiencing as a result of the baby that I was carrying. During my quiet meditation that morning, I reflected on the goodness of HaShem to the people of Israel, and a river of calm swept over me. The presence of the Lord was peacefully strong over and around me, there was no room for fear, being held secure in the embrace of heaven.

Whatever Joseph was going through would be taken care of, for sure. We would simply need to trust the angel's words and believe that this was part of the divine plan, not some reckless mistake that would ruin our credibility.

The sun had been up for some time, the children had been fed and I had commenced the day's activities together with Maria, when my betrothed arrived at the cottage. Had he worked up the courage to face his fears and approach me about it? Would he still be angry, or could he accept this as the will of HaShem?

Joseph stopped at the bench seat and greeted us with a warm but timid "*Shalom*," seeking acceptance to join us. I looked over to Maria, and her cheery smile approved that I could leave my duties and spend time with him to discuss things further. I had confided in Maria and Clopas about the situation, and they were quite aware that he may take some time to cool off after learning about this. So I put down what I was doing onto the table, reached out my hand to indicate that we should leave to discuss things privately.

Joseph was initially quiet, and apparently solemn, though he was still hard to read — given the immense emotional struggle of the last two days. Coming to the edge of the village, we stopped under the shade of a tree, and he opened up, hesitantly, at first.

"Mariam, I must first apologise … for how I responded to your arrival home. I was excited to see you … but surprised at the same time. Are you able to … Can you forgive me … for the way I reacted?" His eyes showed a depth of sincerity that expressed genuine sorrow and confirmed that this was no made-up sense of sympathy. Here was a true and steadfast man, ready for reconciliation, wanting to restore the broken relationship.

Taking the hands of the carpenter, I searched his eyes to locate the depths of the words that were coming from his heart, and responded with my own look of acceptance to indicate that there was nothing stopping us from continuing — that he truly was forgiven. There was nothing that I wanted to keep over him, as in fact the heavenly peace continued to overshadow me, and I wanted that to envelope him as well. There really was nothing to fear.

"Joseph," I started, "I can understand how you felt, though I did not know any other way to tell you. And I was saddened to see how this affected you, I mean us, how it affected us during the last few days." He cut me short, raising a finger to my mouth, not wanting me to talk further. There was something more he needed to say, and it was bubbling up from him so all I needed to do was listen.

"When I ordered you to leave, I could not believe that HaShem would allow this. After all, the vow from our betrothal meant that if something like this occurred then I would divorce you. And when it happened, I was angry at HaShem and angry at you. It's not what I was expecting at all. This is not what married life is about."

This was the first time that I had heard Joseph speak about being angry, though it had clearly struck like a coiled snake in response to the situation that presented itself.

"I was so hurt and angry about this that I went to the synagogue and took a vow to break our betrothal. This seemed like the only logical decision to make, given that I made our vows before the Sanhedrin in Jerusalem. At least the priests would respect my decision, and I would keep my integrity."

My thoughts raced, trying to keep pace with what he was saying and work out a plan to raise this child as a single mother. It would not be easy in this society, which despised single parents, and I would be left without the means to support myself. Perhaps I could stay with Clopas and

Maria, and allow Joseph to be free to live his own life? Or return to Elizabeth?

Joseph continued. "When I considered this, and resolved that we should not be together, I had the matter settled in my heart and intended to meet you this morning to give you my decision." My face jumped back and my eyes flipped up at what he was saying. Was he here to tell me that he was breaking the betrothal?

"But then, last night, I had a dream. This is not something that usually happens. This encounter was so real, that I have the picture clear in my mind and it has changed what I was going to do this morning."

He took his time, searching for the right words to say, determined to finish the story.

"In my dream, an angel appeared to me. He said, 'Joseph, son of David, do not be afraid to take Mariam as your betrothed.'" At that, I realised the reason for his change of heart, just like the angel had told me the news of my pregnancy, Joseph had likewise received a visit from heaven.

"He continued, saying, 'The child within her was conceived by the Holy Spirit.'" This explained how I had become pregnant without knowing a man, and he was able to accept this word which aligned with what I had told him. This baby was going to be no ordinary child, or mistake.

"The angel continued to tell me that you will have a son, and that I was to name him Jesus. His name means that he will save his people from their sins." The baby's name was the same which the angel gave me during my encounter, some three months earlier. This could be no co-incidence that we were both given the name independently.

The responsibility for naming the child laid with the father, and formed part of the circumcision ceremony — eight days after child birth. That would be another six months away, and we would need to work a lot of things out between now and then. Our lives would need to change in such a significant way now that I was with child, and our standing in the community would be questioned and judged every day by those around us. That is, unless they came to believe the story of the angel about his conception?

Joseph bit his lip, wanting to keep the story flowing, while also drawing it to an end. "So, after seeing the angel, I accepted that it was HaShem's will that we continue with the betrothal, that is, continue to get married." I breathed a sigh of relief, as this now aligned with the peace that I was experiencing, and Joseph had finally agreed with me about it. This meant that we could work towards living a normal life together, or so it seemed.

"But," he said, "I have made a vow."

We had already discussed our betrothal vows, and had put this matter to rest. Together, yet independently, we had to let HaShem be HaShem and have His way over our lives. This was something different.

"I mentioned that I visited the priests … and made a vow." Oh, yes, he did.

"Although we will continue with the betrothal, and be married at some future time, I will be unable to consummate our marriage. I need you to understand and respect that this is no ordinary vow that I have made, and it has serious consequences." My mind paused, racing to comprehend the impact of what he was sharing. Had he really been that angry so as to vow against it? Oh HaShem, what does all this mean?

"Though we will be married, we will raise the baby as a true father should. To everyone else, we will look like a married couple."

Behind his words were a series of actions that I had not understood at the time, but which came to reality later. Jesus would grow up to be known as 'The son of the carpenter', although this was only in title. Since the baby had no earthly father, this was going to make the registration of the baby's name somewhat difficult, when it came time.

Our world was changing faster than we could hold onto it.

Although the peace of heaven was guiding our hearts and decisions, I could see that living in this small regional community was not going to be easy. Our move to Emmaus was starting to appeal to me in a very big way. Maybe we would find relief when the baby was born?

We hugged, sharing the solemnity of the moment that had just passed, and spoke nothing further on our way back to see the others.

Chapter 24

Census

The six months leading up the to birth was a mix of awkward peace and patient waiting. We were caught in a time lapse that was playing out in ways that we could not control — although we had both allowed and agreed with the divine acts at the time.

HaShem knew that we would allow Him to plan and control our lives, having given ourselves up for His service since our early days, but we did not realise how this would work itself out in practise. Bubbe would sometimes remind me, "HaShem's ways are not our ways; His thoughts are above our thoughts." And so it was in this case as well. Whatever level of governance that we thought we had over our lives was now handed over to the ways and will of HaShem.

When we broke the news of my pregnancy to both Clopas and Maria, other than the private moment I shared with Maria the night I returned, we also discussed the planning for the next six months — how that would be orchestrated, given such a delicate nature of the pregnancy, especially in such a town as Nazareth where news travelled fast and people were equally quick to judge. There was no doubt that Joseph and I would become the town gossip, and would have to live with the decision to keep the baby and our relationship intact.

Clopas eyed us carefully, taking in everything we shared — from the visit of the angel, independently, to both myself and Joseph, of my hurried visit to Elizabeth and her baby, and working through Joseph's unanticipated response to my pregnancy. Of all the people that had the right to eject me from the town, surprisingly he had no form of judgement against me, but held onto my words with a sense of loyalty. Stroking his beard, and knowing that he held a level of power over me that no-one else had at the time, he gave me assurance.

"Mariam, we know from your experience with us that you are a humble young lady, and that this is not something that you would make up. We are willing to have you stay with us, and we will support you during this time."

His words were soothing to my soul, which had ached at the thought that things could go terribly wrong, although the angels words were the only assurance that I needed to be able to continue to trust in HaShem and see how this would unfold over time. I glanced up to face him and Maria directly, knowing that they were already gracious to have me live with them during erusin. Their faces displayed a radiant grace, reflecting the openness of their hearts to accept both myself and Joseph, and the yet to be born baby Jesus. There was no greater security that I felt during this time than to be with my family, where home was a place of respite from the eyes of the world.

Life returned to normal, or at least a state of routine, where I could take on the role of assistant to Maria once again and teach the boys lessons in life and history. Each morning I was able to enter into my quiet time of peace and reflection, allowing me to dwell on the scriptures, pray and occasionally fast — though I was careful to maintain a proper level of control over the food I ate.

Maria was more of a support and help to my practical needs on a day to day basis, than I felt that I was to her in the running of the household. Having already had the two boys, she was intent on educating me on the process of good health and management of the birth — when that time was to come. She provided a source of comfort to me in our sisterly arrangement, proving that she was one that I could confide in, and who took the time to understand me.

As my older sister, I warmed to her charm and the way she handled situations around the home and the marketplace. Our bonds grew deep and our hearts knit together as we shared stories from our past over the timber table in the cool of the afternoon, which seemed to shape the way of our friendship over time. Her quirky smile almost always gave me a laugh when she was being serious with the boys, asserting her voice of authority with her shoulders leaning forward and hands on hips, she would give me a wink across the room to let me know that this was not simply an outburst of anger. I would bite my lower lip to stop myself from laughing, and take away the seriousness of the situation that she was dealing with at the time. Later I would need to use this approach, I reasoned, with my own boy, so I watched her actions closely.

It was around the eighth month — my belly protesting loudly that the changes to my body were not to be hidden from society — that a murmur commenced in the town, and

Joseph brought us the news about it. The authorities had issued a decree, stating that a census of the Roman empire was to be taken, from the first week of the new year.

Joseph and Clopas considered the consequences of what this might mean, given that I was going full term around that time — I would be in no fit state to travel, it would seem.

"The edict stated that all men must present themselves in the town of their birth for the roll call." Naturally this applied to the betrothed and married couples, and their children. And since Joseph was from the royal line of David, we would need to travel to Bethlehem in Judea — just like the first night of our betrothal.

This was not going to be an easy journey, and it made no sense to leave until it was really necessary. We decided that we would travel in the last week of the year, from the day after the Sabbath, and hoped that we would have sufficient time to arrive in Bethlehem prior to the next Sabbath. It could not have been a more horrible situation to be thrust into, especially since my baby was due at that time.

On a practical note, we would travel by donkey to allow me to easily dismount if required, and Joseph would walk. And we would take the path of our initial journey, from Nazareth through Jericho and then to Bethlehem. This allowed an extra day for travelling, and to rest along the way, if required. This time we would not need a chaperone, given my physical state, and there were already many other townsfolk that were planning to travel the distance with us back to their home towns — which were varied throughout the land of Israel.

The final few days in Nazareth were focussed on our mental and practical preparedness, with Maria providing a verbal checklist of things from time to time to ensure that we had considered as many options as possible for what lay ahead.

"Tomorrow, the day of your journey, are you sure you will be alright?" She was intent on giving me as much assurance as possible, given that my baby could come at any moment. Being the Sabbath, we had just returned from the synagogue and were enjoying a meal together before departing first thing in the morning.

I assured her, "Yes, we will be fine. I have HaShem's peace over me, and I don't seem to have any anxiety in my thoughts or heart about it. We will be covered in His grace, with angels surrounding us."

What they didn't realise is earlier that morning I had meditated on the psalms, and this verse had come to mind:

> "He will order his angels to protect you wherever you go.
> They will hold you up with their hands so you won't ever hurt your foot on a stone."

Would I really be in shape to travel the distance?
What would happen if the baby was to come early?

Although these thoughts came like darts into my mind, the peace of heaven guarded me and there was nothing to be afraid of. Joseph and I prayed together with Clopas and Maria, entrusting the journey to HaShem, and we would be sure to travel carefully until we reached Bethlehem, in time for the census.

At the conclusion of our meal we held hands and sang a traditional song of thanks for all the good things that HaShem had done for us, and for remembering Israel.

Joseph prayed asking for travelling mercies so that we would not fall into bad company along the way, and to keep the baby safe.

We sat and talked until the boys fell asleep in front of the fire, that is, including Clopas and Joseph.

In a whisper, Maria assured me that the journey before us would go without fault. "All things will work out according to His plan. Just trust Him." I'm not sure if she was trying to reassure me, or settle her own thoughts and anxiety, but I accepted it with a smile.

As I put myself to bed that evening, I looked around my room which had been my place of solace for the last year and a half. I had grown to like it here, a place of acceptance, family and belonging. But what challenges lay ahead of us that we were yet to learn about?

Chapter 25

Arrival

The fresh spring air cupped against my face, and although winter was officially over our journey wasn't. We had travelled the distance from Nazareth to Bethlehem over the last six days, with Joseph leading my donkey all the way until we reached his hometown. This was not a trivial journey, as I was heavily pregnant and we could not afford to slow down until we arrived.

We had planned to reach Bethlehem before the Sabbath, allowing the full six days so we could keep the requirements of the Law. Today was the last day of our travels, and we needed to arrive before sundown so as to avoid the Sabbath. And this was not an ordinary Sabbath, we would be welcoming the start of the new year, Nisan 1, once the sun had fallen beyond the horizon.

These circumstances made our journey even more extraordinary. I was dreaming with eager expectation, upon our arrival, that it would be refreshing to put my feet up, rest my back from the long journey and take a hot bath at the local inn to sooth my body.

Our trip was not something we had planned while I was in this state, and it would have been better for me to stay in Nazareth with family instead of risking injury along the way. However the edict required family groups to be counted according to their ancestral divisions to determine the rate of taxes that should be applied.

This made the little town of Bethlehem heavy laden with out-of-towners who were obligated to be present for the census. Those who were well respected or well-known were able to find accommodation, while the rest found lodging where-ever they could.

It was no surprise then that there was no lodging available in the inn, as the village was not used to such a great influx of people all at once. My dreams of relaxing in a hot tub vanished like a mist and my husband-to-be set about finding a suitable resting place with his relatives and extended family who resided in the town. Meanwhile I sat in the village square with the donkey until he returned to collect me.

From the first day of spring, the birthing of the lambs provided renewed life into the village. It was three weeks since they started to drop, and I felt that my baby was to come anytime during this lambing season too. Indeed my lower back started to hurt. Was this simply from riding the colt to get here? The spasms had grown in intensity, and then start to relax — allowing me to breath normally for a while — and they were increasing today, of all days.

Finally, he returned. Joseph has many friends and family connections in this town, I was sure he would be able to persuade someone to take us in. If this baby was to come tonight, I needed to be in a place with family who could help.

"Mariam, I talked with as many relatives as I could find in this short time before sun-down, and it was hard to convince them that we needed a place to stay as they were already taking in others from afar." Joseph's voice sounded partly distressed and melancholic, as though he had failed me. But then he put to me a proposition that needed my careful consideration.

"There is a small stall on the edge of town, outside our village. It belongs to my cousin. They are keeping the special lambs in there with their mothers. He has offered it to us, until we can find another place of rest, if we are willing to accept it."

The disappointment of not being able to bathe soon vanished with the hope that we could rest for the night. It wasn't ideal, but it was the only place on offer at a time when we needed it. I knew we had to accept it, and gave an agreeable nod for Joseph to help me to my feet.

The stall wasn't too far away, about 15 minutes by foot, and we were able to create space towards the back by pushing aside the nursing ewes. This provided us a small amount of roof shelter, keeping us partly protected from the cool of the evening.

It was enjoyable to see the newborn lambs standing next to their mothers with their tails wagging as they drew from their mothers milk; we watched as they spent their time together. The smell was something that I was not too familiar with, the experience was new and refreshing despite the way I felt from our travels. Meanwhile we spread out rugs on the soft earth to form our usual night-time layers of bedding and rustled through our bags for the last of our travel food and water.

The tight pangs in my lower back and side continued to seize me, and as the night grew on Joseph could see that the birth was imminent. Here in the stall there was a heavenly peace that covered the sheep and their lambs, where we could all find our rest. But circumstances seemed to indicate that our rest was likely to be delayed tonight.

A wave of exhaustion mixed with joy, flushed over me, as if the world was about to change forever, the words of the angel Gabriel came to mind. "He will be very great and will be called the Son of the Most High. HaShem Elohim will give him the throne of his ancestor David, and He will reign over Israel forever."

"O HaShem," I prayed, "is he really coming tonight?"

Looking around, this place wasn't fit for a king.

This was no traditional birthing suite, and there were no midwives on hand to help with the delivery. At best, the clay channel provided a source of water for the sheep that used the stall. It wasn't hygienic, and we had limited amounts of fresh clean water on us, to wash down after the birth.

The feed trough, a timber manger that contained the remnants of grain, sat near the entrance. We might be able to use that as a cradle after the birth to lay him in. Due to our travels we brought minimal clothes for the newborn, though Maria prescribed these absolute necessities before we left, and not much in the way of additional clothing for ourselves. We were ill-prepared for this!

The lambs in this stall were dedicated to HaShem for the upcoming ceremony and celebrations. Separated from the rest of the flock, they were to be kept unharmed by wrapping them in cloths and set aside with their mother ewes. This way they could be offered without spot or blemish, an acceptable Passover offering — just fourteen days from now. At best, we may need to use these lambing cloths to wrap up our child, there was really no other clothes to wrap our child at this point.

The rest of the flocks in the fields were kept under close watch by shepherds who protected them from lions or bears who sought an easy meal. At least here, in the stall, they were with their mother, kept calm, safe and protected even when no shepherds were around.

The pangs in my lower back increased again, and the joyful sadness of this birth reached into the depths of my heart, knowing that here in this stall, with these sheep, tonight would be born the lamb of HaShem, the Saviour of the world — just as the angel had spoken.

Time passed, and my breathing increased to pant through the contractions that were now quite regular.

"Joseph," I called in a soft voice, who was resting next to me.

"He's coming!"

Chapter 26

~New Year~

The secluded location was an unintended private birthing suite that was to become extraordinarily busy that night.

Having raised Joseph to seek assistance, he rushed into town in search of a midwife. He had not gone far when he encountered a woman from the hills, who enquired where he was going. In an unexplainable turn of events, she was the one that was needed at this time.

Joseph did not want to stop while the birth was imminent, so he mentioned in passing, "I need to find a Hebrew midwife," not knowing that she was a midwife.

The lady smiled, asserted herself, and asked, "Where is she that needs assistance?"

"She is in the cave, nearby," pointing in the direction where he had left me earlier. "I am a midwife." she explained, and together they travelled back to the stall. Along the way, she was intrigued as to why we would choose an animal stall for the birth, and asked, "Is she not your wife?"— not at all intending to be offensive, but the admission would require some time for explanation. Was there a sense of shame that he did not want to care for me like other women who gave birth?

Joseph replied with my story, which he assumed everyone knew. "This is Mariam — from the Jerusalem Temple. She was educated in the house of the Lord, and I received her as my wife by lot. We were betrothed when she conceived by the Holy Spirit."

Astonished, the midwife became puzzled. Was this true, or a fabrication? Together they returned to catch me panting short breaths as the contractions increased. The midwife came to my side, holding my hand in assurance, and helped me keep pace with the birth. It was reassuring to have another woman there, and especially one experienced in child birth. Finally I could relax and let her provide the directions I needed to continue.

It was not long after that the cave filled with a holy glow, and a bright cloud overshadowed us. The cloud became such a great light that we could not bear it, and we held our arms across our faces to avoid being blinded.

Finally the light intensity decreased, and we managed to see without having to cover our eyes. It became apparent that the birth was over, and the child was found resting on my breast. "What an extraordinary sight! What a glorious day!" The midwife was astonished, and her attendance at the scene became one who was merely a witness, rather than an active participant in the delivery.

Joseph was also nearby, watching things unfold, but unable to participate due to the great light.

It was now late, the moon had passed, the Sabbath had begun, and the new year had commenced.

This really was such an unorganised time to have given birth; the census was only days away, and the number of people in town had increased ten-times above normal levels.

The midwife, whose name was Salome, gathered the swaddling cloths to wrap up the newborn and placed him by my side in the feed trough, allowing us all to get some rest.

A holy hush came over the stall, the night quietened, and the sounds of the lambs occasionally broke the still night air that surrounded us. We were exhausted and needed rest. There were to be no more disturbances tonight, I reasoned.

But I was wrong.

It started with a low commotion afar off, with the tingle of bells that were tied to their staffs as they travelled. A mob of shepherds had been sent in search of the cave, and arrived before dawn while the morning star shone brightly in the sky above.

We were startled awake by their excited tones. Sleep was to escape us this evening. Joseph rose to meet them, keeping a low voice to ask why they were here. Why, in all the nights of history, were they sent to this distant cave on the edge of a remote rural town? Finally, discussions ended, and Joseph led them quietly, two at a time, to my side.

There, asleep in the manger beside me, they saw the baby wrapped in swaddling cloths — just as the angel had told them. They could not contain their joy; earlier that evening a band of angels had appeared from heaven and announced the arrival of the promised Saviour, with a sign being that they would find him wrapped snugly in strips of cloth and lying in a manger.

"But how did you find us?" I asked in a quiet voice so as not to wake the baby. "Oh, that was easy," said the lead. "The innkeeper saw that you were on the verge of giving birth, and the story of your situation travelled very quickly throughout the town. When we arrived they pointed us to this cave where they said we should find you."

I mused at the thought that we had so easily become the talk of the town, as though we were the only news to discuss over their evening dinner.

"Besides, this is where we bring the special lambs, donating only the best to be kept here for *Pesach* in a few weeks' time. We are all familiar with this cave."

Joseph looked directly toward me, our eyes locking together as their words presented us with a sense of future destiny for the child. A tingly sensation crawled up my spine, indicating that there was likely to be more reasons why the baby was born here. Maybe we weren't just the unfortunate ones without accommodation? Perhaps this was part of a greater plan?

Finally, the sun started to break the horizon, it had been a big night. We motioned that we needed rest, and Joseph dismissed the shepherds so that we could once again find sleep.

Meanwhile the men entered the little town and shared all about the nights events with everyone they ran into, who became astonished at what they heard. Later they returned to the hillside to take care of their flocks, grateful for the sign that they had been given and praised HaShem for all that they had seen and heard, just as the angel had told them.

As I lay down again, the people and events from tonight's activities gave me plenty to think over for the coming months and years.

What did all this mean?

I drifted off to sleep with a sincere smile on my face, with the baby in the makeshift cradle next to me.

The promise of a Saviour had been fulfilled.

Chapter 27

~Eight Days~

We became the talk of the town overnight! When the shepherds returned to the village and shared what they had seen and heard, it caused quite a stir. Even the manager of the local inn had heard what had happened and was interested in my welfare, and felt somewhat apprehensive that he was unable to provide us lodging the previous day. As a result we had a continual stream of people visit the cave to verify the stories that were circulating around town.

We would happen to stay among the sheep for another two nights until the census began that week. And that in itself began to be an issue that had played on Josephs' mind. Was he to enrol me, and the baby, as his wife or as his daughter? Everyone by now had become familiar with the situation: that a virgin had given birth, seemingly testified by angels and corroborated by local shepherds. He found it hard to say that I was his daughter, despite our apparent differences in age. And he felt uncomfortable declaring the truth about our betrothal, since we had a baby to declare.. He was able to attend the census alone, given the circumstances, waiting in line until the table had been cleared ahead of him.

The official didn't want to be messed around with illogical debate; they were there simply to capture the information and maintain records of the people. Joseph's situation didn't help his cause in this matter.

"So what is it then?" demanded the enrolling officer. The census required the man of the house to confirm his dependants, which included his wife and children.

Joseph shrugged away shyly, not knowing how to answer. Should he lie to conceal the situation, or openly declare that both the girl and the baby were his? It was difficult. He replied cautiously and remained committed to stand by his integrity. "She is my betrothed. We are not yet married, but will do so in the coming days. And she has had a baby, though I am not his father."

An angry flush swept over the face of the officer. How long would people evade his questions and simply tell the truth? His form did not have a way to record this. The officer thought for a moment, and finally made the decision on behalf of Rome.

"Right, this is what we will do. The baby will be known as the son of Joseph, though you say you aren't his father but will raise him as your own. So we will record him and her with you under the line of King David." Joseph sighed with relief, at least he didn't need to make that decision on his own.

"We are not collecting anything other than the facts at this time. This is just the assessment. Now, off you go, son." Clearly the Roman knew his authority, and wanted no further argument or disputes. This was otherwise going to be a long day if all cases presented like this.

Upon his return, I was keen to learn how his visit went, and what would happen from here. Joseph explained that we were registered under Rome as 'husband and wife, with child' so the census form could be completed. We all had a wry giggle as Joseph explained how the delicate situation was overthrown by the adamant official who was left with no choice other than to make a blunt point about it.

"Son of Joseph, hey?" I teased, jiggling Jesus on my lap. Again Joseph blushed and looked to the ground, accepting the title, though he felt uncomfortable about it. The baby would know no difference at this stage.

Upon finalising their registrations, those people who had been visiting from out of town immediately commenced their return home, allowing rooms to become available at the inn for us to relocate to instead of staying in the animal shelter. So we travelled back into town until we were to register the baby in Jerusalem.

The innkeeper, who had previously been unable to provide us a room, welcomed us back as long lost family members — now that his source of income were leaving for their own homes. The shepherds stories that were circulating added a cheap form of entertainment to those who were staying with us, allowing people to talk to the now-famous couple in person, though we desperately wanted to keep our situation private. And yet, this is how things unfolded; it didn't seem that it would become any easier over time. From now on Jesus would be 'the son of Joseph', though this was all tongue-in-cheek by those who knew us.

We were able to stay at the inn for a further week, which provided enough time for me to rest and recover, and we could prepare for the trip to the Temple. I, for one, was keen to return and see not just the progress of the rebuilding, but to reconnect with Bubbe, my mother figure and mentor. It was about eighteen months now. I longed for her smile, and craved for her embrace — that is, if she were to accept the situation that I was now in. We would have much to talk about!

The trip to Jerusalem was one that we were to take according to the law; boys were to be circumcised on the eighth day. We decided to travel the day prior into Jerusalem, rest overnight, and undertake the ceremony the following day. Joseph, myself and the baby all banded together for the walk and left the tiny village for the days walk ahead of us, arriving before sundown to settle for the night. We left a small number of belongings at the inn, where we would stay two more nights, and then we would relocate more permanently to the house at Emmaus, which Joseph had commenced.

It was the eighth day, and the sounding of the bells from the temple indicated that public duties could commence and that the morning rituals had been completed. My mind returned to the days when I would assist both priests and people with their duties and obligations, as prescribed by the law. It seemed such a long time ago — things were so different for me now, and yet it also felt like 'just yesterday'. Our last steps here together were in the Sanhedrin's hall, to complete our betrothal vows. And today we would face some of the same men who had secured our appointment. This time we returned with a baby in our arms. Would they be surprised? We decided to enter quietly, so as not to create a scene, entering through a side entrance for the dedication.

A priest spotted our entry from across the hall, catching him off guard at the sight. Joseph, he recognised, as well as myself, but why were we holding a baby? His face reflected a sense of outrage, or fear, or disgust — we were not certain what he was thinking at the time — though he clearly did not understand what was happening, and had likely assumed the worst.

The last they saw of us was the wave of my hand as we departed the courts for Bethlehem. They were expecting us to return at a future time to secure the marriage, which had not occurred, to their memory. Holding the baby in my arms created a new tension that put him off guard, and he scurried to get help from another priest.

A small band of men quickly developed around the table where we stopped, and the inquisition began. We had prepared ourselves mentally for questions that would be similar to what Joseph experienced in the census, however this was not like anything that we expected.

Joseph began to explain the situation, to the best of his ability: "During the course of our betrothal, Mariam had a vision of an angel that told her that she would be pregnant by the Holy Spirit. In a similar way, I was instructed by an angel to take her as my wife." Although we rehearsed together, his nerves were quickly revealed that he was under immense pressure.

Being of the religious order, he expected them to accept the story, and to proceed with the ceremony, however it became evident that that this created more issues than we anticipated. Didn't they know that this was the girl that they called 'the servant of the Lord', who was faithful in all her duties in the temple? Didn't she display a life of credibility while she was here? Why would they now think that she had discarded her faith after all the time in the Temple amongst them?

An uneasy tension had developed amongst the men, who were now discussing how to handle this. Clearly they were obligated under law to perform the circumcision ceremony, and could not refuse them from doing so. However the child was to be registered amongst the tribes of Israel and both the father and mother were to be recorded. Returning to the bench, they came with confronting questions that they demanded honest answers — as though we would be hiding the truth in some way. Further, we would be put to the test, as directed by law.

Annas' angry voice demanded an answer. "Tell us again — honestly — who is the father of this child?" They had not accepted the story of the angelic encounters and the resulting pregnancy; that is, they could not write that Joseph was the father of the child. They disagreed with Rome's decision to call the baby 'the son of Joseph' as clearly this did not make sense from a registration perspective.

We were left speechless, how many times would we need to state our story and tell them the truth? Why couldn't they accept what we were saying?

I remained silent, allowing Joseph to do the explaining, although he felt that since the child was mine I should have done the talking. "As we have said all along, the angel confirmed that Mariam would become pregnant through the power of the Holy Spirit. To prove his words were true, he mentioned that Elizabeth was already pregnant, and Mariam confirmed this with a visit to her home."

The priests all knew about this since Zechariah was one of their own, and had created a scene at the Temple when he exited as a mute when he fulfilled his duty. The priests mused among themselves and finally decided to accept what we were saying, though they were uncomfortable with it.

"So you are saying that there is no earthly father for this child, and that he was conceived as a result of an angelic visit. It seems that HaShem is doing miracles these days, and while we consider that your story may be true, we find it easier to believe that Joseph would be the natural father of the child…"

"But he's not!" I exclaimed. The band of men were interrupted by my interjection, I had spoken out of turn and put them on edge. A hesitant wait forced them to hold their breath before continuing their assessment.

"In this case we will register the child as from an unwed mother," and with that statement there was a serious overtone of distaste and disapproval from all the men, who were beaming intently at me, until they resumed their discourse and returned to speak to Joseph directly, "and we will proceed with the circumcision in this way."

They finally agreed that the baby would be circumcised, which was also a huge relief to both of us. But there were more conditions to be laid.

"We want to test the truth of your story. Our law requires that you drink this cup of bitter water." Annas knelt down to gather the dust from the temple floor, and sprinkled it into the cup. "If what you say is true, then there will be no consequences and you will remain healthy. However if this is simply a story to cover your own personal sin …"

There was a definitive pause, and his piercing eyes made me uncomfortable.

 "May the people know that the Lord's curse is upon you when he makes you infertile, causing your womb to shrivel and your abdomen to swell. Now may this water that brings the curse enter your body and cause your abdomen to swell and your womb to shrivel." To which I replied, "Amen. Amen," and drank.

Although I had seen this ceremony performed a few times at the temple on previous occasions, I had never considered that I would be going through it one day. And not in the present circumstances, either. I turned to face my accusers and blinked twice to indicate that I was willing to subject my body to their curse — if one should ever develop — and handed back the cup.

A sense of satisfaction swept across the faces of the gathered priests, giving them the knowledge that my story would be tested by HaShem Himself, and they would be free of any misalignment of their duties. Next, they turned to Joseph to continue with the circumcision, assuming that my role had now been complete, since Joseph was now the responsible owner of the child since they did not believe my story.

We were shuffled off to a side room where an elderly man had been waiting patiently for the milah (the process of circumcision), with a flint knife, a resting blanket and clean up items. The process only took a few minutes, and I held his little fingers tightly during the occasion to let him know that I was not far away. The baby let out the usual screams, and was wrapped snugly in his own baby blanket to be handed back to me. I liked how he was such a cuddly baby, and how he nestled in my arms, as we returned to the priests for the final part of the ceremony.

Upon our arrival, they had prepared a celebratory item that would be provided as a gift during the naming of the baby to conclude the milah ceremony. A tallit — or prayer shawl. Its rectangular blanket-like features would be worn by men over a tunic, and in this case it was provided as a baby blanket. The corners had the standard tassels, or tzitzits, which displayed knots and threads as a visual reminder of Yahweh's commandments.

Before the exchange took place, Annas asked one final question to Joseph. "What do you wish to call the baby?" The name had already been preselected, having been given to both of us separately from the angelic visits prior to his birth.

Joseph took a breath, eyed me carefully to proceed — for which I raised an eyebrow to give him approval — and said, "His name is Jesus, for he will save his people from their sins." The priests took his comment as a vivid blow to their authority, and spat with a snarl on the ground. He added the last bit which the angel had mentioned in the dream, unintentionally flowing from his mouth, which produced an immediate reaction from the priests. I giggled under my breath, realising the formalities of the situation had been interrupted by a verbal slipup. Joseph's face turned pale. Was the hand of HaShem involved in this?

Then Annas, carefully handing over the tallit, slowly declared, "Blessed be the boy Jesus," in traditional Jewish ceremonial style.

Accepting the blessing, we felt a mixed sense of duty, fear and anticipation as the exchange took place.

Although we had fulfilled the requirements of the law, why did we feel such judgement from the priests?

We returned to the inn, discussing the course of events along the way.

Chapter 28

~Forty Days~

We did not envisage that the eighth day would be so traumatic. Families celebrate it with gratitude for bringing a first born son into the world, without the threats and suspicions that we encountered. Even the experience with the bitter water — though I was quietly confident that there would be no repercussions — was not a pleasant experience. Though on a positive note the priests carried out their duties and blessed us with the prayer shawl, which we would use to swaddle the baby Jesus in, and he would have it as a keep-sake while growing up.

Up to this point we had been careful to carry out every requirement of the law and returned to the inn with an expectation that we would find more suitable accommodation so as to work out our future together. We decided to stay in the area of Bethlehem until the forty days of my purification had been completed, allowing me to remain in seclusion and stay with Joseph's family. We already had the privilege of their hospitality on the first nights of our betrothal, and they were pleased to take us in for a lengthier time.

We relocated to the spare rooms offered by Joseph's relatives where we planned to stay until the ceremony had been completed. There we were given the freedom to stay without too much impact on his family, who were happy to provide for us now that the other 'out-of-towners' had departed back home after the census. Joseph stayed in a spare room within his family's sleeping quarters, and I shared a private room with the baby at the end of the dwelling.

Their generosity towards us was impeccable; providing not only accommodation but also lavishly shared their lives with us. It invoked in me a sense of longing to return home to be with Maria and Clopas; I realised I missed their conversation and lively tones, along with my daily routine. For now, however, we were able to stay locally until the Temple visit, and then move to where we felt was right from there.

After childbirth a purification offering was required, which provided the mother forty days to herself, allowing her body to heal, and also put a mandatory distance between herself and her husband for that time. The ceremony required us to take a second trip to Jerusalem to offer a pair of turtledoves to HaShem.

The house at Emmaus was only half built when Joseph had to return to Nazareth and would require more extensive works before we could safely enter the home. So during this time we agreed that Joseph should leave me in the care of his family to continue the house during the weeks leading up to my purification.

We decided that once the offering was completed, and if the house was ready, then we would move permanently to Emmaus to start our lives together and raise the child. This would provide a sense of relief from the Nazarethan community who had already expressed their disapproval toward me as an unwed mother, making it difficult to settle back into Joseph's hometown. At Emmaus we could have an opportunity to start married life without the trappings of the old community.

As my time drew near, Joseph arrived back the day before to ensure that all would be well for our journey the following day. There was really nothing we needed to pack, other than food and water, as well as the small cage with the turtledoves that we would present for the offering. This trip did not require a donkey, and we decided to walk there and back by foot, with the baby swaddled to Joseph's chest. It would take only a few hours, and we set off just after day break to arrive in the early morning, the sun was not yet high in the sky.

The temple was unexpectantly buzzing with activity, as *Pesach* had finished weeks ago and *Shavuot* (the Feast of Weeks) was still a while ahead. We faced up, again, to the priests — who inspected me upon arrival and determined that the curse seemed to have no effect on me — and presented the birds for the ritual. They were cooing quietly within the cage, unaware of their fate, a reminder of the innocence and powerlessness of the procedure. Despite standing near to assist others with this many times as the temple girl, the reality of the procedure was an afront to my feminine identity, with the somewhat unjustified death that the birds were to experience.

An attendant stood by the altar to assist, who accepted the offering and gently broke their necks, allowing the blood to drain onto the altar. Unlike the larger animals brought in for other occasions, the pieces were not cut in half, but instead were offered as whole animals on the altar. Once the blood had finished draining, the priest accepted the birds from the attendant and held them above his head, offering them heavenward as an acceptable sacrifice. Waving them in a circular fashion momentarily gave the acknowledgement that the sacrifice had been completed, and the birds were then taken to be consumed by fire.

Raising his hands over me, the priest declared, "You are now cleansed from the stain of childbirth."

The occasion appeared all too simple, with not much really to celebrate — other than to remove the 'unclean' title from me. It felt freeing, though why should a woman be labelled for giving birth?

Now I was able to participate in life's usual activities, so we crossed the temple courts to return to Bethlehem.

We only made it half way across the grounds before we were stopped by Simeon, an old man that had been given a word of assurance that he would not die until he saw the promised Messiah. This very morning he had been led by the Spirit to the Temple and stood at the entrance, watching and waiting for a prompting as to why he had been called there.

He intercepted us, causing us to halt, and stared at the child in my arms. We paused, not knowing what to expect. My mind raced around the Temple grounds for an exit. Did he intend to harm us, or the baby?

Unconsciously he broke out into a joyful song of praise, dancing in the courtyard. Joseph turned to me with a quizzical expression, as if to ask whether I had planned something secret for today's celebration. I replied with a short giggle, and wagged my head side to side to indicate that this was not a planned event.

> "Oh, Sovereign Lord," Simeon cried, "let me now die in peace, as you have promised.
> For my eyes have seen your salvation which you have prepared for all people.
> He is a light for revelation to the Gentiles.
> He is the glory to your people Israel!"

Joseph and I started laughing together, knowing that this random prophecy was not made up. It coincided with the words spoken to us by the angel, as well as what was revealed to the shepherds when they visited. All these events confirmed that this was no ordinary child, but was indeed a gift from HaShem to the world as the promised Saviour.

Suddenly Simeon's dancing stopped, and his tone became grave and serious. I held the baby closer to my chest. Another unexpected moment from the old man.

I became guarded in my spirit about what was happening. He paused, and looked at me intently, poising himself to share a deeper level of revelation about the child's destiny. And not just for the baby Jesus, his words were also directed to me.

"This child is destined to cause many in Israel to fall, and many others to rise. He has been sent as a sign from God, but many will oppose him." He became overwhelmed with grief by the revelation, and started to weep. After a few deep breaths he continued.

"As a result, the deepest thoughts of many hearts will be revealed."

We did not realise the immense power behind his words at the time. What did it mean when he said, "the thoughts of many hearts would be revealed"? I was pondering these words when he turned to me directly, almost hesitant to share what was being revealed by the Spirit, but he continued.

"You, dear woman, are not separate from this. A sword will pierce your very soul too."

I stopped.
His words left me gasping for breath.

I had heard many prophecies from the Temple while I was there, but none directed towards me with such force as this. I could not let my eyes lock into his, which seemed to penetrate the very depths of my soul. Surely there was nothing more to add? I couldn't bear anything else just now. Let me out of here! People had stopped to stare at us, and had formed a circle to see what might be occurring.

Intentionally, Joseph interrupted, sensing that my face expressed a burden, and rubbed my shoulder to indicate that the interaction should come to an end. This was no ordinary prophecy, and I took it as a warning to be on guard.

Together we headed towards the gates before we could be troubled any further. And as we were departing I caught a glimpse of her coming towards me from the rear of the Temple courts, causing me to stop again.

"Bubbe!" I exclaimed, my sullen face turned bright with joy. We had missed each other on my former visit, but now my heart lit up with the opportunity to embrace and feel like I was home again.

"Mariam, my daughter, I am so happy to see you!" She was radiant with delight to see me, having seen her last at our betrothal, and only then she was a participant in the ceremony. There was so much she wanted to share, and having seen my child she started to express to everyone who passed by that this was the child that HaShem had provided to rescue Jerusalem. She was jubilant and in tears to see both myself and the baby!

Finding a nearby table in the outer courts, where we would often spend our days together after the morning duties had been completed, we were able to share the bread, meat and almonds with Joseph and Jesus under the same tree that we had so many meaningful discussions together. The dappled sunlight sparkled through her hair, and the air was filled with the echoes of the good times we shared contemplating HaShem's promises towards Israel, which were now being fulfilled.

Next, we needed to finish up to return to Bethlehem so that we could arrive before dark, Bubbe turned her focus firmly to me, once again, to share thoughts that she had been pondering earlier.

"Mariam, all these days have been prepared for you for a reason. You are in the centre of HaShem's will for you, but as we have learnt from Simeon's prophecy today, this is not going to be an easy road. So I will leave you with one piece of final advice, for your consideration."

Bubbe was never direct like this, always subtle, and never demanding. I always allowed her words to teach and train me in a way that would help my future life path, and this time would be no exception.

"Blessed," she commenced, "are those who are persecuted for doing right." Her pause was intentional, reflecting on the words of Simeon. "For the kingdom of heaven is theirs." She left it at that. Short and to the point, and with a smile she rose and departed after a lengthy embrace.

"Thank you," I replied, accepting her words as a blessing that would guard my way, not that I was expecting any level of harm to come to me.

We watched her head back to her room, and it appeared she was dancing with a joyous kick in her step along the paved courtyard.

Today was not just a day of purification, but one of blessing, and with warning.

We needed to heed the words of both Simeon and Anna for what was to come.

But what was to become of the child, and what lay ahead for me — his mother?

Joseph tucked Jesus snugly into his chest and we commenced our journey home. Today's events gave us plenty to discuss on our return journey, which I would store up for the future.

'HaShem', I prayed. "So let it be."

Chapter 29

Visitors

We had planned to pack and move to Emmaus two days
after our temple visit, which would give us plenty of time
to say our good-byes to the local community in Bethlehem
and set up a permanent home, which incidentally was
only about a day's walk from where we were already. As it
turned out, our new home would not be too far from my
cousin Elizabeth and I welcomed the thought that Jesus
could grow up near his cousin John. Finally we would be
near my own family, the thought of which lit my eyes with
enthusiasm and ignited my spirit.

The next morning after feeding the baby, I spent time to
meditate and reflect on the good things that HaShem had
done for us, offering prayers of thanks and gratitude. I
was grateful that we were experiencing such rich blessings
despite the uncertainty of the situation we were in. We
felt relieved about this next step to be able to set up home
and start afresh among a community that could accept us
without knowing too much of our back story.

It was mid-morning, and Joseph was rocking Jesus on his lap to put him into an early morning sleep, when a train of camels with a royal pomp of dignitaries arrived at our door. All of Bethlehem appeared to stare as they arrived — and also at us — and we were suitably nervous about the undue level of attention. The camels knelt down to offload the well-groomed gentlemen, who looked rather out of place in this small shepherds town. We were anxiously intrigued as to why they had stopped at our door; and also ready to run at a moments notice, if needed. Joseph eyed them carefully, handed me the baby and went to greet them while I stayed inside the house.

"Sir," a tall man dressed in a royal purple tunic, assumed to be the leader of the group, bowed low in deep respect before Joseph, to commence the introduction. Returning to an upright position, he continued, "We have come from afar, having seen the sign, that a newborn king has arrived."

Joseph's puzzled look invited further explanation as this was not a traditional greeting that we were used to. "Please," he replied, "tell me why you are here. You seem to have come a long way."

At this invitation, the remaining four stepped down from their camels to join the leader and form a group outside the front door. I watched and listened carefully from the window, and could see that these were no ordinary men. They were dressed with dignity, and a display of power flowed from their turbans to their feet, their exquisite tunics providing them with a regal covering. Their arrival could not go unnoticed; they looked somewhat misplaced in this tiny town.

The leader began again, with a very formal and careful choice of words. "Sir, we are from the eastern lands, you may have heard about us — we are the Magi." They waited until we had time to digest their distinguished position, understanding that this was a royal class of elite astronomers whose power lay in accurately predicting future events to advise kings and rulers on spiritual matters. Their class had evolved over many years and civilisations, from the times of Egypt where they were sorcerers and magicians to the Pharoah, having moved north to the land of Syria and Babylon and were advisors to the kings such as Nebuchadnezzar, and had survived the sands of time, here now to identify the latest sign that they had observed.

"We have seen the sign of a coming king, a star that rose from the cluster of stars symbolising your nation. After much consultation and debate within ourselves, not knowing of any other prophecies, we decided to follow the star and see where it would guide us."

Neither Joseph nor I had heard of any new signs in the heavens lately, nor did the local community report any heavenly phenomena that might trigger a discussion over breakfast. Perhaps we were simply not looking for this, the tiredness of feeding and changing the newborn meant that all our energy was focussed on him. But these men of prestige seemed to have a track record and much esteem to suggest that they did not travel this lengthy distance for nothing. Joseph nodded graciously for them to continue.

"Yesterday we were in Jerusalem in the courts of the king, and we asked Herod, 'Where is the newborn king of the Jews? We saw his star when it rose, and we have come to worship him.' Although he appeared intrigued by our arrival, he said that he couldn't help us and had to call on the Sanhedrin to understand what all this might mean, so he had us come back last night in a private meeting to advise us."

Joseph queried, "Do you know what they told him?"

"Yes, they mentioned a certain scripture, a prophecy from their ancient texts, which said,

> "And you, O Bethlehem in the land of Judah,
> are not least among the ruling cities of Judah,
> for a ruler will come from you
> who will be the shepherd for my people Israel."

So he advised us to come to Bethlehem and find you — which was not hard when the star was resting over your house — and later he will come to worship also."

Joseph displayed discomfort at their words, fidgeting his fingers and biting his lip in suspicion. Was this simply a trap sent by Herod to capture the child? We knew how he hated to have his authority challenged, and was an iron ruler to enforce Roman occupation of the region.

The wise men allowed Joseph to settle before continuing. "Sir," they continued, "we have come to bring gifts to the newborn king, and to honour him. After we received this revelation we travelled for many days, to welcome his reign on the earth." They were insistent, and their appearance did not show any form of threat like that of the Romans. Finally he conceded, and looking my way gave a nod towards me to allow them to enter and see me and the child, who was resting peacefully in my arms.

"Friends, you may come in. Please follow me." Joseph opened the door to allow them into the front room where I was seated, with Jesus on my lap. The Magi gathered around us, their faces alight with joy. An incredulous feeling swept over them, a form of conviction that this baby was exactly what had been revealed to them as the king of the Jews, now resting before them. Each face resounded with awe. This was no ordinary moment, but a time of witness to them that they had longed to receive real world confirmation based on their forecasts and study of the heavenly phenomena.

"Allow us to present the king with these gifts." One by one each took out small leather bags of gold coins from under his tunic, and laid them at my feet, the sum of which could not be counted now. They also brought out jars of frankincense and pots of myrrh from the camels' saddle bags, filling the room with an aroma that would normally be found in temples or at weddings or funeral ceremonies. The numerous gifts filled the floor where I was seated, such that we could not move, and together the Magi stared on the baby to soak in the fulfilment of their sacred forecasts.

"Our eyes have seen the king, confirmed by the signs in the heavens. And not only this, your own scriptures have forecast this event. After many years of searching for the fulfillment of this sign that we observed, we have seen for ourselves, and we can testify that this is truly the king of the Jews."

We did not know how to respond, our hearts were filled with gratitude and amazement at their words. We were overwhelmed by their visit, and the gifts, which were heavier than what a single donkey would be able to carry on our planned departure tomorrow. We allowed the men to stay as long as they wanted, understanding that their visit had fulfilled a lifelong dream to see their predictions come to life.

When they had taken a sufficient amount of time and felt that all was completed, they enquired about local accommodation to stop for the evening. Surely this would not be up to the standard that they were used to in this remote rural town, however they decided to stay at the inn. Yes, *that inn* which seemed to welcome notable guests but not unwed mothers. They would stay the night before returning to Herod in the morning to let him know where he too could come to worship the newborn king.

Turning to Joseph once they left, although we were blessed with an excessive amount of gifts, we now faced a predicament: we would need assistance to move. That was something we would work through the following day. For now, we needed to conclude the day with a meal, and process this unexpected visit to see how it all made sense in the long term.

Over dinner we talked about the sincerity of the Magi, along with the accuracy of their investigations that led them to our house, and the resulting gifts that they had brought. As we lay down to rest that night, there was only one thing that Joseph was unsettled by and nagged at his thoughts to keep him awake: that the Magi would be returning to king Herod in the morning, which may result in unwanted trouble.

There was only one thing we could do.

Holding hands, we prayed, "HaShem, we commit these men and the gifts that they have brought to You. And we thank you for the confirmation that they bring for the baby Jesus. We ask that you make it clear to them about what they must do from here, so there will be no trouble brought on us by Herod."

It was a simple prayer, recognising the need for protection and mixed with our thankfulness for the events that had transpired throughout the day.

I retired to my room and Jesus rested comfortably next to me, blissfully unaware of the concerns that we carried. For now, we needed rest, as I would be up during the night to feed and change the baby.

And tomorrow we would travel to our new home.

Chapter 30

Settled

The following day required extra assistance from friends to help pack a second donkey with the gifts that we received from the Magi, taking longer than we expected but we were feeling exceptionally blessed. Whispers from the local townsfolk revealed that the Magi had departed back to their homeland, but not through Jerusalem as anticipated, having had a change of heart overnight. This brought us a sense of relief, knowing that HaShem had quickly responded to our prayers.

It wasn't until a much later time we discovered that the Magi had encountered an angel in a dream, warning them not to inform Herod but to return home by another route. Upon receiving this instruction, they left quietly, heeding the angel's warning, which took them on the north-west route out of town.

Our trip to Emmaus would not take the whole day, but we
more to move than we had originally planned, plus we had
to stop periodically to feed the baby and rest. We arrived
with a fresh breeze in the early afternoon, and Joseph
bridled both donkeys near the front door.

This was the first time I had seen the place that Joseph had
gone to build for us over the last twelve months. I found
it difficult to think what the finished house might look
like when he described it to me. Compared to my room in
Nazareth, this was a kings palace. No wonder he had taken
such a long time to return. I admired his workmanship that
demonstrated pride in his building capabilities, and showed
how detailed he could be.

The doors were intricately carved and swung freely on the
hinges. The orientation of the building allowed the sun to
warm our front room, and the remaining rooms allowed us
to accommodate guests who could stay comfortably, when
required. There were some unfinished rooms that he would
continue to work on while we set up house, but it was
complete enough such that we could move in immediately
with very little extra effort required.

The community was also welcoming, understanding that we
just had a child and were keen to get to know us and invite
us into their homes. We kept silent about the fact that we
were not yet married to avoid any form of criticism, though
continued to live in our own separate rooms. We planned to
formalise our marriage within the next few weeks, when the
time was right and we could do this discreetly. Our warm
acceptance among the community gave us new hope and
confirmed that the move would provide a fresh start to an
otherwise bumpy beginning that we had endured so far.

Finally we had a place to lay our head and find rest for our souls, a place where Jesus could grow up without the community pressure such as what we had endured in Nazareth. Thoughts of finally being established filled my head: I dreamed of having a garden near the kitchen window where we could grow a variety of fresh vegetables, and we could plant citrus and olive trees out the back. This would be the place where our family would be raised.

This was our escape from the realities of the outside world, but we also had an open door for anyone that would need a room or who wanted to stay with us from time to time. Also, being so close to Elizabeth gave rise for Jesus and John to spend time together. With very little other family here, Joseph had done well to be able to give up life in his home town and start anew in an almost unknown part of the world here at Emmaus. I could smell a sense of freedom in the air as we continued to set up house together.

Of course there were still odds and ends to sort out in Nazareth, which would require him to travel back and forth in order to pack up his family home of many years, and the workshop. With the land that he acquired here, there was the opportunity to set up a new workshop where he would train Jesus in his building skills, in time.

It took us until the end of the week to get fully established. I needed to understand how the community functioned in order to locate the local merchants for fresh food supplies and other materials. There was additional bedding required for the baby and myself, and we were waiting on Joseph to finish some household objects to make life more comfortable. It certainly started to feel like home.

One of the more familiar items that made me feel instantly welcome was the front table and bench seats, which in most ways looked just like the set at Clopas and Maria's place. Did Joseph have a hand in making their bench as well, or was this his father's handiwork? Regardless, resting on the bench to give the baby a feed while the sun was setting at the end of the first week gave me a sense of homeliness and assurance that this was where we were meant to be.

I called Joseph over to sit with us, and together we rested on the bench seats until the sun had dropped below the horizon to soak in the peaceful atmosphere of the quiet town.

This was a place we could call home.

The following twelve months welcomed the expansion of the house to include the new workshop, which was being set up progressively as Joseph made a number of trips back to Nazareth for his work tools and timber. There was also the demand for carpenters in the area, so he was busy being called on to create cupboards, chairs, tables, and to perform building works where required.

And we were finally able to welcome a visit from Elizabeth with baby John, who by now was nearing eighteen months of age, running — not walking — through the place and chasing Jesus, the younger cousin. Together they were able to play with the hand-crafted toys that Joseph had made after dinner by the light of the candles, and enjoyed each other's company. Interestingly, there were no bullish standoffs that young boys would normally get themselves into, only the regular rumble-tumble wrestling that we were used to seeing in other families' boys.

After they left the place returned to a normal level of quiet, and I decided that Jesus should sit with me in my quiet times to practise the presence of the Lord in prayer and meditation. From my early years in the temple, Bubbe was convinced that children were more open to receive words from heaven and angelic visitations than adults, though I was not sure why this would be the case. "Start at a young age," she said, "for the kingdom of heaven is theirs." I smile now as I recall her placid teaching, which seems to have given me a good start as a mother.

It was now a year and a half at Emmaus, and we had settled in well. Jesus had been weaned a few months earlier and we had all fallen into regular sleeping patterns. His own personality was starting to reveal itself: a pleasant child, one that heeded instruction, he soaked up the Torah stories and the history of our nation with delight. I was looking forward to see this young man develop into adulthood, and was keen to pass on all I learned and had experienced to him.

The night had become dark and still, and Joseph had returned from a day out and washed. We had finished eating and were talking around the fireplace. It was a regular night with nothing out of the ordinary. I recall us talking how we had arrived at a point in our lives where we felt established and had found favour in the town. There was nothing more we needed, and had been welcomed into the community.

Our private marriage was established a month after we settled, and we chose not to hold the typical week long ceremony with friends or relatives. It was instead an officiation performed by the priests back in Jerusalem, acknowledging that it was time to wed — though this also reinforced the reality that Jesus was born to an unwed mother, and their grievance against me continued. Whatever favour I might have received as the temple girl was now no longer available to me in this position.

We extinguished the candles for the evening and snuggled into bed.

I was lost in the depths of sleep when the quiet evening air exploded into a flurry of activity. Joseph was scurrying around the place for food and belongings.

"Darling, what on earth are you doing?" The candles were lit and the house was alive with the light of day. "You are going to wake everyone up!" I was not cross, just confused as to why he was rummaging through everything in the dead of night. He stopped, came to my side dropping to the floor, with heavy deep breaths and a flurried voice.

"Mariam, we must leave."

Wait.
Stop.
What do you mean, *leave?*

"But Joseph, what is going on?" I needed further explanation, something had obviously disturbed him and the message had not yet come through to my weary head. Grabbing his arm and squeezing it to gain attention, I made him look me in the face to provide further explanation.

"I just had a dream — like the one I had when I was told to take you as my wife." I recalled that he had a vision of an angel, which instructed him to continue to take me as his wife, rather than divorce me quietly and end the betrothal.

"In this dream, the angel said, 'Get up! Get out of here! Flee to Egypt with the child and his mother, and stay there until I tell you to return. Herod is going to search for the child to kill him!'"

Now I was awake.
Now he had my full attention.

Hadn't we been spared from all this when the Magi were instructed to return to their country by another route? The silent air was filled with hurried clanging of utensils, and bags were stuffed with things that we would need, though with the extra little feet the trip would require an additional donkey to help our departure.

Joseph saddled two donkeys which were tied at the front door — one would carry the provisions and sleeping gear, along with some clothes, and the other would carry the baby and other supplies, as much as we could take. Joseph led on foot, keeping a pace that could see us arrive to the border of Egypt within a day.

Once saddled into position, Joseph rushed inside to snuff the candles, and let out a heavy sigh.

Our hopes, dreams and present reality were being smashed in an instant. Did he hear the angel correctly? Why would we be sent to Egypt, when we could easily return to Nazareth and hide among the community there? Joseph was not one to go against orders that had been given, especially since his earlier contact with angels had brought us under the umbrella of protection until now.

Closing the door to say a despondent good-bye to the empty home, we headed into the night towards an unknown land until we received further instructions.

And just like that, our lives were changed — forever.

Chapter 31

~Innocents~

There was no time to pack everything we owned, and barely enough time to gather what we did, before fleeing the town. We saw the sun rise a few hours later, which aided our flight, and it took all day to reach Egypt where we would stay the night and await further direction. Not knowing exactly how long we were to stay, it crossed my mind that this would only be a short stay — perhaps a few days — until the problem resolved. We had no plans to stay for any length of time, and after stopping the night at an inn, we listened for any news that travelled the trade route from home.

We stayed in a town called Raphiah that first night away, which is the entrance to Egypt from the eastern lands along the Via Maris. News travels quickly in this part of the land due to the word of mouth nature of the highway. And news of this type arrived swiftly, given its grave nature.

"Herod's on a killing spree!"

The comment was from a travelling merchant, and Joseph quickly went over and tugged at his tunic to gain more information. The words of last night's angelic visit rang like bells in his head; we were right to flee and escape Herod's jurisdiction. The hairs on his back straightened up and a cold shiver ran down his spine. This was becoming all too real, and his face turned white in a state of shock.

"Sir" Joseph interrupted the man. "What happened back there? Can you tell us more about it?"

The man spun around to find that Joseph was clinging to every word that he was saying, realising that he was the first to bring this story abroad. For once people were listening to him, that he could be the first to release the news to a willing audience, which brought him great delight.

The merchant responded. "Herod sent his men through Bethlehem, Judea and the surrounds. The soldiers doing the killing mentioned that the king was angry from having been deceived."

"Deceived? So he's now killing everyone?" he asked with a nervous quiver in his lip.

"No, not everyone," he explained. Joseph took a short breath and relaxed a little but I could see that he was cautiously on edge.

"Not everyone, just the babies. He doesn't like those babies. So he got mad and wanted them all killed." The man left, apparently that was all the news he carried, and was done with all the questions.

Not only was Joseph confused, but the man's words didn't seem to make sense. What deception caused Herod to kill the babies, and cause an angel to issue the warning for us to flee?

Another merchant stopped, having heard our conversation, and chipped in with additional details. They had been travelling together, and he had more of the background story.

"Herod got angry when he realised that the Magi had tricked him, after a visit to Bethlehem. He said he waited for two years for them to return. He had enough of waiting and learned that they were never coming back. So he called his soldiers together and ordered the execution of all boys that were two years or younger, starting from the region of Ramah in the north to Bethlehem in the south, and into the Judean countryside."

We were both struck with silence, grasping each other's arms tightly and headed back to the inn. Herod wanted Jesus dead! The killing of the innocents was meant for us. How could such a small child intimidate a king? This was not a random killing spree, but a strategic move to remove the one honoured by the Magi to become the king of the Jews. Herod was afraid!

The reality was that we were living in a time when Rome ruled and there were consequences for not following orders. We seemed to narrowly escape this tragedy, but what about Elizabeth? Baby John was also near two years of age, and they lived in the region. This was a threat to his existence as well.

We were not to hear about their situation until a while later, after we had decided that the threat to our lives was too high to return. And besides, the angel instructed Joseph that he would let him know when the time was right to return, although we did not know when that might be.

We learned that Zechariah and Elizabeth's story was to be a mixture of miracles and fate. Having heard that Herod was on a rampage to kill the children, Elizabeth took John and ran to the mountains for a place to hide, however no secret place was found. In her distress she cried to HaShem to be hidden from the soldiers, who were searching for her and the boy. At that time an angel appeared and created an opening in the mountain to hide them inside. She remained there with John, being looked after by angels, until she could safely return home.

Meanwhile Herod actively searched for John and sent his soldiers to Zechariah's house to find him, however he was not at home, nor Elizabeth or the child. Perhaps John was the rumoured king of the Jews? With further questioning, the soldiers discovered that Zechariah had fled to the temple, and was found clinging to the altar asking for mercy.

The soldiers barged into the temple with bloodthirsty demands from the king himself, "Tell us where your child is, or your life is on your own head!"

Grieved, and crying desperately over the altar, Zechariah was determined not to mention anything about the child. "Kill me if you must, though you know that you shed innocent blood. I cannot tell you where my wife and child have gone."

A soldier drew a sword, and thrust it through his side, causing him to fall in front of the altar. His murder was swift, and blood soaked into the ground. Another innocent life lost.

When we heard this news it caused us grief for many days, learning that Herod was bent on maintaining his throne and was fearful of the ancient prophecies about the Jewish ruler that would come to set up a new throne. He had likely been acquainted with the story of Moses, learning that the baby rebelled against Egypt and turned a whole nation away from Pharaoh's control. He was not going to let this happen at this point in history. The Romans had a responsibility to maintain law and order in the world, and would not be usurped by the threat of a rebellious child-king. Indeed all Israel clung to the hope that they would be rescued from their captors some day and establish their own land once again.

It was going to take time before we would settle, and after staying a few days at the inn we went in search of temporary lodging where we could wait for the instructions to return.

Not knowing our story, the locals welcomed their new refugees into their town, and Joseph assisted with local handicrafts and building projects, for which they were extremely grateful.

We took time to establish a place we could call home, although we were sure it wasn't permanent. We intended to return to Emmaus at a later date when it was safe to do so. For now the safest place to be was well away from Judea, away from Rome's occupation. Indeed living outside the land of Israel and in the land of Egypt was the safest place at the time. I smiled to think that HaShem had chosen to act quickly to spare the child that we were responsible for.

And so we settled, somewhat reluctantly and cautiously, into a place that we could call home, and were there for the early years of Jesus' life.

We watched as he played with children from the other culture, and saw him grow and develop into a sensible young boy. Daily we taught him the scriptures and how to live a godly life. We passed on everything that we had learned or been taught from our parents, the synagogue, and of course from Bubbe's source of wise words and counsel.

Despite our circumstances, we managed to live without fear of retribution, and were able to breathe freely again. But the situation we escaped from was always on my mind. There was a sword meant for my child, but instead it pierced my soul. It claimed the lives of many innocent boys, as well as Zechariah.

"HaShem," I pleaded. "Have mercy on us."

Chapter 32

Return

The time in Egypt lasted longer than both Joseph and I anticipated, and we eventually managed to fall into the pattern of daily life like others who were settling in the area. Although unexpected, we made sure that our stay would be intentional, and the townsfolk came to understand the reasons for our flight to settle in their land. As a result, we were able to move freely and became a valuable contribution to their society.

We were there for two years, until Jesus was four years of age, which provided a time of togetherness for me to teach and train him just like Bubbe had mentored me. It was my motherly pleasure to ensure that whatever I had received and learned in my own spiritual training was passed onto him, enabling him to follow in my footsteps. I was rewarded to see that he welcomed everything that I passed on; and he was also good with a saw and a hammer as well!

In my quiet times we studied the scriptures, prayed and meditated on the meaning of the scripture. Then waited for revelation to fill our hearts with deeper understanding and meaning. This was not simply education, but we wanted to ensure that Jesus could establish and maintain his own self-discipline and spirituality from a young age. We were determined to see that Jesus would follow the ways and traditions passed down to us from our forefathers and spiritual leaders.

We were settled, for now, waiting for further instruction, and always being aware of the threat to life and to be on guard.

Then one night those instructions arrived.

An angel appeared to Joseph in a dream, "Get up! It's time to return to Israel, because those who were trying to kill the child are dead." And then as quickly as he appeared, he departed.

This time there was no hurried packing of bags in the middle of the night, unlike the tragic exit from Emmaus. Joseph waited patiently until morning to break the news of the angelic visit, allowing us to continue to sleep through the night. There was indeed no rush to head back so soon, given that we had prepared for an indefinite amount of time anyway. So we planned to return home over the course of the next week, allowing us time to say our good-byes to the local community and pack properly for the return journey home.

Joseph and I agreed that we return to normal daily life at Emmaus, though we were not sure what state it would be in, not having seen it for years. I despised rats and other vermin and hoped that they had not made home amongst the food that had to remain. I guess we would find out sooner or later.

We decided to break the journey and return through Judea to see Elizabeth, just a slight detour off the beaten track, allowing ourselves two or more days to return home. There was no time pressure for us to return, and this meant that we could also become aware of any other changes that might have happened in the region while we were away.

And so we left Egypt, heading east into the rising sun, toward the land we called home.

It was late in the afternoon when we arrived at the door, and Elizabeth was surprised and elated to see us. John also let out a loud squeal to see his cousin. Such a wave of refreshing covered us, and we talked and talked late into the night. There was a lot of news to catch up on.

That night we learned of the tragic circumstances surrounding the killing of the innocents, and of Zechariah's death in the temple. We sobbed and hugged each other as the stories were retold, which seemed as fresh as yesterday in our minds. We were grateful to learn how HaShem's goodness to us had kept us safe from the harmful plots of men, and we both agreed that we were under the protection of angels during the two years that we were away.

HaShem was certainly guarding and protecting us, having confirmed the words of the angels and the prophecies to us over the course of time. But having returned, these were different times now, and we were looking for a sense of security where we would not need to watch our backs.

"There's a new ruler over our region," Elizabeth mentioned quietly over dinner. We shared that an angel instructed us to return because those who wanted the child dead had themselves died.

With curiosity Joseph asked, "Would you happen to know who the new ruler is?"

Elizabeth looked up for a moment, searching her memory to answer his question. "I think it's Archelaus." She didn't sound certain, though we knew that this was the name of one of Herod's sons.

Ironically, it seemed that a parallel relationship had been drawn up during our time away.

Just as we had been teaching Jesus the way of righteousness and holiness, reverence and respect, Herod had been teaching his son how to steal, kill and destroy. Archelaus was to be twice the son of Herod that anyone had ever wanted. He would fulfil his father's expectations with a rod of iron, and implement radical autocracy that would establish him well as a leader in Rome.

Joseph shivered at the thought. Why would we be instructed to return to Israel only to face further harm?

"The best thing," he argued, "would be for me to find out the political situation in and around Jerusalem. If it's as bad as we expect then it might be best to find somewhere else to live." The three of us agreed to this plan — which meant that I could find solace with my cousin for a while longer. Part of the fun of growing up was to share time with extended family, especially when it wasn't planned. This also meant that the boys could have time together as well.

So Joseph left for Emmaus to see how people were getting on in the local towns, and it didn't take much time to understand that there was a widespread fear. He felt it was enough to spend just two nights at our home, and which also provided him time to tidy things up for our return, should we be occasioned to do so. He returned on the third day with the news.

"I can't see that this is going to work, that is, for us to return to Emmaus." He scratched his head, telling numerous stories about what our friends and neighbours experienced over the last few years. Naturally, we became cautious about whether it was right to return home.

"Many people are scared for their lives, because the king rules with an iron fist. This is not some place that we can raise the child."

Joseph sounded despondent, and we felt that we could not be accommodated here in the long term. We couldn't stay with Elizabeth indefinitely, though we were welcome as long as required.

The situation was unsettling, and before we slept that night I took his hand and we prayed together, asking for certainty about where to settle — as the angel had already instructed Joseph to return to our own country.

That night Joseph had another dream, and an angel provided instructed us to return to Galilee. This was out of reach of Archelaus, in the ruling territory of his brother, who was not as cruel. He shared the dream with us the next morning, and having discussed it further, we agreed on a plan. Although reluctant, we would return to Nazareth, to the family home and workshop, and abandon any hopes of our new life in Emmaus.

Considering that we had been living in Egypt for the past two years, and had only stayed a short time in Emmaus, what did we consider to be home for us?

There was no point in me travelling straight away, so we decided that Jesus and I would stay with Elizabeth, allowing Joseph to pack a dray with tools and other household items. Then we would seek to sell the home and workshop to anyone who could use it at a later time. For now, the focus was to relocate the first shipment of goods back to

Nazareth, and when he returned we would travel together with a second dray taking the remainder of our belongings.

That would conclude our life at Emmaus, and I was saddened that it would end this way. The upheaval of the first four years of life may have gone unnoticed by Jesus at such a young age, but we were starting to feel the pressure caused by all our travels. Further, we faced the scorn of the local community on our return, and which was likely to be present upon our arrival. I hoped that we had been forgotten, though I know that Joseph was integral to the town, and that they would change their attitude towards the child that we were to bring back into their world.

All those pressures would return to us when we settled back at Nazareth. But for now, I was content to stay with family who loved and cared for me.

And she was glad to have us there as well.

Chapter 33

Resettled

Joseph had done well to travel quietly back home, locate
and pack a dray full of tools along with some of our
essential belongings to return to Nazareth and meet me
at Elizabeths just over a week later with the empty dray.
He was able to enlist help from two capable youths whose
parents didn't mind them 'going on an adventure' with
Joseph for the couple of weeks that it would take us to
pack and return our items back home. He would send them
with the dray back to Emmaus after our second trip so that
they could travel together for their journey home.

While he was away Elizabeth and I spent time together
watching the boys play, sharing new ways to cook from
my time in Egypt, and generally enjoying each other's
company — knowing that life would soon be different
when we moved back to Nazareth. It was strangely sad not
having Zechariah around, and we reminisced about the

angelic visits and spiritual experiences that seemed to be commonplace between us over the last five years.

Returning to Nazareth meant that we wouldn't have the usual banter between us, something that I would miss. And young John wouldn't have the company of his cousin; their wrestling matches made us laugh a little to see who would be the champion between them. And despite boys being boys and an expectation that there would be tears, we were always surprised when the wrestling match didn't end in fisticuffs. Surprised, but also relieved. Maybe our parenting skills weren't too bad after all? In any case, they always seemed to get on well with a healthy level of respect for each other.

Upon his return, we allowed Joseph and the two youths to rest for a day with us before packing the little we brought from Egypt. We planned to arrive in Emmaus mid-morning, giving us time to pack the last of the household items onto the dray. There was no point staying too much longer in the town, as Joseph had already briefed our closest neighbours with good-byes, and we really didn't want to draw any attention from the rulers who might gain an interest in our return.

The sun was up, and after a quick feed to give us strength for the travels ahead, we headed north and west towards Nazareth, but not like the first journey we had as a betrothed couple. This time felt different. Very different. This time Jesus was a young boy who could walk, but we also placed him on the cart when he got tired, sitting him alongside our household items, whereas previously I had walked and ridden a donkey. The route we travelled this time was through Samaria and up into the mountainous terrain of Nazareth, the shorter route, cutting the overall journey time down by a day or so. Now I was on foot rather than on a donkey, walking alongside Joseph, who was no longer my betrothed but now my husband.

Together we set out to return to the life which we tried to escape, which now seemed like such a long time ago. We had initially responded to the census with a forced visit to Bethlehem, which became the unintended birth place of Jesus, and then moved into our own place at Emmaus to commence our secluded married life together. That was cut short by a frenzied trip to Egypt that lasted a couple of years, and when Herod died we were instructed to return to the holy land. However since Joseph felt uncomfortable returning to our Emmaus home, he received instruction in a dream to return to Nazareth where we would fit back into the community.

At least things were already established there.

Memories of our early life together returned like a flood, and I found myself reminiscing, and occasionally caught myself smiling, which seemed to indicate that I was looking forward to our return. The fear of returning to the community that had not accepted us seemed to fade as my mind drifted onto better times.

Joseph had not sold the house or workshop, so we could return to an already established family home. And there we had the support of Clopas and Maria, along with their boys, who had become close family to me, just as much as Elizabeth was. I didn't realise how much I had missed our early morning conversations together, helping Maria with the daily chores and duties of running the household. And then there was my room which Joseph had built, very lovingly and skilfully, which I called home during the *erusin* period. All these memories filled my mind on our trip home, and I found myself lost in the emotion that came with them.

I could not have been happier living in a place where we felt a sense of privacy from traditional Jewish life. For the town itself, no-one really knew about Nazareth, nor of its history.

Nazareth was a town that no-one visited, or at least no-one wanted to visit. There were no major trade routes along the way, and it was situated in the back hills of the Galilean countryside which had been taken over by foreigners over a century before our arrival. The town was therefore a mixture of Jews and Gentiles, with constant striving between the different people groups to establish or maintain their own cultures.

Some thought the name 'Nazareth' was derived from *neser* which meant sticks or branches, which were common in the area. However others nicknamed the town *Nazar* which meant that it was a town that was consecrated and devoted. This was not to be confused with the Nazirites, or *nazir*, a consecrated one to the Lord, though the rhyming of names gave everyone pleasure when discussing the meaning of the town. There was also the play on words that others gave it: *zara* or *zara'*, which provided reference to the scattering of seed, or euphemistically to the bearing of children.

We really didn't know why or how we ended up back where we started.

The events of the last few years were not something we had planned, and we could only heed the angel's instructions and move when we were instructed to. We would need to once again allow our hearts to open to the little town, swallow our pride, and aim to live peacefully among our relatives and established townsfolk. This would take some getting used to, and we would need to be careful how we integrated back into the community.

It would take time.

The return journey took three nights, and we arrived on the edge of town in late afternoon to find Clopas working the fields with their boys to bring in the harvest, with Maria nearby providing assistance when required. The golden sun shone brightly on the sheaves making them look exceptionally white.

There were hired labourers too, bringing in a bountiful amount of grain that would be threshed and stored before it got dark. In the distance Maria had caught sight of our arrival, put down her basket, and headed our way. The men and boys propped themselves up to question why mother had left, but were quick to realise our return, and continued to work without interruption."

"Shalom!" It was so good to have a Maria hug. *"Shalom!"* she replied.

Her face was fresh and flush with delight as I introduced my now four-year old boy to her, and I could see they immediately felt a bond towards each other. Joseph had momentarily stopped the cart, but when he saw that we intended to take more time than a quick hello could provide, he nodded to me and continued the walk into town towards home. Not that he intended to be rude, but wanted to continue to get home and unpack first, and then allow time later to re-establish with family. There would be plenty of time for that, I reasoned, and I needed to soak in the happiness and emotion of the moments that I had craved while we had been away.

My heart took in the atmosphere, the freedom, the smell of the fields and the pleasantness of my sister whom I had longed for; I didn't realise how dry my life had been, and coming back was like entering an oasis in the desert.

This was where we were going to call home. It felt right.

"Come with me, let me introduce you to the boys." Maria requested. I didn't hesitate, and together we traversed the fields towards the now tall lads who were very efficient at harvesting the grain.

"Simon, Jude — come, please." She waved her hand in a downward motion, signifying them to stop work and be acquainted with the new comer to the family. They arrived, somewhat begrudgingly, although relieved that they could take time out from their present heavy work activities. "Boys, you remember Aunt Mariam, right?" They nodded in agreement, and my goodness it was hard to recognise them as the younger ruffians that I had met upon my first night there with Clopas and Maria. They were now tall, buff and good looking, and approaching the end of their teenage years.

"This is Jesus, Mariam's son."

Jude stooped down to shake the younger boy's hand to accept him into the family. The obvious age difference wasn't going to deter him from extending a warm welcome as the new older brother of Jesus. "Thank you boys," I mentioned casually with a motherly smile, allowing them to return to work after this brief introduction. Had Joseph briefed his family on his first return trip to set things up smoothly?

"Let's go meet the other two," she mentioned, and we continued to walk through the open fields until we reached James and Joses who were standing upright, waiting for us to interrupt them. These boys, around the same age, were from Clopas' previous marriage, and both he and Maria insisted that they would be a family of four rather than two families of two. And now that we had arrived, Jesus would become the new younger brother. We would became one blended supportive family spread over multiple locations.

The oldest, James, had the responsibility to ensure that the younger ones toed the line. He inherited a natural position to maintain orderliness within the mob, and they were expected to listen to him. As a result he had grown into a natural level of leadership where the younger brothers looked to him. It was interesting to see how he eyed Jesus closely upon our arrival, likely trying to determine where he would fit into the pack. Joses, whose proper name was Joseph, got the nickname so that they wouldn't accidentally mix up his name with Uncle Joseph, who was now my husband.

The new family relationships would require some time and patience to develop.

As the sun neared the edge of the horizon I realised that daylight would soon fade and the men would need to stop work soon and break for the day. "Let's catch up again soon," invited Maria.

I would love that, I reasoned. "Yes, we certainly will catch up again soon, we have a lot more to share!"

She returned a pleasant smile, and gave reason for us to hurry. "It's time for you to help Joseph, who will be waiting for you."

"Yes, you are right. Though I'm sure he doesn't really need my help to unpack!" The two youths were fully able to help unload the dray, and they would be staying the night. I smiled cheekily to show her that I was not taking this too seriously, but wanted to give her assurance that I would help Joseph set up house.

After a final embrace, and Jesus joining us by grabbing the lower part of our tunics, we headed back home and to the workshop. There a new life was awaiting us.

It would only take a little time to resettle into home, and introduce our little one to the people who would be our neighbours.

Although it began to feel warmly familiar, I knew this time it would be different.

Having a child under the circumstances that we did, along with the miraculous stories from our last four years together, was probably something that this remote village might not be ready for. Would they be in a position to accept us now?

Or would we become the talk of the town, again?

Chapter 34

Dispute

Settling into Joseph's family home didn't take too long, though there were some obvious differences. Previously I was staying with Clopas and Maria and had my own room; now we were living under the same roof where many of his generations had lived. At the time Joseph was my betrothed, but now my husband. And there were no plans for the sound of little feet running around the place at that time.

The early years of our married life passed very quickly and we slipped into the rhythm of the local community, who were more accepting of us than we anticipated, or feared. Although we had been constantly travelling for Jesus' first four years of life, we soon settled into a place we could call home — back where we started. But it wasn't without trouble. And trouble seemed to be closer to home than we anticipated.

We watched as Jesus grew into a young boy, being now around eight years of age, and we became a blended family as we integrated Jesus alongside Maria and her boys. Joseph's daughters would occasionally appear to stay for a night or two with their husbands and children, dropping in for events such as *Rosh Hashanah* to celebrate the coming of the new year, or the Day of Atonement, *Yom Kippur*. This always brought a smile to Joseph's face whenever family planned to visit. He was very much a loving father and the pillar of family life. Precious memories.

This year we planned to celebrate *Yom Kippur* with all of Joseph's extended family and Clopas' family. All up there were twenty people spread between the two cottages, with some sleeping in the workshop. This was a designated holy day that would bring us closer to HaShem through the process of confessing and repenting of our sins, and seeking forgiveness for the things we had done to others.

Traditionally, we were not required to visit the Temple on *Yom Kippur*, and instead we would fast and humble ourselves over the twenty-four hour ceremony at the local synagogue. The following day our families would join together to give thanks and reflect on HaShem's mercy for atoning of our sins and trespasses against each other.

There were three annual pilgrimages that traditionally required a visit to the temple, which also aligned with the harvest times in Israel: *Pesach*, with the barley harvest; *Shavuot*, with the wheat harvest; and *Sukkot*, the festival of tabernacles. The festivals were also considered to be days of judgment. On *Pesach*, judgment is passed on grain, determining how much will grow until the late spring. On *Shavuot*, judgment is passed on fruit, determining how much will grow during the summer. On *Sukkot*, judgment is passed on water, determining how much rain the land of Israel will receive in the winter.

Given the holy nature of the day, we assembled early outside the synagogue, along with the rest of the Jewish community, to begin the fast for *Yom Kippur*. As this was the holiest day in Israel, we would stop work and gather together in extended prayer services during the day.

Ten days earlier, on *Rosh Hashana*, we commenced a time of repentance to repair our relationship with HaShem. This culminated in the repair of our relationships towards others on *Yom Kippur*. The date was set in stone, literally, as the date Moses returned the second time down the mountain with the second set of tablets.

Historically, this day was a most holy day and a day of humbling. It was recognised as the most holy day of the year. We were expected to observe it with a clean heart during the course of the celebration.

So we were reeling in shock and left speechless when the dispute occurred.

Hadn't our family learnt to adopt humility to ensure we didn't miss out on the covenantal blessings of this day? The children had been involved in all our cultural feasts and celebrations ever since they could walk, and now that they were adults it was expected that they hold fast the traditions as they became leaders in our community.

James, son of Clopas, was to lead part of the ceremony at the synagogue later in the day, reading the book of the prophet Jonah. Other leaders would read from the *Torah*, the books of Moses, usually Leviticus or Deuteronomy, to focus on the message of repentance and reaffirm the responsibility of the covenant between HaShem and his chosen people. As a young man, he was preparing to be married and was being groomed to be a leader in our community. This required him to spend time with the local leaders to learn how to handle matters of religious importance. He was approaching two years under the direction of a Rabbi and he appeared to master the teachings and traditions that had been passed on, responding to what he had learnt.

People were seated around the synagogue along the benches and on the floor, according to their rank and level of wealth, and a solemn hush filled the assembly hall as the meeting commenced. After the usual greetings, the Rabbi welcomed James to the floor. This was James' big moment and he read from the book of the prophet Jonah. Everyone listened intently as the story was retold: how HaShem gave mercy to a repentant Gentile nation, but how Jonah sat in self-pity and misery under the vine that quickly grew up to provide him shade from the scorching sun.

Concluding the reading, James finished the final verse with HaShem asking the prophet, "Shouldn't I feel sorry for such a great city?" allowing a period of silence before proceeding to give his interpretation of events.

As he finished and took a breath, the Rabbi nodded for James to proceed with his own thoughts and interpretations of the scripture, which would provide a backdrop of the events for *Yom Kippur*. Eyeing the room carefully, he began his speech — just like his father had done on many occasions prior to this.

He started confidently. "Friends, we draw upon this passage today to find strength in the forgiveness of HaShem towards the city of Ninevah." A definite pause added dramatic effect. "They repented in sackcloth and ashes when Jonah decreed the destruction of the city." With further pause, the room kept quiet to allow him to continue his observations. "In this we see the picture of HaShem's grace, how He responded to the actions of the people. Instead of destroying the city, He spared them." The story paralleled the way we were to take an attitude of repentance to enter into HaShem's grace and forgiveness.

Puffing his chest, we were expecting James to bring the focus of his interpretation to how we should adopt a life of repentance, like the Ninevites. Instead he changed focus onto the actions of the prophet.

"Jonah was a man, just like us, and called by HaShem to declare judgement over the unrepentant city of Ninevah. He was commanded to bring this message to the city — but instead he ran from his calling, the first time." Once again he paused for dramatic effect. "The passage describes how the sailors threw him into the sea, and pleaded with HaShem that they would not be responsible for his death, and the sea calmed down instantly when it received him."

He did not need to retell the story, but he was making a point, so the Rabbi motioned for him to continue.

"When he conceded the visit to Ninevah, we learn the true heart motivation of the prophet. He boldly proclaimed the message that he had received, which he passed on during his three day walk throughout the city. Instead of judgement falling from the sky, like the fate of Sodom and Gomorrah, everyone from the king to the lowest slaves turned in repentance and believed the message they heard. And HaShem likewise repented of the works that he was going to do, and did not overthrow the city."

A solemn silence enshrouded the synagogue. People inwardly acknowledged the need for repentance, and had started to humble themselves, with quiet prayers emanating as murmurs throughout the room.

Had they missed the point?

James stood vertical on the platform and raised his voice to the unexpecting assembly. "Jonah was an angry prophet. And we too should be angry at sin!"

The prayers stopped, interrupted by the outburst, wondering what was going on. Even the Rabbi looked as though he didn't know where this was headed. I turned to Joseph, his face was aghast, just like mine, at the developing situation. The solemnity changed to a frantic panic, though no-one dared to move.

With an angry finger, he pointed right at Jesus, who was seated on the floor near myself and Joseph, and screeched at the top of his voice, "There's the product of unrepentant sin, right there!" All heads turned towards us, and with confused looks they waited for the words of judgement that were to follow.

My heart pounded so loudly that I couldn't hear myself think, and became dizzy with nausea. Joseph gripped my hand firmly, he was looking for a way of escape to get us out of the room and head home. There was nothing more to be said here today, and there would be no explanations to be had with anyone.

Was James speaking what the community had been secretly murmuring about since our return? Even though he was family, wasn't he aware of the miraculous events that brought Jesus into the world? Didn't he believe the stories that we shared?

The crowd erupted in a roar, siding with James at the thought that we had been harbouring unrepentant sin which was evident to them in the form of the boy child that had grown up in their midst. The room filled with indignant cries of "Shame! Shame!" and we rushed to the exit, dragging Jesus by the hand to free ourselves from their wild cries and run home.

We really did not know the cause of all this, and we quickly understood that it wasn't just the community that looked upon as sinners, but now we had enemies within our household as well.

Life in Nazareth was about to change in a significant way.

My heart felt betrayed.

Despite helping to parent the boys alongside Maria, earning their trust and the right to hold a position equivalent to their mother, todays outburst meant that James held no respect for us or his brother, and it would be unsafe to assume that we could continue life together this way. Had the other boys also been contaminated by judgement from the community? Was it even safe to belong here any longer?

We waited at the house until Joseph's daughters and families arrived. Tears swelled in Joseph's face, along with the others. The focus on repentance for holiness was shattered by the provocative judgement that revealed the true heart of the community.

Should we have stayed in Emmaus, where we would not have been ambushed with such accusations and thoughts?

No, we would not run away, though life would certainly have become easier, we assumed.

We felt that this is where HaShem had led us, being perceived as the safest place in Israel, to raise the boy. We would now face this issue at every turn. If they weren't to believe the story and the miracles, then we wouldn't be able to convince them otherwise.

The situation gave rise to the three of us becoming a closer family unit, forcing us to give some distance from Clopas and Maria — although we had their full support — and it was apparent that it was their boys that challenged the concept of the holy birth.

So our intimate daily contact with Maria and Clopas stopped abruptly, and Jesus instead spent his days with Joseph, taking on the trade as the carpenter's son.

But even that was used as a saying against us.

Chapter 35

~Father~

It took some time to get through the emotional struggle that evolved as part of the *Yom Kippur* incident. Clopas and Maria spent a considerable amount of effort to mend the rift, challenging the mindset of their boys to ensure that violent and angry outbursts were not tolerated in their family — but they found it hard to sway them from the view that the community was right to judge us in this way.

Everyone had become fixated on "the virgin and her illegitimate son," assuming that there was no attempt to hide the product of her sin. James continued his war against us, going so far as to stir up trouble to put me to death, arguing, "The law of Moses says that women caught in adultery are to be stoned." There was no mercy in his tone, and he echoed the sentiment that lurked in some sectors of the community. What made this exceptionally uncomfortable was that this trouble came from within our family, and we were otherwise forced to live with it.

Other kids in the village soon took to taunting Jesus, mocking him as they played together, saying, "so you're the *carpenter's son*," and, "you son of a *whore*." My soul bled each time I overheard their childish insults, rolling in puny fetishes of laughter as though they had every right to judge.

I'm sure they didn't realise the level of pain that they were inflicting on him, or on us, and despite this we aimed to keep the peace without retaliating. There simply was no point trying to explain our situation further, since we had already shared the truth of the matter in many ways and at many times, and it seemed to be rejected by those who should know better. If they refused to accept the word of angels, then other facts didn't matter either. We were, in the eyes of HaShem, vindicated of any wrong doing, and could rest with ease each night because we knew the holy calling to which we had been enrolled — despite the awkward appearance that our family resembled.

As a result we took every opportunity to leave for ceremonies that required us to travel to Jerusalem. This also gave us a way to intentionally demonstrate our commitment to the laws and traditions that we embraced. And it gave us all a small amount of relief from the inherent persecution that we endured on a daily basis.

Each year we travelled for any of the three celebrations, which required our personal appearance, to the Temple for *Pesach* and the Festival of Unleavened Bread, as commanded by the Torah:

> "You must celebrate the Festival of Unleavened Bread.
> For seven days the bread you eat must be made
> without yeast, just as I commanded you.
> Celebrate this festival annually at the appointed time
> in early spring, in the month of Abib, for that is the
> anniversary of your departure from Egypt."

The walk generally took a period of four to five days when walking as a group, which we commenced after the Sabbath. We headed to Jerusalem in the lead up to *Pesach*, taking the easier track down the Jordan River rather than the rocky back hills through Samaria. This allowed us time to talk amongst family and friends, and to prepare for the celebrations ahead. This trip was not only to celebrate the week-long festival, but since Jesus was twelve years old we were also to discuss his coming of age. As we were travelling quite a distance we would normally buy one of the special Bethlehem lambs that had been prepared for *Pesach*, without spot or blemish, according to the law of the Lord, rather than bring our own lamb from Nazareth.

The city was normally full of people, and this year was no exception, where visitors from the towns would occupy the homes of friends and relatives and generally book out every room that was available in the district. Bethlehem, Emmaus, Bethany and other surrounding towns were within the limits of a comfortable days walk and were overflowing with people, and all came together to celebrate this joyous time of remembrance.

Given the intimate nature of the visit, and staying with others from the community, we let Jesus select his own friends from amongst the relatives while we sought our own time with those we wanted to see.

This trip there was someone who I could not find: Bubbe. I searched for her upon our arrival at the Temple, wanting to see her gracious smile and reconnect over the times we shared. However, different to our last visit, we learned that she had passed on to *Olan Ha-Ba*, the world to come. For the last few years I noticed that she looked a little older than before, a little more frail, her joints had become stiff and she was hunched over. On my last trip she passed me a good-bye smile, and a wink, suggesting that her time on earth might be coming soon. So when I became aware of her passing I had to settle myself, knowing that she had fulfilled her life-long calling, having blessed the lives of many people during her time in the Temple.

Pesach finished and we ate bread without yeast to celebrate the nation leaving Egypt in haste. This first part of the week-long festival symbolised freedom from sin and the need to put away the old self, with all its bitterness, hatred and judgements — and to reconnect with HaShem in humility and with respect. The time spent with family and friends was rich with cultural adornments, and gave us a holiday away from home.

As the festival drew to an end, the band was called together and we headed back to Nazareth on our traditional route through the Jordan Valley. Eating together around a campfire that night, I performed the usual roll call to confirm that everyone had regrouped, and to my surprise I could not find Jesus. My heart began to beat hard and cold clammy sweat poured from my hands; had he been taken and killed along the way? Did they want to get rid of him, like they did to our patriarch Joseph, who was thrown in a well and sold to Ishmaelites?

"Joseph, have you seen Jesus?" I called. We did a more extensive search together through the clans that we were travelling with, earnest to find where and with whom he was staying that evening, but we did not find him. He asserted that we would need to return to continue the search in the city, but it was already too late and we were too tired to travel tonight. So after a rough night's rest we departed the group in the early morning and returned to Jerusalem, anxious to find him.

His disappearance caused us to search frantically from door to door, seeking anyone who might know his whereabouts, and the first day resulted in nothing. Our fears were developing into trauma, our stomachs sick with the thought that someone had taken our son and disposed of his body. After another night of disturbed rest and lack of sleep with friends, we decided to head back to the Temple and retrace our steps. Perhaps someone might have seen him there and see where he might have gone after leaving town — although with so many people he could easily have been missed in the crowds.

We entered the Temple courts, and to our surprise — and relief — and annoyance — we found Jesus sitting among the religious leaders, listening to them and asking them questions.

"Joseph, wait!" I called under my breath to stop him from marching in to take control of the situation we had fallen victim to. Together we paused at the court entrance. This was the same location where Joseph and I had met on the day of our betrothal, where we exchanged a sacred acceptance of each other, before heading out of town. "Let's see what is happening." I requested. "We can be thankful that he has not been not hurt, or killed."

Joseph took a deep breath and clung to my side, leaning against the wall near the entrance, and stroked my hair gently. He was concerned that it had been three days without Jesus with us, not knowing what had happened, and he began to comfort me to set my heart at peace. After a while we had seen enough to understand what was going on, and slipped in to join the leaders and listen to the discussion.

Jesus seemed innocently excited and alert, with no consideration that he had caused us any grief. And in fact he had done no wrong, though we were terrified that something more sinister had unfolded and had been scared for his safety. If nothing else, we were feeling the guilt of not being responsible parents, and assuming that he was old enough to look after himself.

"Son," I called from the side of the group. The meeting stopped, and the men turned to me to see why a woman would interrupt such a learned gathering. Around fifteen of the leaders, scribes and others from the Sanhedrin — those whose responsibilities were to maintain the ideology and theology of our law — were intently listening to Jesus while he asked them questions, for which he also provided them answers.

Jesus stopped, and waited for me to speak further, the group also focusing in on me. I continued. "Son, why have you done this to us? Your father and I have been frantic, searching for you everywhere." My throat gulped, which seemed to echo through the temple courts like a gong, catching their attention for a moment. Was I just being an over-protective mother? Did they care more for Jesus than myself and Joseph?

My mind was aflutter with various thoughts, not knowing how this might end up, though I was grateful that our son was safe and we could continue the journey back together, where we could contend the issues of daily life.

As though seeking my permission, Jesus responded carefully, asking, "But why did you need to search?" We were baffled at his question; did it show a level of disrespect that we were unaware of? Was he questioning our authority like other teenagers, who seemed to show contempt for their parents? Before we could answer, my heart shook silently, resonating with the thought that he had commenced down a path that would lead him astray from the core principals of our beliefs.

He didn't wait for me to respond, and continued. "Didn't you know that I must be in my Father's house?" There was a long pause while we waited for him to fill us with more background information about that statement. Joseph grabbed my hand tightly, and I gripped his equally hard. What was he really saying?

The pain of rejection has been always evident from the taunts he received from the community, as well as our own household. But his response came as if in a form of insult to Joseph, openly rejecting him as his father. I looked up to see a mix of grief, sorrow and anger flush across Joseph's face; though he knew that one day Jesus would need to realise his own destiny — and the shadow of his earthly past would fade away as he embraced the calling on his life.

Clearly, the man whom I married was upset; it wasn't simply the taunts and accusations from the community, but now it realised itself as a form of separation from the son we raised.

Joseph was no longer being called "father", and that hurt.

The group didn't understand what was going on; they observed the conversation without the full backdrop to which we lived every day.

Having said this out loud, there was no harshness in his voice, and no intent to degrade the loving relationship with Joseph or myself. Jesus was revealing to us that his relationship had now shifted from earthly to heavenly, knowing that his true Father was in heaven and that he had a calling to fulfill on earth.

The Temple leaders sought to consolidate this somewhat awkward family situation, and grouped themselves together to allow us to process what was happening.

Jesus was now entering an era that was not something we understood, and it wasn't until much later that we knew the significance of his statement to us at that time.

I pondered over this for many years, and it wasn't until Joseph's passing that Jesus' words took on a whole new level of significance.

Chapter 36

Passing

An icy coldness swept a chill across my heart, sending a shiver down my spine. We dreaded this day — the day we would have to say good-bye. The shock of this event created numbness inside, ensuring that I was emotionally dead.

> We gathered at his bed when he died.
> A solemn time of grief and mourning.
>
> He was our rock, our protector.
> We expected him to live forever —
> That death could not touch him.
>
> It was too soon for him to pass on.
> And now we hold only memories.

Joseph showed no sign of illness, his physical strength had not declined, until a few days before being called home.

There he had resigned to lay in bed, under the power of an illness that was not common in our area. He was sapped of energy, not able to move, his feet had grown cold and his body shivered. I tucked a blanket around him to keep his body warm, but he shivered none-the-less.

We called his daughters and their families to the bedside, arriving in time to form a family circle, allowing them to take one last look at the one they loved. The room was filled with sadness and grief, but also peace. To those who had assembled, we could see that the gold had lost its splendour and the silver had been worn down by use. We gathered around this man — this great man — who gained our full respect. He filled our homes with craftsmanship, and had earned our trust. And in these last hours he was surrounded with family who had come to say good-bye.

From the bed he let out deep sighs and his heavy breathing indicated that the struggle for life was nearly over. He groaned in agony, and we were unsure how to provide any form of relief. We had to simply let the process of death fulfil its duty, and watch until he released his last breath.

Joseph had never been sick at any time that we were together; his strength had never failed, and his eyesight had not grown dim like other men his age. He was quite a capable man, and respected in the community. At the end of his days we could find no reason why his health would decline so rapidly. My mind turned to the miraculous events that surrounded the birth of my son, and wondered if the angels would appear to take away the soul of my husband and escort him to his forever home.

The young children, Joseph's grand-children, were outside playing unsupervised, old enough to look after themselves, and their squeals occasionally sent a message to the bedside vigil that new life was already surrounding us while it was only a matter of time before life ended inside.

Gathered at the bedside in front of the group, I shared a good-bye speech — knowing that he was already standing at the gates and was simply waiting for permission to leave.

"Joseph." I swallowed, finding it hard to string the words together. "You were called to be by my side to raise the boy Jesus. Through our years, you have been my friend, my confidante and my supporter." Tears flooded my eyes, having released these words from my lips, and waves of emotion washed from my head to my toes.

My throat choked up and I needed to clear it before going on.

"You spent your life in service for others, and were obedient to the commands of angels." Pausing, I recalled the miraculous times we shared together: where an angel instructed him to marry me, and also to rush to Egypt to avoid the killing of the innocents, and then the instruction to return home. I gave a brief smile, knowing that we shared these difficult but intimate moments together, squeezing his fingers gently before I continued.

"We will miss your weathered hands, your lofty headed hair and your gentle voice with words of assurance that you gave us. We didn't always know the things that were going through your mind, or residing in your heart; we guess that you had your own reasons at times not to talk about the things that you were going through."

Although he could hear my words, I wasn't expecting any form of acknowledgement, though the occasional groan suggested that he was grateful for the kind words being shared.

I continued on behalf of the family. "What we will miss most about you is your loving and caring touch, the way you handled all relationships with dignity and respect. We have been blessed by your presence and we will remember those good times that we shared together."

This was the collective thought from the grieving community by his bedside, while waiting for the sighing to end. Jesus, who was standing next to me, put his hand gently on his chest, and sensed that his spirit was ready to depart. I asked if everyone could please leave the room so we could say our private good-byes. Graciously, they let us alone and waited outside.

The room took on an air of stillness, reminding me of the little stall where we had been surrounded by the special lambs at the birth of Jesus. Just the three of us, as it was in the beginning, twenty-two years ago. And here, now, just myself and Jesus watching the final stages of life play out on the righteous man. There was a moment when his breathing slowed, whereby we thought he would breathe his last, however instead, in a faint and gentle voice, he spoke.

"Mariam," his voice was weak, but none-the-less carried a familiar tone, spacing out his words. "We had a good life. I did everything that HaShem wanted." His eyes teared up; he had run the race and was coming to the end. "It wasn't easy, most of the time." I felt exhausted listening as he exhaled his words. Yes, the calling we shared was not something that we would call an ordinary marriage, though his care for us demonstrated that it wasn't simply out of duty, but of genuine love and commitment towards me.

I accepted his words, rubbing my hand up and down his arm, grief flooded my eyes with salty tears that stung my face, forcing me to wipe them into my hair. We held the moment until he called Jesus to his side, and when he was ready he garnered strength to raise himself painfully from his resting place.

"Son," he called. I let go of his arm to let Jesus replace me. When he realised his physical strength was over-ridden by the pain in his body and that he was not capable of maintaining the position, he slumped back down again. Jesus' firm hands partnered with Joseph, interlocking his fingers to help him find a comfortable position in the bed again. We waited for what Joseph might say next, allowing silence to fill the gap until he was ready.

"Son, my call is completed." By this he intended that his angelic assignments had been finished — there was nothing more to be done, and he could hand over all earthly things to the first-born.

"I pass onto you our family trade." He stopped to breathe, choking from a mixture of grief and a knot in his chest, becoming fully aware that Jesus was looking intently at him, accepting his words. They had shared times in the workshop that I was not privy to, where only a father and son could appreciate the context of what was being said. But it wasn't just the workshop that he wanted to hand over. There was now the responsibility to appoint the head of the house, and for Jesus to accept this mantle of leadership — with all that was required in that position.

Somehow he found the found the words, and the strength, to make the appointment.

"The angel called you the son of the Most High. I know you could not call me 'father'. I am pleased you have your Heavenly father." His message laboured under short breaths, and not complete. Waiting for a pause, he continued by eyeing Jesus directly, and then turned to me.

"Your mother. Your mother…" the grief swelled in his throat and prevented him from speaking, until he was able to swallow, and release his words. "Your mother, she is now in your care. You … must look after her now." His energy was sapped, slumping into the bed again.

With eyes closed and wet with tears, his chest beat out sobs of sorrow, and together we passed our attention to Jesus, who was standing between us. From now on he would be responsible for my protection and provision to ensure that we had a stable home and enough income from the business to ensure our daily life would not be interrupted. Joseph's breathing slowed again, he was now at the finish line.

We listened for the quiet of his breath to be the only silence that the room could hold, then Jesus responded. "Father," a long pause allowed the two to connect in a way that they never had attempted to do during their adult years. Joseph's chest resonated again with a sob, allowing the words of Jesus to bind them together for the moments that remained.

"I have heard your request, and accept your mantle. From now on, I will step into the role you are handing to me." I observed the two of them share this holy bond and commitment, and Joseph gave a single nod of his forehead with his eyes closed. There was really nothing more to say, or do. This was the end.

"Father, this is my final good-bye. You are free to leave. I entrust you to the care of the Most High, that He will carry you safely to your heavenly home."

And with that, I was called to pray the release of his soul from his body, though it wasn't me but Jesus who prayed. Together we placed our hands on his chest, and the presence of the Holy Spirit filled the atmosphere, which became bright and airy. Heaven was responding in a way that we experienced many years ago, enveloping us with a shroud of brightness, as though the room was filled with angels.

My tears coughed into a chuckle, and an unexpected smile swept my face, brightening my eyes. My countenance lifted from the grief that we were experiencing into a form of bubbling joy. This wasn't a traditional death, it was a birth, as though a new life had just been born, and we were there to experience it.

Jesus squeezed my hand gently, "Mother," he said, wiping the tears from my eyes. "He's gone."

And we headed out the room to share the news with those who waited outside.

Chapter 37

Sent

The years that followed Joseph's passing provided us a new routine, along with a new set of challenges. His presence was missed around the home and workshop, people would look to their toes instead of checking in with us whenever we moved around the village, and our little synagogue wasn't really the same now that he was gone.

Without Joseph, we had to establish ourselves with a new form of independence.

On the Sabbaths that followed, I watched to see if the synagogue leaders might take the opportunity to induct Jesus under Joseph's mantle, however that did not occur. Without Joseph there and under this new paradigm, Jesus would instead be tested by them and have to earn his place in the community. They would demand an exemplary life and to follow the Rabbi's directions without fault or waver.

But from those who should have practiced forgiveness, that never came.

Privately I sought acceptance for Jesus to be trained under a Rabbi, just like James and Jude had been adopted as their disciples, but there was no willingness of behalf of the leaders to have him as one of their own. Instead, I encountered resistance to this notion, and my senses grew weary from their decisions that showed a continual flow of discrimination from their leadership.

Jesus was not like Joseph, and nor were they willing to train him. And that was clear now. Further, they did not accept him as a man in good standing in their community, because he had technically not passed through the rite of passage that would call him a man.

Jesus' coming of age celebration did not occur during Joseph's lifetime, and nor could it, because the role of inducting boys into adulthood was traditionally done by their father; and in this case it was clear to family and community alike that Joseph was not the father of Jesus. It didn't help that Jesus happened to reinforce that during his pre-teen visit with us to the Temple.

Even Elizabeth was feeling the changes, as though a new season had commenced. John, having essentially grown up without a father, led a life of solitude under the care and attention of his mother. He had an inner stirred passion for righteousness — living a right life in the eyes of HaShem — which translated into practising things in different ways. Instead of wearing fine clothes, he wore a jacket of camel hide — inverted so that the bristles rubbed against his skin.

As a Nazarite, John had a divine calling and was consecrated from birth to fulfil vows of abstinence from wine and alcoholic drinks; he would not marry and instead he was called to be single; and he could not touch dead bodies. Propelled by these conditions and the inner stirrings of the Holy Spirit, and now around thirty years of age, John commenced ministry.

He positioned himself at the Jordan River, calling people to repentance by confessing their sins, and to demonstrate their change of heart by stepping into the waters of baptism. Thousands came to hear and see the prophet, but not all were there to get baptised. Some people simply came to watch the spectacle, while others were there to stir up the crowd and dissuade them about his methods and lifestyle, saying that his supposed religious actions didn't line up with 'the way it's done around here'.

At that time Jesus arrived as part of a larger crowd to accept John's baptism, and it took some effort to persuade John, who laboured against him saying, "I need the baptism that you offer! Why are you coming to be baptised by me?!" But Jesus was resolute with his decision, and replied, "We need to do it this way, for the sake of righteousness."

John stopped, thinking of his own commitment to righteousness, and received a witness in his spirit that this was the right thing to do. He had to allow his cousin to be baptised under his hand.

"Please," Jesus urged, "accept my confession as an act of good conscience towards HaShem." Having settled the matter in his heart, John baptised Jesus in the Jordan River, along with others.

But this was no ordinary baptism.

As he rose from the water the heavens opened, and the Holy Spirit descended on Jesus in the form of a dove, settling on him. This unexpected event caused all who saw it to marvel, revealing the interaction between heaven and earth as a divine testimony that the baptism of Jesus had been accepted.

Suddenly there was a roar from the skies above. Some said it thundered, others said that it was like a river in flood, and a voice spoke the following words, "You are my dearly beloved son, and you bring me great joy!"

The valley echoed with the sound of this voice, resonating the announcement like the long blast of the shofar during *Yom Kippur*.

Traditionally, these words are only announced by a father over their son at their coming of age. Jesus looked heavenward and smiled; his Father's voice showed divine acceptance. This was a sign from heaven, sealing his call to ministry. Looking through His father's eyes, he was now considered a man, and passed through this rite of passage for all to see and hear.

The angel's announcement many years ago to myself, to Joseph, to the Bethlehem shepherds, and others at his birth was now at hand. The prophecies given to Zechariah, Elizabeth, Simeon and Anna were coming true. And it seemed that his baptism was a form of new birth.

This was his time.

The news of the thundering voice at Jesus' baptism accompanied him where-ever he went. This was heaven's endorsement of his ministry, providing him authority to speak and act. He no longer needed the approval of men.

Straight after this he was led by the Spirit into the Judean wilderness, south along the Jordan River Valley to a secluded location in the hills, where he fasted for forty days. From here he could view the holy land where the young nation of Israel had crossed the Jordan to take the town of Jericho. Hidden amongst the caves, Jesus practised the teachings that I had passed on to him from Bubbe during my early years in the Temple: recalling the scriptures that he memorised; dwelling on the goodness of HaShem in prayer; and waiting for divine favour to strengthen him from the heavenly source.

The practice of fasting, coupled with daily prayer and meditations, and a period of time — usually a few days, or a week — was common practise to seek the face of HaShem by rejecting life's usual comforts. In this case, Jesus listened to the desire of the Holy Spirit who led him to fast for an unusually longer time than he had done previously. It is unknown what occurred while he was away, however the significant change in the level of his authority and power was noticeable.

On the days that followed, he returned to the region of Galilee, walking in the power of the Holy Spirit. He began visiting synagogues and taught regularly from the Torah and other scriptures with authority that confounded the leaders. And in fact everyone praised his teaching, as he taught not as their own. Along with John's call to repentance and Jesus' teaching, the area of Galilee was stirred up. The incumbent leaders were indignant — they did not like others working the ground that they had ploughed.

Shortly after this Jesus returned to Nazareth, having arrived home to be with me the day before the Sabbath. I listened intently to hear what he had been doing in the towns and synagogues after his baptism. My spirit soared to the heights of heaven to hear the good things he had done, though feared that there would be undue attention and persecution from those he challenged. Hadn't he been through enough during his time in Nazareth? Finally he could start to live without fearing those who called themselves leaders, and fulfil his calling in life.

I was glad that we could spend time together since he had been away for some time, and news of his miracles and teaching travelled throughout the region. The next day we planned to attend the local synagogue, and then return back for lunch where I could be 'ima' to him again. In all things I was exceptionally proud that he had made the decision to leave home and step into his next phase of life.

Our overnight chat included Maria and Clopas, who were likewise delighted to see him. They recalled the stories of him being a youngster in the workshop, under the shadow of Joseph, as the carpenters son. And had sided with us to form a layer of protection from the community's comments that had been circling since the early days of our return. Despite the actions and attitudes of their sons toward us, they remained faithful and stuck close to us through some very tough times.

They accompanied us to the meeting, and we took our traditional seats inside. Arriving at the usual time and place, we chose a seated position along the rear wall, and waited for the service to begin. Just as in times past, an attendant called everyone to order and invited the synagogue ruler to the front.

It was time for the meeting to start.

The reading that day was from the prophet Isaiah, and with nervous hesitation, the scroll was handed to Jesus, with the invitation to read just like they heard him speaking in the other towns around Galilee over the last few weeks. Their reluctance was based on their position and attitude, as he had grown up in their town; and their invitation was to see if he would meet the stories that circulated from other towns — and not of their favour.

This was the first time he was invited, or allowed, to read from the scriptures in his hometown, and he accepted the invitation carefully. Stepping onto the platform, he was handed the passage which happened to confirm his calling. It wasn't just the words he spoke, but the effect it had on the entire assembly, causing everyone to tremble in awe.

Waiting for the room to become silent, he spoke.

> "The Spirit of the sovereign Lord is upon me,
>> for he has anointed me to bring the gospel to the
>> poor.
> He has sent me to proclaim:
>> that captives will be released,
>> that the blind will see,
>> that the oppressed will be set free, and
>> that the time of the Lord's favour has now come."

When finished, he rolled up the scroll and handed it back to the attendant, and returned to his seat. All eyes in the synagogue watched him with intense scrutiny, and delight. His words carried an air of authority and revelation that was missing — causing the local leaders to be incited by it.

The room filled with an eerie silence, as they waited for him to share his own thoughts on the passage, but he appeared hesitant. Looking to the synagogue ruler for approval, he was given permission to speak. Rising from his seated position, he began to speak. "The Scripture you've just heard has been fulfilled this very day!" and sat down again. There was nothing more he wanted to add; the scriptures opened a divine communication between heaven and their souls for them to accept the word, should they choose to do so.

The room almost broke into applause with his comment, and everyone spoke well of him and was amazed by the gracious words that came from his lips. But the leaders of the synagogue were not convinced, and some snarled, "How can this be? Isn't this *Joseph's son?*"

The angry slurs bit into the memories of his childhood, where on *Yom Kippur* James stood to accuse Jesus of being the product of illicit sin. It had become apparent that this wasn't his own idea, but the teaching of the Rabbi that had adopted him.

Having remained seated until the murmuring grew into a hostile debate within the sanctuary, Jesus rose again and stood to address the situation. This time he would confront the attitude of the sanctuary rulers that had divided the people for so long.

He started, "You want me to do miracles here, just like you heard me do in Capernaum, don't you?" The room went silent with an air of caution, as Jesus probed the reasoning of their hearts. Eyeing the room and knowing those who despised him, he spoke, "I tell you the truth, no prophet is accepted in his own hometown."

His words cut the air to expose the discrimination that lay in the heart of this synagogue.

"We don't do things that way around here!" the synagogue ruler exploded.

Certainly Jesus had earned the title of Rabbi early in his ministry, with demonstrations of miraculous powers through healings and by commanding evil spirits to leave, but they wanted none of that in this place. Their icy faces stonewalled the prophet, and their bodies stood erect to assert a dominant position, insisting that he had no right to tell them how to run the meeting.

"Let me tell you this," he paused, waiting for the room to come to a point where they would listen to Him again. "There were many needy widows during Elijah's time, when the heavens were closed for three and a half years, and a severe famine devastated the land. Yet Elijah was not sent to any of them. He was sent instead to a foreigner — a widow of Zarephath in the land of Sidon."

The faces of the rulers turned from icy shale to hellish red. This was a direct attack, suggesting that they weren't worthy of hosting the word of the Lord, and they became irate.

But Jesus continued further, calling out their pride. "There were many in Israel that had leprosy in the time of Elisha the prophet, but only one was healed: Naaman, a Syrian." Jews despised the Gentiles, and especially in this area which was a battleground between the two cultures.

When they heard this, the people in the synagogue were furious. They jumped up and formed a mob, forcing him to the edge of the hill on which the town was built — intending to throw him off.

However, through an unseen force he was able to pass right through the crowd and went his way, and left for Capernaum.

The angry cries shouted at him with raised fists as he departed.

There was to be no "mother and son" time today.

And that hurt.

But the greater hurt was to see the ministry and calling of my son rejected by the leaders.

I could no longer live here, in this shallow town, and would follow him into Galilee, and Maria would help too.

Closing my eyes, my memory stirred tears to roll down my cheeks as I recalled the Temple leaders forcing me to marry, despite my vow of devotion to HaShem, to serve him only. Although I dedicated my life to full time service, and I demonstrated this with my whole being, the very leaders whom I respected expelled me from their midst.

Was it happening again?
Was this happening to Jesus?

I didn't want to see his life wasted with insults and opposition that could bring him harm. Or for him to attract undue attention to himself, opposing those who ruled us in the name of HaShem.

Together Maria and I would look out for him, and make sure his ministry would be unhindered. His calling shouldn't end in tragedy, but it seemed to be heading that way.

So packing the few things we needed, we shook the dust from our feet in Nazareth and headed to Capernaum to be close to him, and see his ministry in action.

Chapter 38

~Family~

The ministry of Jesus grew popular in a very short period of time. People rushed from towns and villages to see, hear and experience the self-proclaimed Rabbi who was healing many people, casting out demons with a word, and even raising the dead. Those who were deaf could hear again; those with blindness had their sight restored; those who were paralysed were healed and could walk again.

This was not a passing magic show that happened to be travelling from town to town with the merchants. Jesus displayed miraculous power among everyday people to demonstrate that something significant was taking place, and it got their attention. The Jewish leaders debated his words, but could not defy the Spirit's power by which He claimed to be working. People recovered from diseases without the problems recurring, and demonic spirits left instantly — and sometimes dramatically!

If this were simply an act to gain attention then the healings would simply be a slight of hand, with deceptive claims that a healing had taken place. But instead these signs continued to amaze the crowds, with the claim that he had the authority and power from HaShem to work among them. It was truly a remarkable time, and everyone was pleased with the appearance of the new prophet.

This was a new paradigm.

"Either that, or he's crazy!" James slurred angrily. "This is his way of getting back at us, bringing dishonour to our family name!"

The family had gathered to discuss the situation, pooling together at Capernaum to work out how to bring Jesus back under control. As the oldest of the brothers, James demanded that this nonsense had to stop. He was becoming known all over the district, not following traditional Jewish customs which required propriety and respect.

"Mother Mariam, we need him to stop. He is out of control!" He was insistent, and eyed his brothers and sisters to gain their approval to assist him to do a 'quiet arrest' and take the troublemaker back to Nazareth. It was becoming obvious that unless they stepped in and stopped Jesus from doing any more of those supposed miracles that it would ruin the family reputation. "We have to save him from himself!"

The others that came were cautious about the plan, but ultimately agreed to travel with James to take charge of their youngest brother, and prohibit him from acting any further. The ultimate decision to proceed would require one person in authority to give approval, and that was me.

"Mother, the plan is to go to where he is working and take him back to Nazareth. But I'm sure he won't come without a struggle, and we don't really want to cause a scene. We need you to call him out, then we will carry him away. Can we trust you to be involved?"

Immediately I felt sick; my stomach churned to think that the family had assembled to take him away from what he was doing. Had we really come to take charge of him, instruct him to stop, and escape the threat of harm?

I was thrust into a situation I did not want to be involved in. But I also did not want to see any threats carried out against him. From James' perspective, Jesus was creating a situation that was going against the methods and teaching passed on from our synagogue, gaining attention for himself, "A form of pride that requires humbling," he exhorted. James didn't care for the history I shared about my encounters with angels and the calling on Jesus' life; nor the miraculous ministry that was unfolding in front of everyone. By being associated with Jesus, James felt the pain of rejection from the authorities and knew that he needed to stop this at all cost.

His face showed frustration, indicating that this situation was out of his control. My own soul felt that we should not try to restrain the ministry of Jesus because I knew that whatever happens to him would need to fit with HaShem's divine plan and calling. Did I have the right to interfere with the plans of heaven?

James waited long enough and clapped his hands together to awaken me to his demand. "Are you in?"

I honestly did not want to answer, my eyes watered as I pondered the significance of the outcome that would unfold. Would I allow James to set such a trap to take Jesus away? Or could I be silent and allow them to do what they felt was right, without me being involved?

There seemed to be no way out of this.

If I didn't consent, they were going to do it anyway, and Jesus might be treated without dignity in their attempts to shut him down, which would create more of a scene in front of the crowds. Then we would certainly look like a family of lunatics.

There was really no choice in the matter.

I had to go along with the plan, even if it was just to keep a sense of harmony among the family so that no harm could be done.

"Okay, I'll come."

My heart skipped a beat as I gave consent, and taking a quick breath I needed to compose myself again as I provided authority to put the plan into action. From this point on they needed to listen to me and do things my way, so I asserted how this would work.

"But under one condition."

James stopped grinning, knowing that I had now taken charge and that his band of coerced supporters would only participate on my command. He eyed me carefully, trying to stare down my position to allow him complete freedom in how this should work. But knowing that he could not do this without me, he nodded for me to speak.

I started, almost tripping over my words, "We will arrive at the house, and seek to call him out. If he does not want to come, then we will not create a scene. Instead …"

James' face twisted and contorted to show that he wanted more forcible action than simply a mother's words of invitation to a wayward son, and his fingers started twitching as he sensed he would lose control of the tiny band of rebels who were now starting to submit to my maternal authority.

Allowing him to take a few deep breaths, I continued.

"Instead, we will wait outside the house and call for him. I'm sure he will respond to his family." The siblings tended to agree with me, knowing that if we were to have any chance at making this plan succeed then they would need my help. Not that they all agreed to this, but consented to help James fulfil his mission.

James bit his lower lip through his beard, and although not completely happy with my words, it was agreed: we would attempt to get Jesus to come with us, away from the crowds, and allow his mind to take a rest from all the things that were going on. We would reason with him as a family for a few days, and try to talk some sense into him.

"Agreed. Let's go." James was once again taking control of the family, ushering us along before any objections could be raised by the others.

We travelled across town to see a large crowd spilling over into the streets. He would be nearby, so we approached someone and they pointed towards a small cottage that was overflowing with people. We travelled together as a family, that is, the siblings along with me and Maria, and pressed as hard as we could to get through the door, but we were prevented from getting in.

James called out, asking to pass a message onto the miracle worker inside the house. "Tell him that his family are here to see him, and we are waiting outside."

Somehow a messenger was able to bring the request in to the healer, so Jesus rose and arrived at the door to check and see that it really was his family that was waiting outside. His face displayed a sense of amusement, and we were not sure from his expression whether he would comply with our request or use this as a teaching opportunity. He seemed to prefer the latter, and stepped back inside the dwelling to continue with the people, as if to ignore our presence.

"Who is my mother?" Jesus asked. The crowd looked across the room towards each other, thinking that Jesus had misplaced understanding and could not work out who his family was, who were standing restrained outside, waiting.

His query cut my heart like a sword.

I writhed in agony and buckled over, as though struck from an unknown enemy.

I'm your mother! Aren't you going to listen to me?

My heart pumped loudly and deafened me; my soul raged that I was being dismissed from my natural position of authority.

When the boy Jesus rejected Joseph at the Temple, this exposed Joseph to a new level of personal pain. From this point on, Jesus started to become his own man and embrace the calling that he believed came from his true Father. Joseph had often discussed privately with me how this caused him to hurt, though he knew that his role was more of a protector and guardian until he would step into the ministry that would be his life calling. Throughout Joseph's life he carried this burden of this grief; the wounding causing him to step back and allow Jesus to develop his own identity.

And now Jesus' words wounded my own soul.

I had not expected to feel their pain so sharply, so pointed. It wasn't just the words themselves that created the grief, but the meaning behind them. That is, he was denying my role to call him to order, and instead was enforcing his own authority to ignore his family.

Inside the little cottage, the people looked confused. If they knew the emotional struggle that was taking place outside the door, they might not have wanted to be part of this lesson.

Jesus made eye contact with everyone in the room and then continued. "And who are my brothers?" James, Joses, Simon and Jude all objected at the statement, spitting at the ground while taking a gasp of air. He was preparing to be defiant and dispose of his family in front of everyone; the statement seemed to be fuelled with bitterness. Was he rejecting them also, like he did to his father, and now his mother?

Jesus eyed those surrounding him, and pointed towards them all. "Look, these are my mother and brothers."

His finger touched everyone who earnestly sought him, who were present in the room, and in his usual style he turned the message into a life lesson by waiting for them to contemplate his words.

Then he continued. "Anyone who does the will of HaShem is my brother and sister and mother."

My heart cringed at what this implied.

Had we failed him?
Did he really want to cut off his own family?
Had he really gone insane, or hungry for power and attention?

Embarrassed and humiliated, there was nothing more that we could do. It became clear that he was intent on staying with the crowds and dismissed any association with his family.

In essence, Jesus was publicly saying good-bye to whatever family attachments that could have lay hold of him. And there was nothing more that we could do to change this situation.

The life lesson was for us, not just his followers.

We would have to learn to live without Jesus as a regular family member.

He was not intent on listening to us anyway, and the burden of rejection caused me a heavy heart.

And so we left.

But I was starting to break.

Chapter 39

~Pierced~

It seemed for the most part that Jesus preferred to keep us at a distance. We had heard him say that to become his disciple you would need to hate your father and mother, wife and children, brothers and sisters — even your own life — and this hurt us all deeply. Had all the years of rejection in Nazareth made an impact on him? Was he taking out his resentment on us? The idyllic memories of his future glory and reign were being challenged in a way that we did not expect. My sense of maternal control was no longer effective.

It took some time for us to understand that he was asking everyone who wanted to be his disciple to choose him ahead of their closest relationships. "Will you choose to follow me, or submit to your family? It's your choice!" This was a challenge that caused people to question their values and allegiances. And in my case, the pain of Jesus' separation from me caused my heart to ache in pain and sorrow. Was he really casting me away? Did he really want to abandon me at this time?

"And if you do not carry your own cross, and follow me," Jesus had said, "then you cannot be my disciple."

His words echoed through our minds as the stomp of cruel Roman feet jarred our ears. Our hearts shook in fear, our bodies shaking nervously as we coiled into a ball on the ground, and our eyes streamed with tears at the horror that was unfolding before us.

The Via Dolorosa was in an uproar, the sweaty soldiers pushed back the crowds with brutal swipes, and yelling, "STAND BACK!" pointing their spears at us. Women shrieked and sobbed nearby, and the crowd screamed abuse as well as cheers as the condemned stumbled down the street to Skull Hill.

Death ruled the city, and chaos reigned.

Last night I shared the meal with Maria and other friends as we recounted our nation's hurried flight from Egypt. Jesus shared the meal with his Twelve in a large upper room, leading them in the traditional Psalms that were sung throughout the evening. And afterwards they headed to the Mount of Olives to pray — though Judas had been tasked with other duties, it seemed.

Today was the Day of Preparation.

We had bought lambs from the Temple merchants the previous day, and their occasional bleats could be heard echoing down the street until the ceremony. They would be slaughtered outside to re-enact our release from Egypt, and the blood of lambs would be painted on the lintels over the entrance to our homes. We would roast the lamb and eat it that evening, nothing would be left until morning — or it would need to be burned.

We were visiting Jerusalem for *Pesach*, along with Jesus and the Twelve, which had been prepared in the upper room of John Mark's mother, one of the regular disciples.

Passover required us to lay our hands on the lamb, transferring our transgressions so that they wouldn't be counted against us. In a practical way it enabled us to receive HaShem's forgiveness by identifying with the sacrifice.

That's how *Pesach* was performed under normal circumstances.

However this wasn't a "normal" time.

The Temple leaders had been angered to the point of murder, and they needed to stop this rebel who opposed their authority. In an impromptu overnight trial, the Sanhedrin agreed to condemn Jesus to death, but this would require assistance from Rome, as they had no authority to put anyone to death.

Further, being the Day of Preparation, the Jews needed to stay clean so as to eat the Passover meal that evening. This meant that it needed to be completed before sundown. And the following day, being a Sabbath, would be no work either.

The Sanhedrin had approached Pilate in the early morning, demanding that this rebel be killed due to a violation of their religious order. Eventually he submitted to their demands, with sentencing to be performed by crucifixion, after initially refusing to be swayed. So Jesus was taken and flogged, then driven to the cross.

Finally, the Jews had a victory.

They could shut the mouth of the one who rose up against them, the one they hated.

After years of having their authority threatened, this day marked an incredible release. His presumed authority would be stripped, and his body would be cast into a grave just like an ordinary criminal. There would be no way he could oppose them.

Once he was crushed, they would celebrate *Pesach* and rejoice in their personal victory tonight.

This was their time to celebrate.

"KEEP MOVING!" The soldier screeched to the condemned to continue down the hill.

My feet froze, shouldering the burden of my son's grief as he shuffled from the weight of the crossbeam to stumble and fall before me. His body bled from the flogging he'd received, which Pilate had inflicted before insisting that he be released. Blood flowed freely down his face, dripping on the ground before me as his hand pressed against the ground to keep his body upright.

Mother and son locked eyes for an instant that covered a limitless eternity. Surely this could not be the one destined to glory, who was declared by angels to save the people from their sins?

Two others were being swept down the hill in the procession.

Earlier their charges had been read and accepted by Pilate as worthy of death: the first, insurrection against Roman authority; the second, a murderer. There was no room in this society to harbour these people.

In Roman tradition, these criminals had the lintel forcibly removed from their homes, which became the cross beam to which they were nailed. This sent a strong visual message to anyone who might rise against Rome, that their house and family would be affected. I don't know where they got the beam which Jesus carried as he picked himself up before me, though it may have come from the home of Barabbas.

The shuffling downhill to the place of the skull took longer than expected; the thirty-nine lashes had cut deep into His flesh and bone and muscle, making it difficult to walk. If only I had been there to intervene! How I wish he had listened to his family, he could have been spared all this agony and pain, and become the respected saviour that everyone had hoped for.

Arriving at the site, the soldiers thrust him backwards to the ground — there were no niceties in their approach. A roar of laughter erupted as this provided a source of brutal entertainment, knowing that they were soon to take pleasure in watching the final breaths from the criminal's last hours on earth. They revelled in death, and dying.

I stood a distance away from the cross, my friends covered me with their shawls to console me, drawing me away from the pit where the clanging of hammers rang in our ears; unlike others, we weren't there to be entertained. Huddled together at the rear of the crowd, along with one of the Twelve and other followers of Jesus, an eerie cold wind blew causing me to shake and shiver, our tunics quivered in the breeze.

This was the time when darkness reigned.

The main stay of the cross dropped into the pre-dug hole, and ropes were attached to hoist the beam and its victim into place. This spectacle was what the Jews longed for, and would silence the man that opposed their secret society. Certainly Jesus wasn't one of them: He was a despised outcast; an illegitimate son of one who once served in the

Temple. He would never join their ranks, though he had intrigued — and angered — them for a very long time.

THUD!

The main stay fell into the hole and the soldiers hoisted the cross beam, with the daggling body attached, up the post and into position.

This was a messy process. The ground had darkened from years of blood that drained as they were nailed into position, and hoisted up for everyone's entertainment.

The clang of hammers rang out again as other soldiers secured their feet into position on the pole, crossing one leg over the other as the long rusty nails were driven hard through the flesh.

The intent was torture, not immediate death, which would provide time to revel in the last-breath's struggle for life, and watch as a mixture of blood and air bubbled from their mouths.

I cried, and wept, and ached.
But I had no more tears to give.

Sorrow flooded me.
Grief struck my heart.

My son.
My son.

What have they done to you?
Why didn't you listen?

You were destined to bring life.
But how can that be, now?

There is nothing left for me.
I need this to end.

There is no light in my soul.
Darkness surrounds me.

My breath is rough.
And I choke on the sweaty air.

I find it hard to think.
How long must this go on?

Son, I need you before your last breath.
Son, I need to hold you one last time.

My senses were numb.
My lips quivered as all hope was lost.

Maybe it had been hours. The initial entertainment now
turned into a waiting game.
My small group of supporters pressed around me, and we
walked to the foot of the cross.

Groans above us indicated some sign of life was still present.
But this tragedy would not finish with a miracle.

Unlike his birth, there were no angelic visitations to herald
his death.
Although he might easily have called upon his Father to
do so.

A cough and splutter caught our attention.
Jesus' finger stretched out to me.

"Woman," he called.
I looked up, straining through my own personal pain, to see
his face.

"Here is your son."
Standing next to me was John, a beloved disciple and was in
my support group.

John edged close to me and wrapped his arm around
my shoulder.

Looking to Jesus, he closed his eyes to accept the instruction.

"And here is your mother."
The role of the eldest son was passed on.

There was no other will or testimony required.
I was adopted into his house from that day, to be cared and provided for.

Grasping his feet, the naked bloodied form on the cross could do no more.
I held them with bursts of tears as the end of life drew near.

We shuffled away from the cross, and waited.

A loud cry.
Exhausted.

"Tetelestai!"

It was finished.

The heavens cracked like a whip while thunder roared across the sky.
And Jesus' head sank, lifeless.

We waited.

The air quietened, and the cold breeze stopped blowing.
The eery darkness subsided.
Life ended.

A soldier later came to inspect the bodies.

Seeing Jesus already dead, he called another to pierce the side with a spear.
And having done so, blood and water flowed, saturating the ground.

"He's dead."

This announcement blackened my mind.
And I was numb to any more emotion.

The spear sliced my soul.
It is finished, indeed.

My heart exploded under pressure.
Grief filled my dry eyes.

Sadness stripped my face of all dignity.
I could hardly stand.

All earthly meaning vanished.
I could see no future.
My life ended there.
On the cross.
With Jesus.

Chapter 40

~The Tomb~

It was mid-afternoon and tomorrow was the Sabbath, so the entertainment needed to end.

One had died, but the other two were not yet at that point, so to hasten the process the soldiers brought hammers and smashed their legs. Their end of life soon followed with splutters and gasps, and finally there was silence.

It was daunting as we watched and waited for this spectacle to end. In the middle was the one who was promised to be the next king of Israel, and either side of him hung the broken bodies of criminals. All seemed to want the same thing — the struggle for power over Rome, or so it was thought.

They were nothing but outcasts of society, and now a mess to be cleaned up.

I could not watch this much longer, and the eeriness of the hour caused us to come together and console each other away from the scene. Our shared grief and shock was evident to the soldiers who were preparing to lower the bodies to the ground and throw them into unmarked graves or burned, and they ushered us to the end of the cesspit where we would not be an inconvenience to them while they completed the job.

I couldn't allow the body of my son to be discarded like this, where there would be no honour or dignity or respect held for his name. "John, John," I tugged at his coat, straining my voice to grab his attention. He leaned into me, ready to meet my need in his new role. "Mother, what is it?" he asked gently and quietly.

I held back for a moment, my voice not knowing how to ask this question. My confidence had been crushed, I needed someone to help with my immediate needs. And right now the only thing that concerned me was a proper burial. So I asked, "Where will they take his body?"

John looked into my eyes; releasing heart-felt compassion that gave me comfort in that moment, when I needed it most. His dark hair covered his face, and light from the afternoon sun splashed across our faces as though a storm had just passed over us. And with a squeeze of my hand, he slipped away to find out.

Permission had been sought, and granted to Joseph of Arimathea to take the body of Jesus and place it in a tomb. He was joined by Nicodemus, and together they had opposed the other's decision to put Jesus to death. They were part of the trial that occurred overnight, members of the Sanhedrin.

"But he's done nothing against the law!" they insisted, trying to overturn the pre-assumed verdict. The overnight jury were not to be deterred. They needed to fully agree on the charge that they would bring to Pilate, and these two were delaying the procedure by arguing against them.

Finally someone claimed, "He said, I am able to destroy this Temple and rebuild it in three days.'"

"Is this so?" questioned Caiaphas. "Aren't you going to answer? What is this that these testify against you?"

Jesus stood resolute and kept his peace, angering the high priest by his silence.

"I adjure you," demanded Caiaphas, "in the name of the living G-d, tell us whether you are the Christ, the son of G-d!" The steamy air became silent as the demand was placed on Jesus to answer.

All eyes looked to their prisoner, awaiting a response.

It came, firm and clear, and this would give them what they wanted.

"It is as you say."

The high priest tore his clothes, squealing with victory at the admission, "Do we need any more witnesses?"

The room erupted.
They got their man.

This would end his threats.
This would secure their reign.

The faces of Joseph and Nicodemus were forced to admit defeat in their mission to save the man whom they respected to be the promised messiah. They had openly denied allegiance to the society, and would no longer have a seat at the table which they attended for many years.

Together, the pair were now outcasts — they had chosen to follow Jesus.

Here at the cross, the body was lowered by soldiers who tore the nails from the disfigured hands and feet, allowing the body to slump to the ground. There was no life or form on the Jesus we knew. The two secret disciples rolled the body into a sheet and with the help of others they placed it in a nearby tomb.

A virgin tomb.

John returned to collect me, along with the other women, and together we shuffled to the burial spot, passing through a garden nearby. My group of supporters had been with me since Galilee, and now we stood outside where the body was laid.

This was it.
The final resting place.

No more miracles.
No more healings.
No more evil spirits.

His time amongst us was cut short.
It was clear to me that he did not fulfil his calling.
His lifeless body was of no use to Israel as future king.

And now I was left with a heart full of broken promises.
Where were the angels now, in my time of grief and despair?

We stood and watched until the sun gave no more light.
But there really was nowhere to go home to.

The tomb was freshly cut, and a large round stone placed at the entrance which would be rolled down the gentle incline to prevent tomb raiders from interfering with the corpse once interred. Having heard first-hand the threats from the Sanhedrin, Joseph considered that this would only end in tragedy.

Planning ahead, he had arranged to cut a tomb in the side of the hill. At least he would be able to honour Jesus with a proper burial, despite the plans of others to destroy him. But oh how he hoped that things would not go awry! How he wished that Jesus could remain among them forever!

The amount of spices they brought was incredible, and heavy — more than enough to prepare a body and remove the stench of rotting flesh. But this was not a normal burial, and these were not normal spices.

The men worked hard to prepare the body until it was too dark inside. Joseph stretched out the long linen sheets along the solid stone bench, and Nicodemus spread the aloes and myrrh over the full length of the body, embalming it from head to foot. Then they rolled it back and forth completely sealed. A cloth bound the head of the deceased.

Respectfully, the pair bowed as they stepped backwards out of the tomb.
There was nothing more to do now.
The Sabbath commenced.

Unlatching the chock, the stone artfully rolled in front of the entrance so that it became completely sealed. There was now no way in or out of the tomb without significant help from others to roll back the stone.

We stayed outside while the men finished their burial procedure.

The five of us waited for closure: myself, my sister Maria, Maria from Magdala and Salome. John nestled himself between Salome and me, resting an arm across our shoulders, showing love for those whom he now called 'mother'.

The sun dropped below the horizon, and the secret disciples left.

A feeling of loneliness rattled within my heart.
There were no crowds present.
Just me, and my girls.
And John.

All my hopes and dreams, dissolved.
My eyes ran dry tears.
I could not breathe.

This was the end.

"Jesus, Jesus. Why did you do it?"

I waited.

No miracles now.
No angelic visits.
No response from heaven.

There was no answer.

The grave was silent.

$\mathcal{E}$pilogue

The three days that followed were the lowest and darkest period of my life. I could not find the strength to eat, and was unable to be consoled. I felt as though my life been wasted to raise this boy who had given us high hopes, only to see it end in tragedy. I honestly did not know how I would make it through.

Somewhere it is written, 'Weeping may last the night, but joy comes in the morning.' This has been my story, and it has not been easy. The days and weeks that followed were soon replaced by times of joy, as the birth of the church had begun!

After three days, reports surfaced that Jesus had risen from the dead, which shocked and amazed everyone. And it wasn't just hearsay, Jesus himself appeared to us as we waited in the upper room, and at many other times, to prove that he truly was alive. This resulted in many coming to believe that he was the promised Messiah. The message I received from angels at the time of his birth stirred my heart with sincere gratitude, and my despair changed to hope.

The risen Jesus was sure to show the world that even death was not going to stop HaShem's mission, who had planned long ago to seek and save those who were lost and reconnect them to Himself. Through this and other revelations, Jesus openly revealed himself to the world, though this time his brothers didn't come to taunt him. They soon changed their thoughts to believe that he was not the illegitimate son who wanted revenge, but one who was sent into the world as their Saviour.

James, who earlier accused Jesus in front of the town, had a significant turn-around after all this. Although he openly opposed and humiliated him, he later repented of his own judgements and honoured the one he accused. Later, he became a foundation in the early church, well respected by Peter and the other apostles. In fact they turned to James for godly counsel and advice, as one who knew and trusted the living Jesus.

After Jesus' resurrection we waited in the upper room, praying and searching the scriptures for everything that had been written about the Messiah. We held little value for the things of this earth, and shared freely with those who had a need. And during this time Jesus continually met us in various forms to explain the things of heaven, and how that was to come about on earth once he returned to his Father.

These events continued for forty days after his resurrection, when he led us up onto a hill, blessed us, and then ascended into the heavens. He said, "Don't go anywhere, but stay in Jerusalem. I have a gift for you from my Father, just as

I told you previously. In just a few days' time you will be baptised in the Holy Spirit."

And it was in that upper room, the same which he had eaten together with his disciples, that we met and gathered. We were gifted hospitality while many people gathered to hear the stories, pray and read scripture, and wait for the gift that Jesus promised.

I was able to share the training that Bubbe gave me in my early years with others, teaching them to pray expectantly and to listen to the voice of HaShem. The events from my past faded into insignificance; I was no longer remembered as the Temple girl, nor taunted as the outcast single mother.

Through all these things I have yielded to be HaShem's servant. Through the good times, and the bad.

And for that I have been exceedingly blessed.

Keep looking to Jesus, the risen Lord.

Mariam, of Christ.

Theological Backdrop

The theology of Mariam, Joseph and Jesus has be a long-debated topic for theologians just as much as it is for anyone with an interest in Christianity. This book has been written along the following lines with concepts derived from canonized scripture as first preference, a selection of apocryphal writings as a second preference, then from Jewish history and stories, legends and wider sources. I have been careful to weigh up the information to present *a most likely scenario* granted my small theological training and limited time and resources, which I hope aims to provide an insightful and thoroughly enjoyably stimulating version of events. Here are some explanations as to why I carried the storyline in a certain direction at times. Please allow me the grace to create the storyline despite the many differences in opinion and understanding.

How did Mary become Mariam ?

The New Testament presents the predicament of *the three Marys* in various places when describing important events, so I firstly wanted to see differentiate *Mary the mother of Jesus* from *Mary Magdalene* and *Mary the mother of James and Joses*.

There seems to be a fairly simple explanation in scripture that provides clarity around this topic. The way that the name *Mary* is written has been translated to the generic English word Mary in all three cases of the use of the name, however the Greek has been written in a variety of ways.

Mary Magdalene is almost always given context that this Mary is from Magdala, and her Greek name is written as Maria. Also, due to her position within the group of people she is almost always referred to as Mary Magdalene to distinguish her from the others.

Mary mother of James and Joses is similarly written as Maria in Greek, and is sometimes called 'the other Mary' or 'the mother of James and Joses'. And there is also Mary the mother of John Mark, as listed in Acts, and she is clearly identified by this attribution (Acts 12:12).

For Mary the mother of Jesus, her name in Greek is Mariam and sometimes Marias, (which is derived from the Hebrew name *Mariam*) and is written distinctly different to *Maria*, used by the other two (or three) Marys. For clarity, and to introduce some historical context, I have used the Greek form of her name *Mariam* throughout this book, for the most part.

The role of Joseph

When we are presented with the annual Christmas events showing a young and mature Joseph and Mariam with their child, this is a very unlikely (but romantic!) notion of how the Holy Family was brought together. It makes a great kids story in the twenty-first century but heralds far from the truth of scripture and extra-biblical context to which I have written from. Scripture and apocrypha tell us that Joseph was a much older man that was previously married and with at least two sons. This line of thinking has been captured in my former books *Via Crucis Via Lucis: The Way of the Cross, The Way of the Light* as well as *The Advent*. I have had to lean deeper into how this arrangement worked to provide a more historically considered account of how Josephs' role with Mariam was handled.

The Holy Family has long been presented as a married man and wife who have the Christ child, along with other children — unless you follow Catholic tradition — which holds the firm belief that Mariam only gave birth to Jesus and did not have any other children; thus considering her womb as a holy solace for the Saviour alone. This is hard for Protestants to accept due to several scriptures like "Jesus' mother and brothers were outside" (Matt 12:46), as well as the traditional role of a husband to his wife, once they are married, to engage in normal marital rites, that "they had no sexual union until they were married." (Matt 1:25)

If Mariam was to only give birth to Jesus alone, then I needed to search scripture to determine how this may have presented itself in other ways, and whether any of the former assumptions were true. For instance, if Joseph was an older man and not a young man, then his role and expectations for his betrothed might not be as strong (although we would expect that he would have had inclinations towards his wife!) I have had to read and search the translations of the Biblical texts closely to get a better picture of Joseph's role, which I will share here now.

The first acknowledgement by scripture is that it was difficult for the New Testament writers to officially state that Joseph was the father of Jesus. Mariam scolded Jesus saying, "Son, why have you treated us like this? Your father and I have been anxiously searching for you." (Luke 2:48) Jesus responded by saying, "…shouldn't I be in my Fathers' house?" (Luke 2:49) His point seems emphatic, and a general reading of this scripture will often miss the intent of the message that Jesus is stating here. Jesus was declaring out loud that Joseph was not his real father; His real Father was in Heaven and this was His House in Jerusalem. *(Let's address the elephant in the room, shall we?)*

Matthew traces the genealogy of Jesus through to Joseph, but adds the line "Jacob was the father of Joseph, the husband of Mariam. Mariam gave birth to Jesus, who is called the Messiah." (Matt 1:16) Special emphasis was given to Mariam, along with other women of notable significance in the lineage of Jesus in Matthew's gospel. The association of Mariam with Jesus the Messiah, rather than Joseph being the father of the Messiah, should not be easily dismissed.

Luke further emphasises the mystery of Joseph's role when he writes, "He was the son, *so it was thought*, of Joseph." (Luke 3:23) The link between Joseph and Jesus was not that of a blood relative, and apparently more of a legal responsibility, or caretaker, as the angel had directed.

"… an angel of the Lord appeared to him in a dream. "Joseph, son of David," the angel said, "do not be afraid to take Mariam as your wife (or betrothed, more on this later). For the child within her was conceived by the Holy Spirit. And she will have a son, and you are to name him Jesus, for he will save his people from their sins." (Matt 1:20, 21)

The angel places emphasis on Josephs lineage with respect to being of the line of David, so he was certainly required from a legal standpoint to confirm the prophecies about the Messiah being of the royal line of David. (Refer to *The Advent* for the prophecies about Jesus.)

The word for *husband* (Matt 1:16, 19) can be translated in Greek to be 'betrothed' or 'future husband' or simply 'any male' and to distinguish an adult male from a boy, according to Strongs Concordance G435 (aner, ἀνήρ). This term is used by the angel who directed Joseph to take Mariam as his *wife*. (Matt 1:20, 24) The Greek word for 'wife' is Strongs G1135 (ghyne, γυνή), which can also be translated to mean a woman of any age, a virgin or married woman or even a widow, or *betrothed*.

So a possible interpretation (without trying to stretch the limits of imagination too far) is that the angel directed Joseph to take Mariam as his betrothed. It is understood that he took her legally to be his wife in obedience to the angels' direction, but he may not necessarily have consummated the marriage in the normal way. There are a few reasons for this that we should consider.

First, he was quite old (around 89 years of age) when he was appointed by lot in a ceremony to take Mariam as his wife. Apocrypha mentions that he died at the age of 111, and we know that Joseph wasn't around when Jesus started his ministry around the age of thirty. The years of his age presented in "Joseph the Carpenter"[1] marks the death of Joseph to be when Jesus was 22 years of age.

Second, he was willing to participate in the divine appointment and obeyed the voice of the angel at least three times. That is, i) take Mariam to be your betrothed, ii) flee to Egypt, iii) return to Israel. He was also warned in a dream to settle in Galilee after he was afraid to return to the region of Judea, and we could assume that this was from an angel as well.

a)   "As he considered this, an angel of the Lord appeared to him in a dream. "Joseph, son of David," the angel said, "do not be afraid to take Mariam as your *betrothed*. For the child within her was conceived by the Holy Spirit." (Matt 1:20)

b)   "After the wise men were gone, an angel of the Lord appeared to Joseph in a dream. "Get up! Flee to Egypt with the child and his mother," the angel said. "Stay there until I tell you to return, because Herod is going to search for the child to kill him."" (Matt 2:13)

c)   "When Herod died, an angel of the Lord appeared in a dream to Joseph in Egypt. "Get up!" the angel said. "Take the child and his mother back to the land of Israel, because those who were trying to kill the child are dead."" (Matt 2:19, 20)

d)   "So Joseph got up and returned to the land of Israel with Jesus and his mother. But when he learned that the new ruler of Judea was Herod's son Archelaus, he was afraid to go there. Then, after being warned in a dream, he left for the region of Galilee." (Matt 2:21, 22)

If the marriage was never consummated through sexual relations, we may interpret "But he did not have sexual relations with her *until* her son was born" (Matt 1:25) to mean that Joseph never had sex with Mariam. The word "until" in Greek (G2193) is a definition where something continues up to a certain point in time, and Matthew has used the word intentionally in this phrase. It is possible that he may have intentionally vowed not to have relations with Mariam, and yet continue with the marriage.

It was awkwardly known at the time of their betrothal that Mariam was pregnant and that Joseph was not the father. Joseph would have been both angry and afraid, but he wanted to do the right thing by both HaShem and man by divorcing her quietly and not putting her to public disgrace. But we see it was HaShem's intent that he take her. Was this to ensure that the Messiah was raised in a godly household, and that Mariam was protected?

Matthew's use of the word "until" appears to quietly dance around the issue of the couple raising a child whilst not legally married, and taking the responsibility (and the mocking of it) directly on the chin. Luke is more direct in his gospel account, stating that "Jesus was the son of Joseph, *so it was thought.*" (Luke 3:23) If we were to interpret these scenarios together in the cultural context of the day that demands that *sex outside of marriage was not accepted* then it would likely tar the rest of the gospel story that demonstrates that Jesus is the Messiah. So I'm assuming that this situation has been mentioned quietly, and downplayed to allow the rest of the gospel to have more air time.

These dynamics would have been at work when Jesus remained at the Temple and the company had commenced their return journey back to Nazareth. He was found three days later talking with the religious leaders, and replied to his parents, "Didn't you know that I must be in my Father's house?" His statement is emphatic, directly claiming his true Father was God Himself, rather than Joseph.

These scriptures, circumstances and awkward word choices tend to indicate that although Mariam and Joseph were betrothed and likely to have married, it appears that they may never have had sex, and therefore did not have children together.

Was Joseph simply a caretaker or guardian?

If the role of Joseph was to be a sort of caretaker or guardian to Mariam, then he was obedient to the directions given to him by the angel so that God was able to achieve an outcome through him.

It is also interesting to note that the angel ordered Joseph 'to take' Mariam, and the Greek word is Strongs G3880 paralambano (παραλαμβάνω), which means 'to join with one's self a companion, to receive something transmitted, to receive with the mind'. The word is used moreso to discuss a companion and less inference about someone you would marry.

A general word for 'a man', 'a husband', 'of a betrothed or future husband', 'distinguishing an adult man from a boy', 'any male' or a 'generic use of the term to identify a group of both men and women' is Strongs G435 aner (ἀνήρ), used in Matthew 1:19.

Similarly, a general word for 'a woman of any age whether a virgin or married or widow', or 'a wife' or 'of a betrothed woman' is Strongs Greek G1135 gyne (γυνή) is used in Matthew 1:20.

A word of higher intensity — if it had of been used by the angel — would have been 'to marry' which is the Greek word in Strongs concordance G1060 gameo (γαμέω) which literally means 'to get married, to give one's self in marriage, to give a daughter in marriage'. This word was never used in the Bible to confirm that Joseph married Mariam, in a literal sense, and instead the less definitive word selections (that are not translated into English sufficiently) and a focus on traditional (perhaps Western?) marriage rites has replaced what I believe is the intended meaning of the texts.

So one way to interpret the charge to Joseph by the angel was to accept and receive Mariam as a companion to himself, which he did while in the state of being betrothed. It's unfortunate that Luke does not elaborate on this situation, which is covered by Matthew alone. I've assumed in this book that they eventually did marry, though I have reason to believe that they never married and could easily have been in a state of being betrothed during their lives together, and which never led to marriage — which would support the Catholic doctrine of the perpetual virginity of Mariam.

I have therefore leaned towards the opinion that they were married but that never had relations due to Joseph's vow, and his age being significantly greater than his wife contributing to this theory.

Rewriting the scriptures to accommodate the original intended meaning might appear to be something like the below:

a) "Joseph, to whom she was *betrothed* (G435), was a righteous man and did not want to disgrace her publicly." (Matt 1:19)

b) "As he considered this, an angel of the Lord appeared to him in a dream. "Joseph, son of David," the angel said, "do not be afraid *to take* (G3880) Mariam as your *betrothed* (G1135). For the child within her was conceived by the Holy Spirit."" (Matt 1:20)

c) "When Joseph woke up, he did as the angel of the Lord commanded and *took* (G3880) Mariam as his *betrothed* (G1135)." (Matt 1:24)

But didn't Mariam make a vow?

There is good reason to believe that Mariam had already made a vow of celibacy to the Lord before the time of her appointment to marry to Joseph. In this case it would easily explain many things about her role with Joseph, the virgin birth and her special relationship with Jesus.

I have offered an alternative opinion as a storyline in this account of Biblical fiction, that it was Joseph who made the vow without needing to mention that Mariam made something similar. Perhaps there were two vows operating, and the gospel writers chose to be overly silent about them both? In any case, the shock announcement of the pending birth to Joseph demonstrated that he did not expect to see these set of events occurring. In this case, let's assume that it is okay for Mariam to keep some secrets to herself, and not have to reveal all at this time.

Didn't Jesus Have Other Brothers and Sisters?

The Bible mentions clearly that Jesus had brothers and sisters. (Matt 12:46-50; Mark 6:3; Matt 13:55; John 7:3,10)

> "He returned to Nazareth, his hometown.
> When he taught there in the synagogue, everyone was amazed and said, "Where does he get this wisdom and the power to do miracles?"
> Then they scoffed, "He's just the carpenter's son, and we know Mariam, his mother, and his brothers—
> James, Joseph, Simon, and Judas.
> All his sisters live right here among us. Where did he learn all these things?"
> And they were deeply offended and refused to believe in him." (Matt 13:54-57)

Doesn't this mean that Joseph consummated the marriage and that Mariam had other children with him?

It's a fair point, and in a Western culture context with 2,000 years of history after the fact, we would argue that the normal thing for a married man to do would be to have relations with his wife that result in other children. But if Joseph went on to fulfill a role as a caretaker of Mariam then the other brothers and sisters are likely to have been notionally referred to as His siblings and are more likely to have been cousins or at best half-brothers - not directly related - but *treated as family*, in the context of the culture that they were in.

The meaning for 'brother' in Aramaic also includes by default the notion of non-blood and non-direct relatives, which is likely to have been the case since there are numerous sources of tradition, extra-Biblical and apocrypha that support the listing of the names of Jesus's brothers as being from other parents, and not Mariam his mother.

Apocrypha mentions that Joseph had previously been married and that he had children of his own. When living in Nazareth they likely lived with Clopas, Joseph's younger brother, who also had children of his own and whose wife had passed away, but he had remarried. Thus it would have been an extended family, rather than a nuclear family, that Jesus grew up in. And in this case, 'brothers and sisters' were treated as family although they might not have been directly blood relatives of the parents that were raising them.

Mariam and Jesus as the primary focus

The Biblical texts emphasise the mother-son relationship, and Joseph is almost always presented as a sideline supporter instead of the role of father. Similarly, scripture does not state emphatically that Jesus was the son of Joseph, or that Joseph is the father of Jesus. However many scriptures present the dual relationship of "the mother and child" together. For example:

a)   When the wise men came, they "saw the child with his mother Mariam" (Matt 2:11)

b)   When the angel warned Joseph to flee to Egypt, "Joseph left for Egypt with the child and Mariam, his mother" (Matt 2:14)

c)   "Get up!" the angel said. "Take the child and his mother back to the land of Israel, because those who were trying to kill the child are dead." So Joseph got up and returned to the land of Israel with Jesus and his mother. (Matt 2:19 -21)

Who named Jesus?

The angel directed Joseph to name the baby Jesus: "And she will have a son, and you are to name him Jesus, for he will save his people from their sins." (Matt 1:21)

"Eight days later, when the baby was circumcised, he was named Jesus, the name given him by the angel even before he was conceived." (Luke 2:21)

"And Joseph named him Jesus". (Matt 1:25)

How old was Jesus when He died?

Luke mentions that "Jesus was about thirty years old when he started his ministry". (Luke 3:23) General Christian tradition has taught that Jesus had a three year ministry, which would make him about 33 years of age. However this hasn't taken into consideration the extra-Biblical and historical accounts, and Jesus' actual age at the time of his death was never published.

The timeline of events has been researched to show approximate timings of the life of Jesus, placing his birth around 6 BC and his death around 30 CE, which would have made Him around 36 years of age. Mariam would have therefore been about 50 years of age at the time of his death.

Recall that the Jewish leaders rebutted Jesus when He said that He would destroy this temple and rebuild it in three days, saying "It has taken forty-six years to build this Temple, and you can rebuild it in three days?" (John 2:20) so the Temple was rebuilt during Jesus' lifetime was a known historical fact, and they were protective of it. They didn't want some young upstart (a.k.a. Jesus) taking over their pride of place that they had worked hard to put together.

Who were the children of Joseph?

There are differences of opinion about the listings of the brothers of Jesus listed in Matthew 13:55 and Mark 6:3 (James, Joses, Simon, and Judas). The commentators make mention of the two pairs of names James and Joses, in contrast to Simon and Judas), and there is a firm consensus that they are from two different parental figures.

Some attribute one pair to Joseph's earlier marriage, and the second to his brothers earlier marriage — both having lost their first wives. Another line of thinking — which I adopted in this book — was that one pair of boys was from Maria the wife of Clopas, and the other from Clopas.

This means that we wouldn't know who the children of Joseph were, and in this case I have assumed that he had daughters, simply because girls were not considered as significant in the family line as men in that period and as a result there is less chance that they would have been recorded in historical documents. This also brings out a softer and more compassionate side of Joseph when he is instructed to marry Mariam.

Why do you think James caused an issue?

Reading the epistle of James towards the end of the New Testament, he focuses strongly on the practise of humility, repenting of anger, and drawing near to God. The Bible indicates that 'even His own brothers did not believe Him' and tried to remove Him from the people during times of ministry.

I'm led to believe that James had an amazing turn around from his own personal attitudes and actions towards Jesus when he realised that Jesus was who He claimed to be, and as a result the book of James provides a strong contrast of his own personal testimony from what he was before he met Christ and the resulting way of life that he led afterwards.

If James was one of the twelve apostles, could he also have been a non-believer?

James and his brothers did not accept Jesus and tried to reduce the religious stir that He was making, so clearly his brother James was not one of the twelve apostles listed in Mark 3:16-19 (and elsewhere) which lists James as being the son of Alphaeus. In this series of names, Mark puts a gap between Simon (Peter) and his brother Andrew by inserting the brothers James and John, who were also brothers.

Matthew (also known as Levi) was also the son of Alphaeus (Mark 2:14) and James is also identified as the son of Alphaeus

(Matthew 10:3, Mark 3:18, Luke 6:15 and Acts 1:13) which would make them brothers, or at least half-brothers.

The listing of names in the books of Matthew (Matt 10:3) and Acts (Acts 1:13) aligns Matthew (the tax collector, also known as Levi) next to James (son of Alphaeus), demonstrating their familial relationship. However Mark's gospel does not intend to group the apostles according to family relationships but rather by a perceived level of authority within the group, which is why they are not listed in order of family groups, otherwise we would see Peter and Andrew grouped along with Matthew and James.

This also means that James (son of Alphaeus) was not "James the Less" as some have believed because James the Less was not in favour with Jesus during His ministry years, and as a result needed a conversion experience to become the apostle who was well known in the early church, and who wrote the book of James.

The other James, who was the brother of John, was an early martyr in church history (Acts 12:1,2) whereas when the New Testament mentioned "Mary the mother of James and Joses" (Mark 16:1) this refers to the half-brother of Jesus whose mother was Maria, and who rejected Jesus during His growing up and ministry years.

Why do you think Joseph built a house in Emmaus?

A lot of commentators build a scenario around Josephs absence based on apocrypha that states Joseph was abroad building houses and returned home to find his betrothed pregnant. It would make sense that he went to build a house for the two of them to raise Jesus, and in an area that avoided the sting of the label that he was willing to accept in the situation that the Lord put him in.

I chose Emmaus as it was in the area where Archelaus was ruling (Matthew 2:22) which was in the region of Bethlehem and would have reconnected Joseph with his grass roots, but Joseph was scared to return there due to the poor reputation that he had in place of his father Herod, so instead headed back to Nazareth, which fits the greater storyline of the Biblical account.

After Joseph dies, there may be reason for his brother Clopas and wife Maria to have moved from Nazareth to Emmaus and hence take over the house that Joseph built, which would line up with Luke's account of the couple who walked to Emmaus and had the revelation of Jesus after His resurrection. It would have been a beautiful gift for Jesus to be revealed first to his brother Clopas and Maria, the ones who raised Him along with Mariam, from a young age.

Who was Q?

There is a lack of knowledge about who collected the stories of Jesus, Mariam, Joseph and the early church and as a result Biblical scholars consider that an unnamed person or people group, notionally called "Q," were responsible for keeping the records in written form which were then circulated.

The possible identity of Q, in my opinion, is Clopas. This is based on the tradition that both Clopas and Joseph were known to be strong religious leaders in the community, who would have had an interest in preserving tradition. As I've asserted in this book, with Mariam and Maria living together for many years to raise Jesus and the four boys they would have had a very close knit set of stories that they would likely have had written down to capture the stories surrounding the birth of Jesus, the visit of the Magi, the hurried trip to Egypt, et cetera.

Clopas was in a unique position to be able to witness the life of Jesus unfold, test the stories against what he held personally from experience and write them down to be preserved for future reference.

It is also evident that Peter and Mariam pooled their stories, but this was most likely from the time of Jesus' ministry and not His early years, and would have contributed to the later body of stories surrounding Jesus.

Timeline of Events

Who	What	When	Where	Why	Source
Anne and Joachim	Mariam's conception and birth	21 BC	Unknown	God required a vessel to carry the promised Deliverer who would fulfil the promises of scripture to give birth to Mariam.	Apocrypha John 2:20
The Temple	Rebuilding of the Second Temple by Herod the Great of Judea	20 BC	Jerusalem	Construction lasted 46 years	Historical records
Mariam	Grew up in the Jerusalem Temple while it was being rebuilt	18-9 BC	Jerusalem	Mariam was dedicated to service of the Lord in the Temple at the age of three	Apocrypha/ Catholic
Joachim	Mariam's father passed away when Mariam was 8 years old	13 BC	Jerusalem	Buried in the Valley of Josaphat	Coptic tradition

Anne	Mariam's mother passed away when Mariam was 9 years old	12 BC	Jerusalem	One year after the death of her father, her mother was also passed away and was buried by his side.	Coptic tradition
Mariam	Betrothed to Joseph	8 BC	Jerusalem	The priests needed to remove Mariam from the temple prior to her physical maturity, to keep the temple clean for worship	Apocrypha/ Catholic
Joseph	Appointed to be betrothed to the virgin by lot	8 BC	Jerusalem	Among the single men, Josephs' staff budded during the ceremony and he was appointed to marry the temple girl	Apocrypha/ Catholic
Mariam	Staying in Nazareth while betrothed to Joseph, but not yet pregnant	8–7 BC	Nazareth in Galilee	It's likely that Mariam had no other family so she stayed with Joseph's family in Nazareth, most possibly Joseph's younger brother Clopas (who had at least two boys of his own).	Luke 1:26, 27
Mariam	The Annunciation	7 BC	Nazareth of Galilee	Angelic visitation to announce that Mariam will get pregnant	Luke 1:26

Who	What	When	Who	Why	Source
Elizabeth	Mariam's visit to Elizabeth	7 BC	The house of Zechariah	Mariam rushed from Nazareth to see her cousin Elizabeth who was pregnant, to confirm the angel's words.	Luke 1:39, 40
Mariam	Mariam's baby had been conceived	7 BC	Zechariah and Elizabeth's home	When the baby leaped in Elizabeth's womb, she declared that Mariam's child was blessed and that she was a mother.	Luke 1:41, 42, 44
Mariam	Returned to Nazareth	7 BC	Elizabeth's house	Mariam stayed up until the point of birth of John the Baptist, and left just prior. Likely to have returned for Yom Kippur, The Feast of Atonement, on Tishri 10.	Luke 1:56
Mariam and Joseph	Nazareth	7 BC	House of Clopas	When Mariam returned to Nazareth she was three months pregnant, and gave the shock announcement to Joseph	Matt 1:19
Joseph	Royal lineage of King David	7 BC	Lineage	The Messiah was prophesied to be of the line of King David, so Joseph had to fulfill this role.	Matt 1:20 Luke 1:27, 32, 69 Luke 2:4, 11

Joseph	Nazareth of Galilee	7 BC, while Quirinius was governor of Syria	House of Clopas	Joseph may have lived with Clopas and his wife and two boys, and Mariam.	Luke 2:4 and Apocrypha
Joseph and Mariam	Bethlehem, the town of David	7–6 BC	Possibly a relative's house	After they arrived in Bethlehem, Joseph possibly arranged to stay with a relative in a short term stay arrangement	Luke 2:4, 5
The Shepherds	The birth of Jesus	6 BC Nisan 1	The stable In a manger	The shepherds were told to look for the Christ child in Bethlehem	Luke 2:11, 15
Mariam, Joseph and Jesus	The circumcision of Jesus	6 BC	Jerusalem temple	On the eighth day Jesus was taken to the temple for circumcision and the naming ceremony	Luke 2:21
Mariam, Joseph and Jesus	Place of residence	6 BC	A house in Bethlehem	The holy family would have moved out of the stable into temporary accommodation (the inn?) after the census where they would reside until after the purification offering (40 days from birth of Jesus)	Luke 2:22

Who	What	When	Who	Why	Source
Joseph and Mariam	Jerusalem Temple	6 BC Iyar 19	The Temple	Mariam's purification offering was 40 days after the birth of Jesus, and this puts them in Jerusalem on Iyar 19	Luke 2:22
Simeon	Simeon's prophecy	6 BC	The Temple	Simeon prophesied about the life and ministry of Jesus and also declared that a sword would pierce the soul of Mariam	Luke 2:34, 35
Anna	Anna's prophecy	6 BC	The Temple	Anna shared testimony about Jesus, likely to have received revelation through her years of prayer and fasting in the Temple, as she told everyone who had been waiting for the deliverer to come to rescue Jerusalem.	Luke 2:34, 35
Wise Men sent to Bethlehem	Bethlehem	6 BC	A house in Bethlehem	The wise men entered the house where they were staying and saw the child with his mother. It's possible that Joseph had commenced building a house for the holy family in Judea (perhaps Emmaus?) so that Mariam's and Elizabeth's babies could grow up together and have a sense of family.	Matt 2:9–11

Joseph, Mariam and Jesus	Place of residence	6–5 BC Up to 2 years, until the event *The Killing of the Innocents.*	A house in Bethlehem or Judea	Matthew's gospel does not provide a definitive timeline, only "after the wise men had gone," which could mean that they were in the location for a while, giving Joseph time to build a home for the family in this area. Noting that Joseph had later considered returning to Judea after the flight to Egypt and the primary reason for this would be because he had commenced building a home. (Matt 2:22)	Matt 2:13
Joseph	Escape to Egypt	5–4 BC Jesus' childhood years	Egypt	They left the house where they were staying in Bethlehem or Judea and an angel directed them to flee to Egypt where they stayed until Herod died.	Matt 2:13–15
Baby boys	The Killing of the Innocents	5–4 BC	Bethlehem	Herod commanded his soldiers to kill all the boys living in and around Bethlehem who were two years old or younger.	Matt 2:16

Who	What	When	Who	Why	Source
Joseph, Mariam and Jesus	Directed to return to Israel	4 BC	Egypt	The angel directed Joseph to take the child and his mother back to the land of Israel because those who were trying to kill the child (Herod the Great) were dead.	Matt 2:19, 20
Joseph, Mariam and Jesus	Intended place of return: Israel	4/3 BC		Joseph had planned to return to Israel, likely to be Bethlehem or Judea, and it's likely that he had started to build a house for the family there.	Matt 2:22, 23
Joseph, Mariam and Jesus	Place of residence: To their own town, Nazareth of Galilee	4/3 BC		Luke fails to mention the time in Egypt but Matthew mentions that Joseph had planned to return to live in Israel but when warned in a dream they returned to Nazareth in Galilee.	Matt 2:22 Luke 2:39
Joseph, Mariam and Jesus	Place of residence: Nazareth	3 BC–30 AD	Nazareth	*There* He grew up healthy and strong. Emphasis on 'there' being the place where Jeus was to be recognised to grow up.	Luke 2:40
				Jesus was 'about thirty' years old when he began His ministry, and he could have stayed at home to look after Mariam and the rest of the family until then	Luke 3:23

Joseph, Mariam and Jesus	Visit the Jerusalem Temple every year	During Passover, Nisan 14–15	The Temple	It is likely that Joseph and Mariam wanted to make Jesus known to the temple priests (to indicate the coming Messiah was in their midst) and demonstrate their own commitment to the regulations of the Law.	Luke 2:41
Joseph, Mariam and Jesus	Jesus at the Temple as a pre-teen	Nisan 18	The Temple	When Mariam and Joseph couldn't find Jesus in their company on the way back to Nazareth, they frantically returned to find him with the elders. "Didn't you know that I had to be in my Father's House?" (Luke 2:49) Jesus was bluntly pointing out his true Father was not Joseph.	Luke 2:46
Jesus	Jesus stayed with his parents in Nazareth	During his early years	Nazareth home	Jesus demonstrated his commitment to honour his parents as required by Mosaic Law.	Luke 2:51
The Temple	Completion of Second Temple	16 AD	Jerusalem	Completion of the Second Temple is possible to have finished at Jesus' trip when he was 12 years of age.	[2] Britannica

Who	What	When	Who	Why	Source
Joseph	Joseph's occupation and location of family upbringing	As Jesus grew up	Nazareth	Joseph was a carpenter and lived in Nazareth.	Matt 13:53–55
Joseph	Death	Lived 111 years. Jesus was 22 years of age, according to Apocrypha	Unknown	Not recorded in the Bible however the apocryphal versions relate stories that seem to align with scripture.	Apocrypha "The History of Joseph the Carpenter"
Jesus	Baptism by John	30 AD Age around 36 years	River Jordan	The Father's voice was heard at the Baptism of Jesus, stating "This is my beloved Son, who brings Me great joy." It's likely that Jesus started to draw His disciples together prior to His baptism, because when he returned from the desert they were already with Him. They were also at the wedding at Cana (John 2:2) shortly after His baptism.	Matt 3:17 Luke 3:21

John the Baptist	John exalts Jesus	30-31 AD	Aenon near Salim in the Judean country-side	John emphatically clarified that he was the friend of the bridegroom and not the groom, giving full honour to Jesus in His role as Messiah.	John 3:22–36
John the Baptist	John in prison	31 AD	Assumed to be Nain where Jesus raised the boy from the dead (John 7:11)	While John was in prison, he asked if Jesus really was the Messiah, or should they be looking for someone else ?	Matt 11:1–6 Mark 6:14 Luke 3:20; 7:18–23 John 3:24
John the Baptist	Decollation of Saint John the Baptist	31 AD	Machaerus, east of the Dead Sea	Herod Antipas	Josephus (*Jewish Antiquities* 18. 5. 2) Matt 14:1–12
Jesus	Death on the Cross	33 AD	The Place of The Skull	The physical death of Jesus is recorded as a historical fact. Refer to *Via Crucis Via Lucis* [7] for a better explanation of the timeline of events.	Matt 27 Mark 15 Luke 23 John 19

Glossary

The following Jewish terms are used throughout this book, and are listed here to enable ease of reading.

Abijah — the name of the head priest in the time of King David, whose name means "My Father is Yahweh".

Bubbe — means grandmother, pronounced *BUH-buh*

HaShem — the respectful name of God which literally means "the Name," used as a substitute for God's actual name

Sabbath — is the time observed from sundown on Friday to sundown on Saturday and is a forced day of rest in order to maintain an aspect of holiness

Sabbath restrictions — there were 39 categories of work that were prohibited on the Sabbath (equivalent to our Saturday), which included things like lighting fires, cooking, baking, writing, business transactions, gardening, planting, harvesting, sewing, building, laundry, and distances travelled.

Sanhedrin — the ancient Jewish supreme council and court of law in the religious and political life of Israel

Erusin — the first stage of a traditional Jewish marriage which is known as a betrothal. Unlike a western engagement, it carries deeper legal and spiritual significance. The couple were bound legally but not living together and sexual relations are strictly prohibited.

Kiddushin — the betrothal ceremony, this sets apart the couple and makes the woman exclusively designated for her husband. There is usually an exchange of money or something of value, typically the groom gives his bride a ring. This stage is about legal commitment, such as a contract.

Nissuin — the second stage of the traditional Jewish marriage, following Kiddushin. This enables the full union of the couple to live together under legal, spiritual and physical conditions as husband and wife. This stage is about spiritual and emotional union, moving the relationship from formality to intimacy.

Shtar — The written declaration of intent to marry which is witnessed at the Kiddushin.

Shema — from Deuteronomy 6:4, "Hear, O Israel, the Lord is our God, the Lord is One."

Shalom — means Hello, or more literally "Peace"

Shalom Aleichem — means "Peace be upon you"——

Aleichem Shalom — is the response to Shalom Aleichem, which literally means "Upon you be peace"

Boker Tov — means Good morning, spoken at first be a person to greet family or a friend

Boker Or — response to Boker Tov, which literally means "Morning light" in a poetic form of response to a good-morning greeting

Laila Tov — means Good night

Shabbat — is the Jewish day of rest, called the Sabbath

Shabbat Shalom — means "Peaceful Sabbath"

Gut Shabbos — means "Good Sabbath"

Pesach — means "to pass over" and commemorates the exodus where the Israelites escaped Egypt after the slaughter of a lamb was celebrated for a family, and its blood painted on the lintel of the door posts

With Thanks

The author wishes to thank the following people for volunteering their time, thoughts and energy to make the manuscript sing, polishing out most of the grammatical and syntactical errors, and helping it to become easily read.

Ray W, you have been such a faithful friend and provided a keen eye over all my books to date, and your questioning has got me thinking about whether I have been on the right track at times. Although I couldn't accommodate all your suggestions, your persistence is truly appreciated.

Emma L, thank you for filling your unused time with valuable comments and challenges to make the manuscript a work of art. I honestly don't know how you juggled the triplets along with the challenges of life, giving well over a hundred percent to meet my publishing deadline.

Nat D, I appreciated your sincere one on one about the formation of the early character and identity of Mariam, which got me thinking about how that should be better prepared. I hope this has now given her the image that she deserves.

Brisbane Writers Group, your feedback for several chapters of the book in its raw form was truly inspirational, and caused me to rethink some scenes and word imagery with a more astute eye throughout the rest of the book. I love being part of such a respectable community.

Omega Writers, you have been my early Christian support and encouragement to write and publish books, so faithful and friendly. I look forward to many happy days ahead for all of us!

Rebekah R, I know how hard you work to bring my projects together, giving a careful eye over the typesetting, cover images, font styles and overall presentation. I am sincerely grateful for everything you do to make things great. Many blessings!

About the Author

Brother Brad Smith is a Brisbane-born Aussie and grew up in a variety of church denominations in both the city and rural contexts. He is married and has two adult children, and loves to share with others about the risen Jesus.

The storyline for *Mariam's Memoirs* was adopted primarily from Biblical records and commentaries, with some (or maybe a lot!) of supporting storyline from apocryphal accounts. And for a little flair there has been the generation of some events that cannot be found in either source nor historical accounts. For these instances, the author seeks your grace to allow freedom of expression, noting that this is Biblical fiction, and encourages everyone to take particular note of the version of events from holy scripture which is inspired by the Holy Spirit.

Brother Brad enjoys writing about theological topics, explaining Biblical subjects in simple terms, and has a passion to express the message of the gospel through stories and holds a Diploma of Theology from Harvest Bible College, Australia.

For more information or to make contact with the author, please refer to his website,

www.brotherbrad.com

References and Resources

Books of Interest

1. Sri, Dr E (2006). *Rethinking Mary*. Ignatius Press, Sycamore, IL.

2. Ford-Grabowsky, M (2007). *The Way of Mary: Following Her Footsteps Toward God*. Paraclete Press, Brewster MA.

3. McBride, A (1999). *Images of Mary*. St Anthony Messenger Press, Cincinnati, Ohio.

4. McKnight, S (2007). *The Real Mary: Why Protestant Christians Can Embrace the Mother of Jesus*. Paraclete Press, Brewster MA.

5. Bauer, J (2001). *Advent and Christmas with Fulton J. Sheen*. Liguori Publications, Liguori, Missouri.

6. Sri, E (2013). *Walking with Mary: A Biblical Journey from Nazareth to the Cross*. Crown Publishing Group, New York.

7. Ferrell, A (2016). *Mary, The Mother of Jesus*. Voice of The Light Ministries.

8. Smith, Brother Brad (2023). *Via Crucis Via Lucis: The Way of the Cross, The Way of the Light*. Sure Fire Web Pty Ltd, Brisbane, Australia.

9. Smith, Brother Brad (2024). *The Advent*. Sure Fire Web Pty Ltd, Brisbane, Australia.

Website Sources

1.   Apocrypha, The History of Joseph the Carpenter, retrieved 9 March 2025,
     https://www.interfaith.org/christianity/apocrypha-joseph-the-carpenter/

2.   Apocrypha, The Gospel of the Birth of Mary, retrieved 18 July 2025,
     https://sacred-texts.com/bib/lbob/lbob05.htm

3.   Britannica Online, Temple of Jerusalem, retrieved 25 May 2025
     https://www.britannica.com/topic/Temple-of-Jerusalem

4.   The Gospel of Christ, Was Jacob or Heli The Father of Joseph?, retrieved 31 May 2025 (explains how the Hebrews used the word "son" in different senses)
     https://www.thegospelofchrist.com/knowledge-base/tgoc-kb--dh6hx

5.   The Jewish Holidays, retrieved 16 June 2025,
     https://www.hebrew4christians.com/Holidays/Introduction/introduction.html

6.   Abarim Publications, Meaning of the town name Nazareth, retrieved 14 July 2025,
     https://www.abarim-publications.com/Meaning/Nazareth.html

7.   Bible Gateway, https://www.biblegateway.com/

8.   Blue Letter Bible, Lexicon lookup for the word ἀνήρ in Greek, amongst other words,
     https://www.blueletterbible.org/lexicon/g435/web/tr/0-1/

9.   Wikipedia, Brothers of Jesus, retrieved 24 June 2025,
     https://en.wikipedia.org/wiki/Brothers_of_Jesus

Via Crucis Via Lucis is a 28-chapter devotional journey through the passion and resurrection of Jesus Christ, exploring the 12 Stations of the Cross and the 12 Stations of Light.

From the anguish of Gethsemane to the glory of the Ascension, each chapter offers Scripture, reflection, and insight into the redemptive path Christ walked — and the radiant hope that followed.

Via Crucis Via Lucis invites readers to meditate on both suffering and triumph, embracing the full mystery of salvation. Whether used during Lent, Easter, or any season of renewal, *Via Crucis Via Lucis* provides a powerful guide for prayer, contemplation, and spiritual growth.

Walk the way of sorrow. Rise in the light of glory. The journey of Christ is the journey of us all.

Available online in ebook or softback version from
www.brotherbrad.com

The Advent is a 24-chapter exploration of God's promises for the coming Messiah, fulfilled in Jesus Christ.

From the first whisper of redemption in Genesis to the vivid prophecies of Isaiah and beyond, each chapter unveils a divine promise that pointed toward the birth of the Savior.

The Advent invites you to trace the golden thread of hope woven through Scripture, revealing God's faithfulness across generations.

Whether used for personal devotion, group study, or seasonal reflection, *The Advent* offers rich insight into the longing, joy, and fulfillment found in Christ's arrival. With accessible language and theological depth, it's a perfect companion for Advent or any time of year when hearts turn toward the wonder of incarnation.

The promise was spoken. The promise was kept. The Messiah has come.

Available online in ebook or softback version from

www.brotherbrad.com

www.ingramcontent.com/pod-product-compliance
Lightning Source LLC
Chambersburg PA
CBHW020332120726
47904CB00002B/385